L W Cameron

MUSEUM
PIECES

WILLIAM PLOMER

DISCARD

THE NOONDAY PRESS

NEW YORK

CH 4721

First Printing October, 1954
Second Printing November, 1954

Copyright 1954 by William Plomer
Manufactured in the United States of America
By H. Wolff, New York

Library of Congress Catalog Card No.: 54-11725

Now that I am no longer a widow, now that I need no longer earn at least part of my living, I can write the book I have wanted to write. The question is, What sort of book will it be? How can I know, until I see how it turns out? I think I know what I have to say and how I want to say it. It is a matter of memory, of recollection. I want to look back twenty years or more and isolate certain names and faces and scenes, certain incidents and anecdotes, to trace certain lines of habit and conduct, to catch some fragments of truth about a handful of persons living in varying relations to one another, and in changing conditions.

Am I setting out to write a memoir in the form of a novel, or a novel in the form of a memoir? I owe a little debt, I feel, to the truth, and I intend to pay it: it is my debt, and I am the only person who can pay it. That is more important to me than contriving a plot, keeping potential readers in a state of tension, flattering their prejudices, and so on. And another thing—a novelist generally pretends to know everything. That is something I can't do. I have found life in London during the last quarter of a century so complex and its tempo so rapid that even what one knows best is only known by fits and starts, in bits and pieces. Even the lives of some of the people one knows best are "seen, lost, and seen," like dragonflies on a summer morning—especially the lives of people like Toby, who was so greatly concerned to keep his friends segregated from one another or even completely ignorant of one another's existence.

A reader looking for strong and new sensations may not think my story a story at all, but just a superficial sketch of a totally unimportant and now entirely faded corner of society. Whatever it is, it begins at a moment almost exactly half-way between the two wars, when I received one morning a letter signed "Susannah Mount-faucon." It came from an address in Duchess's Gate. The paper was smooth and ample, the handwriting expansive, leisurely, and a trifle childish, or naïve. Mrs. Mount-faucon, whoever she might be, had expressed herself very politely. She hoped I would not mind being written to by a stranger, but my name had been given her by an acquaintance we had in common, Miss Lilac Evans. Miss Evans had said that I was "an accomplished historian." She and her son much hoped to ask my advice about some family papers, and she would be so grateful and pleased if I would come to tea one afternoon in the week after next, and if I would suggest a day. She was mine sincerely.

The first thing I did, naturally, was to ring up Lilac Evans. I didn't know her very well, and when we had met I had felt a little daunted by the extreme modishness of her clothes and by her poise. I knew that she worked for *Style,* that expensive and glossy fashion paper, separate editions of which came out simultaneously in London, Paris, and New York. I had heard that she was dressed free by one of the best *haute couture* establishments in Paris as an advertisement, and that her shoes, her scent,

2

her make-up and everything were all supplied by the best makers in the same way. She could not very well help being highly conscious of her elegance and of having to live up to it without a pause. Every looking-glass proclaimed it, and wherever she went the eyes of other women were glued to her like embittered limpets. But I had not found her at all condescending, although she must have been as aware as I was, when we first met, that my shoes were merely practical, that my brooch was neither modern nor antique but just demoded, and that I was more than due for a visit to the hairdresser. What I liked about her was that although she was perfect as a mannequin, or clothes-horse, she seemed both intelligent and pleasant. Yet she seemed a little too good to be true, a little too suave. She reminded me of a woman known to me in my childhood and referred to in my family, on account of the extreme smoothness of her manner, as "Butterball." I got into the habit of thinking of Lilac Evans as another Butterball.

If she had said that I was an accomplished historian she was talking through her fashionable hat. She must have used the phrase in order to do me a good turn, or perhaps she really thought it true. She had come to stay at a place in Wiltshire where I was cataloging a lot of old papers. (I had been trained as an archivist, and now that I was on my own again, I took on stray jobs of this kind to augment my income.) She had asked some sensible questions about the work and had insisted on my being photographed and written about in *Style*. The photograph showed me sitting snugly in the muniment room like a maggot in an apple. With a perhaps absurd wish not to appear what I was—that is to say, a youngish intellectual woman, rather plain but quite amiable-looking, alone with a lot of old papers in an old room smelling like a faint agreeable blend of mouldy straw, mushrooms, and tomb-

3

stones—I had taken off the spectacles I use for reading and had hidden them, and I remember that I was trying, as I faced the camera, not to screw up my eyes in order to bring into focus the precise expression on the face of Lilac Evans, who was standing at the photographer's elbow.

I now took up the telephone with some diffidence.

"But of course, my dear," she said, before I could explain anything, "you want the low-down on Mrs. Mountfaucon. What are you doing on Thursday at six? Come and have a drink."

So on Thursday at six I went to see Lilac Evans. I knew it was no good trying to dress myself up, but I did not want to appear too obviously the muniment-girl. Fortunately I am tidy by nature, so I aimed at simple neatness as a kind of protective coloring in her expected setting of expensive simplicity. Lilac lived, as she still does, in a flat in Wilton Place, and the setting was just what I had expected. A French maid showed me into the drawing-room, where Lilac was shaking a cocktail.

"What a charming frock," she said, "so beautifully cut. Who's your dressmaker? Do help yourself to a cigarette."

Blushing with pleasure, I had just time to notice that the question about my dressmaker was merely rhetorical. After a preliminary skirmish of talk on such ground as we had in common, like our encounter in Wiltshire, and after we had settled down with our drinks, which tasted interestingly of some ingredient unknown to me, she opened up.

"Mrs. Mountfaucon," she said, "has been twice widowed. There's one child, Toby. He must be verging on thirty. His name's William, but he's always called Toby— Toby d'Arfey, you know. She had him by her first hus-

4

band. She left the schoolroom, I believe, to marry Toby's father, and he was old enough to be her grandfather. Her second was once a Young Lochinvar type, all profile and polo, you know, but he took to drink and died, quite dipso, only a year or two ago. She sold up the old home, in Somerset or somewhere, and settled in at Duchess's Gate, I suppose for Toby's sake. Whether she is more of a problem to Toby, or whether Toby's more of a problem to her, I'll leave you to decide for yourself."

This seemed the moment for me to ask some bright question, but I couldn't think of one.

"Don't be surprised by her style," Lilac went on. "She goes to Galhauban Sœurs for everything, and between them they've worked out a style of her own—a shade *outré*, it might be thought, but she began life, I believe, as a country parson's daughter, so I suppose it's a kind of compensation. She's a perfect dear with a great air of innocence. You're bound to like her."

"And her son?" I asked. "Does he live under the same roof? What's he like?"

"Toby," she said, with, I thought, a softer nuance in her voice. "Oh, my dear, *I* don't know. He's very good company, at any rate. If he doesn't like people, he's apt to show it a bit too plainly. If he likes them, he lays himself out to please and amuse them, so much so, that he sometimes arouses hopes. I can't say I understand him. He's really rather complicated."

"Not married?"

"If he is, it doesn't show."

I wondered what that meant, and said so.

"Well, I think he rather keeps different parts of his life in different compartments. Although I know him fairly well, I don't believe I really understand him. I'm fond of him, but that's quite another thing."

5

And not, I guessed, from the tone of her voice, a very deep thing.

"It's easy to misjudge him," she went on. "I've heard him called brilliant, I've heard him called a booby. He's an aesthete, but he's tough. He has a feminine streak, but the nicest men often have, don't you think? I said the nicest, not necessarily the most attractive. He travels a lot, he's always in Benin, or Bahia, or Bangkok, or somewhere, but when he's in London he's generally under his mother's roof. He has a talent for painting, but I don't think he's likely to develop it. I should say he's a dilettante, in the best sense. Such people are needed, I think, don't you, the way the world's going? I wish there were more of them."

We went on to talk of something else, and when I was going she said, "You'll be charmed, I know, with Toby and his mother. You'll adore them, they're not like anybody else."

When I had already said good-bye she kept me back to tell me that Toby d'Arfey had lately been dining at a restaurant in Paris, I think the Tour d'Argent, with an eminent soprano, a Negress, as his guest. At another table was a party of Americans, not of the most liberal kind, and dominated by a matriarch, arrogant and overdressed. She made it pretty plain by her behavior that she resented the presence of the Negress. To make her disapproval perfectly clear to d'Arfey and his guest she put up a lorgnon and glared at them. The other members of her party turned to see what she was looking at. This was too much for d'Arfey, who picked up two tumblers, clapped them to his eyes, and stared at her through the bottoms of them until she lowered her lorgnon and averted her eyes.

I liked this story, but I can't say that I came away with any very clear idea about Mrs. Mountfaucon and her son

—not that it mattered very much, because I should be seeing them soon, this dressy widow and her apparently somewhat high-spirited son, and could try and judge for myself what they were like. I had quite forgotten to ask Lilac Evans if she had any idea of the nature of the family papers that Mrs. Mountfaucon wanted me to look at.

It seemed that the widow and her son were looming up in my life. Between my visit to Lilac Evans and my first visit to Duchess's Gate somebody asked me at a party what I was doing nowadays.

"Have you ever heard of a Mrs. Mountfaucon?" I asked.

At this a red-haired woman in her thirties, who was said to be an ambitious but not very successful actress, spread her fingers out in a clutching, clawing gesture that was meant to be humorous but was in fact a trifle startling, and exclaimed, "Oh, my God, if I could get my hands on that woman!"

Seeing my questioning look, she explained, "His mother, I mean! She has of course quite ruined his life. Predatory isn't the word—she's clamped to her prey for life. Poor Toby—a classic case of mother-fixation."

"Oh, nonsense," said somebody. "If a child shows any affection for its parents nowadays it's supposed to be morbid. Why, Toby's nearly always abroad."

"And the umbilical cord is always elastic," said the actress.

I heard later that she had "literally thrown herself" at Toby, and, far from bowling him over, had rebounded like a tennis ball from a stone wall. This possibly explained her vehemence.

"Toby d'Arfey?" said somebody else. "He used to go about a lot with Lydia Delap."

I knew vaguely of Lydia Delap as a girl with an opulent

7

Edwardian background who had turned Bohemian in a nineteen-twentyish way and had written a couple of novels. I hadn't read them but imagined them to be decidedly precious.

"Damn good chap to be with in a tight corner," said a soldierly-looking man who worked as a test pilot for an aircraft company, and he went on to say he knew a man who had been with d'Arfey in Glasgow once, late at night. The two of them had been set upon by a gang of keelies. "D'Arfey rushed at them with his arms going like a windmill and they turned and ran. He gashed his knuckles badly and while he was binding them up with his handkerchief he said, 'If it's poverty that makes them so nasty it's high time they all had a thousand a year.'"

"He has no idea of the value of money," said the actress. "Never had." She seemed to intend an inference that she had had to try and stop him spending money upon her.

"But he has an idea of the value of pictures. I hear he has found a Rubens or something."

"One's always hearing about these discoveries," said the actress, giving a languid pat to her back hair. "And what's the subject? A mare's nest, I suppose."

At this point the conversation was broken up by our hostess, and I heard no more of d'Arfey and his mother. I thought that casual gossip could give one a bewildering view of somebody one had never met. I forget who it was that said that you and I are already six people. Here am I, as I seem to myself; I, as I seem to you; and I, as I really am. There are you, as you seem to yourself; you, as you seem to me; and you, as you really are. But then there are whole series of ourselves as we might have been and might still be; and at any given moment each of us has a kind of aggregate of reputation, always variable. In other

people's casual talk about a man, one catches glimpses of
what he seems like to them. If they like or admire him
or feel loyal towards him they may reveal glimpses of him
at his best, glimpses that may be true or purely fanciful.
And out of envy, guilt, fear, ignorance, or facetiousness
they may either caricature or falsify him, or be too directly, too unkindly truthful about him—and therefore un-
truthful. My confused impression of Toby d'Arfey was
the product of hearsay: I was now to form an impression
at first hand.

TWO

And so it was at a moment, as I said, about half-way between the two wars that I found myself pressing the bell
of Mrs. Mountfaucon's house in Duchess's Gate. The
papers I was to examine had somehow become of less interest than the prospect of meeting Toby d'Arfey. I was
looking forward to that, but felt a little apprehensive
about meeting his mother. I thought the "perfect dear"
dressed by Galhauban Sœurs might prove a dragon, unduly defensive of her young.

The door was opened by a butler younger than most
butlers, and redder in the face than most indoor servants.
His manner was pleasant but slightly uneasy: although I

was expected he had an air of having been disturbed in some private indulgence. He showed me into a long and handsome drawing-room. There was nobody in it and he asked me to wait. The room was not furnished with any uniformity of style. The things in it, of various origins and periods, were all good of their kind, and went well together; one could see that they had either been inherited or acquired by people with taste. I noticed particularly some choice pieces of Empire furniture, not then so fashionable as it was to become in the thirties. It was one of those rooms in which diversity makes harmony—much better, to my mind, than a room done all "in period" or all in the latest fashion. An Aubusson carpet, an Italian cabinet of the sixteenth century, a pair of Chinese vases (looted, I was to hear, from the Summer Palace), an old looking-glass discolored like pond water and enclosed in a much carved and curved gilt frame, evidently Spanish, a case of English miniatures (trim souls with clean linen, big eyes, and small mouths), a seascape by Boudin with a few windswept girls wearing crinolines and looking like doomed butterflies—all these things seemed to understand each other, as if their makers had had a common understanding not to think of war, or of the ups and downs of private fortunes, or of decay, that patient if unresting subverter.

Since my husband's death I had had a flat on my own. It was in the region known in my family as Redcliffia, or Beyond-the-Boltons. There I had for the first time in my life had to take some notice of housekeeping. I had learned how the maintenance of a passable cleanliness and order, even in a small space, means a constant battle, constant hard work, and continual expense. It was therefore with an almost housewifely eye that I gazed at that beautiful room. A sleepy fire and afternoon sunshine were dreamily reflected here and there on some gleaming or muted surface; they filled the room with rich comfort and peace; but when a clock chimed, thinly and sadly, it seemed a reminder of mortality. Whenever I am reading old papers and hear a clock strike, particularly a church clock, it is apt to make me feel melancholy.

The room was dominated by two large and admirable modern portraits hanging on either side of the chimneypiece. One represented a young man in full evening dress. He was prematurely bald, with a clean-shaven, fresh-looking face, and impressive eyes under heavy but not languorous lids. These eyes, which reminded me of those of Degas in his self-portrait, had a look of alert intelligence, slightly sceptical or judging, and the mouth was haunted by a disturbing ironical smile. The face, together with the white tie and white waistcoat, suggested a man who loved pleasure although he saw through it. I remembered the phrase "It's high time they all had a thousand a year."

The other portrait was of a middle-aged woman with a roundish flattish face, heavily powdered, though her fresh pink complexion might have been natural. She wore a large summery hat, and two pink roses were fastened in a rather low and full-bosomed corsage. Her hands, in long white kid gloves, were clasped in a childish gesture that implied not only supplication but eagerness tinged with anxiety, and the face had something of the same childlike look, except for the saddened, experienced eyes, which were much older than the rest of the face: it seemed the face of a Bernhardt without a temperament.

While I was gazing at this picture I was startled by a loud tap. It had been caused by the fall upon a polished table of a heavy tulip-petal from an immense vaseful of various flowers. From where I sat I could see a fine scattering of yellow pollen beside the petal on the glossy surface of the table. Immediately after the petal had fallen the door opened as if at a signal, and there stood Toby d'Arfey. Apart from the portrait, I had little idea of what he might look like, and for a measurable moment I had the impression of a large pair of eyes to which the rest of him seemed a mere adjunct. They were in fact neither protuberant nor inordinately large, but as he had a fair skin and no eyebrows to speak of, and as his fair hair was cut very short on each side of his mainly bald cranium, the eyes, with dilated pupils, made by their darkness a strong contrast with the light blondness of the face and head generally: they were not merely dark, but warmly and darkly glowing, like the eyes of some highly-strung animal. They looked keenly at me, appraising, mischievous, and, I thought, just a shade apprehensive.

Having welcomed me, he told me that his mother would be down in a minute, and so she was. She too was instantly recognizable from the portrait, and though hatless, gloveless, and roseless, she yet had the same summery air. She was not very tall and her head was covered with a loosely curling and straying golden fleece, parted, not too conspicuously, in the middle. I thought at first it must be dyed, but its abundance and formal disarray inclined me to judge it a remarkably well-made wig. Mrs. Mountfaucon's figure was, in an Edwardian sense, good "for her age," and although on the stocky side, its stockiness had been dissembled by an evidently first-rate dressmaker with as much skill as if "the perfect dear" had wished to hide an advanced pregnancy—that is to say, without unduly obvious drapings and air-pockets. Her straight back, small hands and feet, impulsive movements, and winning smile no doubt kept her looking younger than her age. She might have been sixty-five or more.

The butler came in with the tea-things, and the conversation had the affability of any conversation in which the talkers are strangers with a mutual wish to please. I had expressed my admiration of the chair in which Mrs. Mountfaucon was sitting.

"If you love old things," she said, with the quiet triumphant assurance of a card-player laying down the first of a fistful of aces, "I think you'll like to know that you're sitting in a chair that belonged to Pope. He was a *very* close friend, as I expect you know, of Toby's ancestor, John d'Arfey. Yes, and this is Pope's teapot, he *always* had his tea out of this pot."

"That'll *do,* mother," said Toby sharply, as if she had been boasting. But it seemed to me that she was one of those women who enjoy the prestige and beauty of their possessions, which have become as it were part of their personalities. Perhaps this was an irritation to her son.

I was genuinely interested in the associations with Pope. Only lately I had seen what was alleged to be Marie Antoinette's favorite chair, and if all the chairs which have been so called were in fact favorites, she must have spent the whole of her life sitting for a short time only in each of a vast concourse of chairs extending from the cradle to the scaffold, as many as the beds in which Queen Elizabeth is alleged to have slept, as if she were a sloth— which is not what history says. However, the d'Arfey-Pope friendship was in fact close, and Pope may well have been much attached to the chair.

"A few weeks ago," I said, "when I was in Poland, I was taken to tea, or rather coffee, in Warsaw with a woman who said, 'I think you may like to know that you're sitting in Sienkiewicz's chair. This is his coffee-pot,' she said. 'He always had his coffee out of this pot. That's his portrait, and this is the room in which he wrote *Quo Vadis.*'"

The sweetness of Mrs. Mountfaucon's smile suggested at least a certain vagueness about Sienkiewicz, and perhaps a strained tolerance of such an obscure rival to Pope.

"I'm afraid I've never read *Quo Vadis*," I said hastily, as if to mitigate any excessive claim I might appear to be putting forward on behalf of its author. "Do you think," I asked, turning to her son, "one ought to?"

"I'm pretty sure one needn't," he said cheerfully. "A welter, I imagine, of depraved Roman matrons, heavy-weight gladiators, and priggish Early Christians."

Sitting in Pope's chair and talking with a descendant of his friend caused me to see Mrs. Mountfaucon and her son for a moment in relation to the vast and dazzling scheme of European culture. These two, I thought, were beings to be honored; they had the piety that preserves relics of poets. But Mrs. Mountfaucon, a little put out, I dare say, by never having heard of Sienkiewicz, seemed to feel that it was time to trump this insignificant card. With the girlish agility sometimes to be seen in heavy old women, she rose from her chair, fluttered to a cabinet, opened it, and came back with an elaborately jewelled watch in one hand and a plain fat one in the other. I at once suspected Marie Antoinette, but I was wrong: the showier of the two had been given, Mrs. Mountfaucon explained, by Catherine the Great to Sir Ferdinand d'Arfey, the English envoy to Moscow. The less showy watch, she said, had been Dr. Johnson's. When I had duly admired them, she played Pope again.

"At Marsh," she said, "our house in the country, our *exquisite*, dearly loved *gem* of a house, which, alas, we had to sell after Morven's, my second husband's, death, because of death-duties—you know how truly crushing they are—oh, and I dream of Marsh every night of my life—we had a Pope cabinet, a very large cabinet, quite crammed with relics and mementoes. Most we sold, some are in the British Museum, and a very few we kept. Professor Snade Leavenbread, you know, a most *brilliant* man and *the* authority on Pope—but of course you know about him—came specially from America to see our Pope things and he *raved* about them."

"For God's sake, mother!" cried Toby, "Mrs. Valance will think you're trying to sell her something. And I'm afraid your swan, as usual, is a goose." He turned to me. "Professor Leavenbread, I may say, was about as brilliant as a cup of lukewarm cocoa. He was as drab a bore as ever crossed the Atlantic. He had a mind like a card-index, and he wore those rimless pince-nez that used to be known as fairy glasses. You can bet that every time the Prof. utters Pope's name, Pope twirls round in his grave like a lathe. 'Studying up source material' was I think the graceful way the Prof. explained his visit to Marsh."

This was my introduction to the fact that one had to translate much of what was said both by Mrs. Mountfaucon and her son into plainer English. Their vocabularies differed, but had in common, I soon learned, a lack of half-tones.

As a clergyman's daughter and a specimen of that dwindling species, the lady, Mrs. Mountfaucon shrank from giving offence. Thus of a really ugly woman she might say, "I'm afraid one couldn't call her exactly pretty, poor thing, but I know some people think her *interesting-looking*." Of moderate praise she was incapable, so that a fairly pretty woman of whom she approved she would call "*exquisitely* pretty." I shrink from recalling how she would describe a raging beauty. Loyal, fanatically loyal, to those she liked, she was an enthusiast who saw life in vivid colors, and it was perhaps something of an actress in her that made her wish to excite and work upon the attention of her hearers.

Her son was no less given to exaggeration, with this peculiarity, as I was to find—that he would sometimes build up those of whom he disapproved into towering legendary figures moving in a world of outrageous fantasy and casting the longest and most grotesque of shadows. They were generally women. He gave me the impression that he was strongly attracted to women but unconsciously feared that they might despise him.

"Do you think, Toby," Mrs. Mountfaucon asked with real or assumed diffidence, "that Mrs. Valance would be interested to hear about the picture?"

"She might. Try and see."

"It's our Rembrandt, you know."

"If it is a Rembrandt, mother."

"We had a rather murky picture," she said, "left us with some other things by a distant cousin of Toby's, one of the three beautiful Miss Golightlys, you know, one of whom married Lord—"

"Oh, spare us the stud-book, mother, please!" He turned to me.

"The picture, I may say, together with a quantity of motheaten lace and some bound volumes of sermons, was left to us out of malice. We had some reason to expect a good slice of her fortune, but it all went to an ambiguous, or perhaps I had better say an *un*ambiguous female companion, a burning Sappho from Ilfracombe, by all accounts."

"Oh, Toby!" cried Mrs. Mountfaucon, hiding her face in her hands—unnecessarily, I thought.

"The point is that there's some reason to believe that the picture may be a Rembrandt. If she'd known, of course, she'd never have left it to us. We think she left it to us as a dig at mother, of whom she was always jealous. The subject of the picture is Susannah and the Elders, and Susannah happens to be mother's name. The picture was very dirty and it seemed to me that there was some over-painting, so we had it X-rayed, and we now have to arrange for the cleaning. I wish I could show it to you, but it's not here at the moment."

"We haven't said anything much about it to anybody yet," Mrs. Mountfaucon remarked, "so you won't mind not talking about it just yet, Mrs. Valance, will you?"

"I shan't say a word," I said.

"The experts, you know, the big dealers—we don't want any publicity just yet. They're all hand in glove, of course."

"And," said Toby, "we don't want to count our purely putative chickens before they're hatched."

"Lilac Evans tells us that you're a most *learned* historian," Mrs. Mountfaucon said ingratiatingly.

"I'm afraid she has misled you," I said. "It's true I did read history, but I'm only an archivist, and not at all a learned one. Mostly self-taught, I'm afraid. It's just that I like old papers."

"And so you're perhaps very kindly going to look at ours? You shall have a room to yourself, and a key, and come and go as you like—that is, if you're really going to be so kind."

"I should think it's all waste paper." Toby turned to me. "You've only to say so."

"Oh, dear Toby, no, how wicked! Why there are title-deeds going back I don't know how far, and manorial accounts, and a mass of letters, and a charter of Henry III —do I mean Henry III?"

"Ask me another, my dear mother. I should think Mrs. Valance will curse us for wasting her time."

17

"Oh, I hope not," Mrs. Mountfaucon smiled. "Do you know Miss Evans well? She's a very old friend of Toby's. Isn't she exquisite? Quite one of the best-dressed women in London, I always think."

"And so she should be, mother, with all found."

"As an advertisement," Mrs. Mountfaucon explained. "But so convenient. I expect you know she's one of the editors of *Style*. Of course she knows so well how to *wear* her clothes, how to move. She carries herself so well."

I at once straightened my spine. It was a reflex action. A chorus of remembered reprimands from my childhood rang in my ears.

"Jane, don't slouch!" "Jane, must you come into the room in that sloppy way?" "Jane, this is the drawing-room, not the hockey-field!"

"How lovely to have that said about one," I remarked wistfully.

"She has such an *interesting* life," said Mrs. Mountfaucon. "She quite often goes to Paris. She has such poise."

"She had better, it's her bread and butter," said Toby. "She happens to look the part she happens to play for a living. She's a career-girl who has completely subordinated her private life to her public life. No wonder her husband left her."

"I never knew she had one," I said.

"She hardly knew it herself. She's a narcissist. Not frigid, I should say—that would suggest a possibility of a thaw—but just bored by sex, bored to extinction."

With a little bat-like shriek Mrs. Mountfaucon hid her face in her hands again. If she were really a possessive kind of mother, no doubt it was a little shriek of pleasure because there was no danger of Lilac stealing Toby away from her; but ostensibly it was a little shriek of real or assumed modesty. Looking back, I know it was assumed. She was used to her son's plain speaking, she delighted in it; she was just saving her own face—an innocent affectation, and perhaps her only one.

THREE

On my second visit to Duchess's Gate the door was opened not by the butler but by a motherly old soul in an apron.

"That," Mrs. Mountfaucon explained, "was Mrs. Crumpsey. I'm afraid I've had to get rid of Seddons. The other night at dinner, you know, as he handed the dishes, they seemed to float away and then float too near, so that it was quite difficult to time the right moment to help oneself, and one began to feel quite dizzy. I lay awake for hours on Tuesday night, wondering what to do. At Marsh, you know, we had the same butler for thirty-four years, a perfect *angel*. Of course he was there long before my arrival. Toby's father engaged him from a General Somebody, a great hunting man. He was a *miracle* when we had to entertain, as we occasionally did, a regular horde of people. . . . So I lay awake wondering what on earth I could say to get rid of him. You see, if I had said, 'Seddons, you were abominably drunk last night, and you'll have to go,' he might have denied it and become argumentative. And then, of course, I didn't want to hurt his feelings, difficult though it had been at dinner to aim the spoon at the soufflé as he waved it about. So I decided to say, 'Seddons, you were *nearly* drunk last night.' It worked like a charm, and he was as meek as milk."

She paused, with the air of a little girl expecting praise for cleverness.

"How very tactful of you," I said. "And how lucky you are to have Mrs. Crumpsey. She's so comfortable-looking."

"Oh yes, my *dear* Mrs. Crumpsey. Do you know, one morning I went into the kitchen and she said to me quite spontaneously, 'Oh, I do love you so! When I'm with you I feel just as I used to do with my husband.' Of course my darling Toby put the worst possible construction on *that*. . . . She's a widow, you know, with an only son, a perfect *prodigy*. When he left school he came and told her he must have thirty pounds. She didn't ask him what he wanted it for, she's so full of sense and such real delicacy of feeling. He was only fifteen, but he'd always been a good boy, so she took the money out of the savings bank, quite a *large* sum for her, and gave it to him without a word. He'd never asked her for a penny before, she says, and he's never asked her for a penny since. He wanted the money, it seems, to open a business—just think, at fifteen! Before he was thirty he was quite a rich man, owning a small factory, something to do with wireless sets, I think, and a comfortable house, and living on quite a scale. Such a good son! He comes here once a week in a smart shiny car to see her, oh, and never misses. He's the apple of her eye. He used to urge her to retire and live in comfort at his expense, but she always refused. She said that although she was happy that he had got on so well, she preferred to go on living and working as she was accustomed. She told me she was too old to 'change her class.' That shows real strength of character, don't you think?"

I thought it also showed the force of habit, but I didn't say so. It seemed a sign of the times that whereas Mrs. Mountfaucon had not been able to afford to keep up her place in the country, her cook's son had become a property owner.

"Won't you come upstairs?" she said, "and I'll show you how I've arranged the room for you to work in."

On the landing I paused to look at a portrait hanging in a darkish alcove.

"That's Morven," she said, "my second husband, you know. Toby won't allow me to hang it anywhere else. I'm afraid they never got on very well."

I remembered Lilac Evans saying "quite dipso" and "Young Lochinvar type," and craned forward. At first I thought I was looking at a tinted touched-up enlargement of a photograph, but it proved to be a pastel, done perhaps about 1890. It represented the top half of a young man wearing a creamy flannel blazer piped with purple and having an heraldic breast-pocket, an open shirt also of cream-colored flannel, and one of those absurdly small and almost peakless cricketing caps of the period. He was seen against a background of vague verdure.

This portrait had a horribly smooth, a suède-like texture, and though realistic enough to be taken for a doctored photograph, it was at the same time sentimental and made the dashing athlete look soft and dewy. Scanning the perfectly regular features, the peach-like complexion, the clear eyes, the pearly teeth just showing between parted lips as if advertising an old-fashioned dentifrice, the upper lip just shaded with golden down, I realized that he must have been quite uncommonly good-looking.

"His men *adored* him," said Mrs. Mountfaucon with a sigh. She seemed to take it for granted that I should know he had been in a cavalry regiment, but the sigh, I felt sure, had nothing to do with that.

"You must tell me at once," she said, opening a door, "if everything is exactly as you like it," and I saw at once that she had taken trouble to equip the room conveniently for my labors.

I was to spend a good deal of time in that room, so I will describe it. It was on the second floor, at the back of the house, and faced more or less eastwards, because it got a little sun in the mornings. Most of the day, whatever the weather, it seemed to be filled with an even, filtered light. It was free of draughts, and away from the sound of traffic, and there was nothing to distract the attention in the view of some plane trees and the half-hidden backs of some tall houses. The windows were hung with red-and-white striped curtains, the wallpaper was a pale nacre-ous grey, and there was a plain dove-grey carpet. There were no pictures on the walls, and the only ornaments were some rare Meissen figures which, I learned later, had been given to Morven Mountfaucon's father by the King of Saxony. They stood on the mantelshelf with their backs to a looking-glass framed between two slender columns of rosewood, with a pediment of the same. I mostly sat at a large desk with my back to these things, and with the light coming over my left shoulder. Round the walls was an assortment of boxes and trunks, deed-boxes, hat-boxes, and old-fashioned uniform-cases. Those which contained papers had been ranged together.

It seemed to me from the first a perfect room to work in. It was laid down that I was not to be disturbed and that if I wanted anything I was to ring. I was given a key of the house and the keys of the various boxes and was free to come and go as I liked. I had agreed to look through all the papers in my own time, sort them out, set aside anything that seemed to me worth preserving, discard everything that I thought not worth keeping, draw attention of course to anything that I might think valuable, and make a rough list of my findings. I said it would suit me best to come to Duchess's Gate for two or three mornings a week. Mrs. Mountfaucon insisted that I should stay to luncheon whenever I had no other engagements, and if both she and her son happened to be out, Mrs. Crumpsey would be delighted to provide for me.

I had not then been very long a widow, but long enough not to relish particularly poaching at home, as I often had to, like some anchoret, a left-over egg, or boning sardines—the drear and unenterprising sardines of a lone woman roosting in a small flat in Tregunter Road and disinclined to cook for herself.

I like good food, but to cater for oneself alone is not much fun. I am not unsociable, but I had some disagreeable recollections, and there was a danger that I might tend to mope: Mrs. Mountfaucon, by her friendly hospitality, was therefore doing me a human kindness, and she did it entirely without emphasis. Although grateful, I was just a shade uneasy. I had rightly or wrongly formed the idea that she did what she could to keep her son, when he was in England, as much as possible to herself. Did her cordiality to me signify that she did not for a moment consider me as a possible attraction to her son? Was I so utterly undangerous? Or had she gone even further, and thought of me in fact as a possible attraction but of some unappetizing kind like a "steadying influence" or something of that sort? I should not like to give the idea that my mind was at once much occupied with these speculations; I simply want to record that they did occur to me,

23

and I think it natural enough that they should have done so.

As I now began to come often to the house and as I was soon treated almost like an old friend by Mrs. Mountfaucon and her son, I quickly became familiar with many details of their domestic and social life, and I got used to their characters and their behavior, though I sometimes found Toby's behavior to his mother disconcerting. They undoubtedly had a knack of attracting somewhat farcical or at least tragi-comic persons and events. For instance, Seddons the butler was replaced by a parlormaid, whose name was Laceman. She was of medium height, thin and pale, frustrated-looking and a little stiff. She seemed to me to have that withdrawn and shuttered look one sees in the eyes of those who have been injured by life, and I imagined that her stiffness and even haughtiness came from shyness and was defensive. She had a slightly hunted look. Mrs. Mountfaucon was just right, I thought, in her manner to Laceman, but Toby was distant towards her, and with me that told against him.

Before Laceman had been two days in the house she told Mrs. Crumpsey (who repeated everything to Mrs. Mountfaucon) that she was a countess in her own right. Laceman explained that she had come down in the world and therefore did not use her title or her real name. Mrs. Crumpsey asked her what these were; Laceman said she would "prefer not to say," so of course Mrs. Crumpsey did not believe in her claim. Nor did Mrs. Mountfaucon, but she did not say so. She said gently to Mrs. Crumpsey that it was quite likely that Laceman had had some disappointment in life, as many people do, but so long as she did her work properly there was no need to worry about her origins, especially as she had good references.

"For all we know," said Toby, "it may be true. We

know the peerage has its ups and downs. But it looks to me like a compensation-fantasy."

"Oh, my dear Toby!" cried Mrs. Mountfaucon. "A *what*?"

He turned to me.

"Mother loves to pretend to be extremely simple. She's a *fausse naïve*. . . . What I mean, mother, is that she feels insecure and so she tries to keep up her morale by trying to impress other people with her importance."

"Poor thing," said Mrs. Mountfaucon, and added, with what seemed unusual concision, "there's evidence that she has been a parlormaid for a long time, but not that she has ever been anything else."

It was not long before further light was thrown, really thrown, upon Laceman, whom Toby had taken to calling "the Countess." Her bedroom had a window overlooking a mews, and she was apparently in the habit of undressing near it without drawing the curtains. Whether intentional or not, the result was that she could easily be seen by passers-by. She soon attracted the attention of a policeman. He can hardly have found the exhibition alluring, because he called to complain of it. This led to the Countess's being gently advised by her employer to draw her curtains in future before undressing: I dare say Mrs. Mountfaucon told her she had been seen "*nearly* undressed."

In conversation with Mrs. Crumpsey about this incident, the Countess said, "Of course I'm a virgin."

"Well, that *is* nice for you," Mrs. Crumpsey had replied, and one could well imagine the tolerant, comfortably resigned, dry, and faintly ironical tone of her voice as she added: "There aren't many of *them* about nowadays."

Laceman seemed to settle very soon into the rhythm

of life at Duchess's Gate. Her finely starched apron crackled slightly when she leaned forward, and she reminded me of the pre-1914 parlormaids of my childhood. She soon seemed to have the poise of an old retainer, but her white, lost look, her dedicated air, always worried me a little, and I always made myself especially agreeable to her, as if to show my acknowledgement of her attentions to me as an outsider who needed them pretty often.

There were a couple of scurrying or loitering daily maids whom I occasionally saw in the distance, on tiptoe with a duster or genuflecting with a dustpan, but Mrs. Crumpsey I seldom saw. She was certainly kept busy helping to keep up Mrs. Mountfaucon's and Toby's almost Edwardian standards of hospitality—Toby's, in particular. Owing, I suppose, to the way he had been brought up he had no idea of the trouble and expense and forethought and skill that are needed, for instance, to produce a good dinner for even a few people, but, just like a man, he expected everything to be perfect and made a great fuss if anything went wrong.

The dining-room, though not large, had a stately air. Its most conspicuous ornament was a large seventeenth-century portrait of a luscious young woman, life-size in a gaping robe of yellow satin against a summer landscape of sultry foliage and melting distances; her hair fell in a sweet disorder of calculated curls about her brow and neck, with a tendril or two straying down towards her unconcealed and globose Restoration bosom. This was said to be a Lely of Louise de Querouaille. Then, near one door, a sword hung on the wall, and when people who had come to the house for the first time were about to pass through this door into the drawing-room Mrs. Mountfaucon usually drew their attention to it, saying, "This was Daddy's sword, you know."

days, expect to see. In it a graphologist might have found a guilelessness unvitiated by experience (or so I fancied), and that attribute which phrenologists used to call "adhesiveness," but I doubt if he would have found any trace of what is called a business sense, or of anything like a calculating disposition. Even in quite a short note from her there might be some surprising misspelling, and I remember Toby once or twice teasing her about her spelling mistakes. She belonged to a class and generation of which some members still occasionally, as in earlier times, thought exact spelling unimportant or even a mark of commonness or pedantry, but she had lived to see exact spelling generally regarded as necessary.

"My grandmother used to say that only governesses and ushers were pernickety about spelling," she explained, "and as I dreaded that I might grow up schoolmarmish, I didn't bother much."

"You may as well admit, mother," said Toby, "that you deliberately cultivated your fancy spellings. It was coquettish of you. You did it deliberately to attract attention."

This gave me a chance to come in on Mrs. Mountfaucon's side with some rather unoriginal remarks about the wild variations in spelling to which I was accustomed in old documents.

"Ah yes," she said, "they had more important things to bother about in those days."

In fact she was liable, even in conversation, to mispronunciations that sometimes resulted in impropriety. I remember a little luncheon party at Duchess's Gate which for once included a rather stiff and humorless couple. I forget who they were or why they were there, but I can see the woman now: she sat facing Louise de Querouaille and now and then glanced apprehensively up at the carmine nipples as if, so Toby remarked afterwards, they

31

had been traffic lights and she was waiting for them to turn green. Mrs. Mountfaucon had embarked on a rather complicated anecdote. The occasion for it was that she had been that morning to pay a visit, in company with her friend Lady Meliora Sperrow, to an invalid relation of Lady Meliora's living in Chelsea, and that Lady Meliora had with her a large dog she was looking after while its owners were away.

"Lady Meliora," Mrs. Mountfaucon explained to her guests, "was a little worried because she had the mastiff, Hector, with her, a really magnificent creature, you know, such a tremendous thoroughbred and as gentle as a lamb, but really a little large for London, don't you think, a mastiff? It seems not quite *fair* to keep him in London."

"Not quite fair," said Toby, "to those of us who have to use the pavements and wish to avoid the sudden glissade that ends in a cracked pelvis. But do come to the point, mother."

"I'm just coming to it, dear. She was worried because her invalid cousin, whom we were going to see, keeps buggeridgers—"

"Budgeri*gars*, mother! Do have some regard for pronunciation if not for decorum."

"Oh dear, have I said something wrong?" Mrs. Mountfaucon put on a hurt, appealing look. "Those little lovebirds, you know." She pretended to disregard him. "Like the most exquisite tiny parakeets—"

"They *are* parakeets," said Toby.

"—and Lady Meliora was afraid they might be afraid of Hector. She didn't, of course, want to agitate the invalid."

"And were they?"

"Oh, but the most dreadful thing happened! You could never imagine . . . Hector, you know, has such a heavy head, the lower jaw especially, and seems to have real difficulty, at least when he is standing up, in closing his mouth."

"Like Ramsay MacDonald," said Toby.

"The awful thing was," she went on, "and Meliora had no idea, that the cousin, who has the most *excruciating* arthritis, sometimes lets the little birds out of their cage so that they can fly about the room, which I may say is so full of potted plants, not really very healthy for an invalid, that they must feel quite at home. It's a regular *jungle*. At the very instant we came in, they were fluttering about the room. Hector was spellbound, and one of them dashed madly into his open mouth. Hector gave a gulp, and the poor little bugger—little love-bird, I mean —just disappeared, all in a flash!"

"Do you mean, mother, that the dog swallowed it?"

"Swallowed it *instantly,* Toby, in a second! We were all too astonished to do anything, it was too sudden. Hector just coughed, and had such an *unbelieving* expression on his face."

Toby laughed.

"Well," he said, "it serves the woman right for keeping filthy little birds in her bedroom and for allowing people with gigantic dogs, deformed at that, by your account, to come and see her. I hope she cuts Lady Meliora off with a shilling—or a brace of budgerigars."

"Oh, but there's no question—"

"Oh come, mother, I'm sure Lady Meliora is a confirmed legacy-hunter."

"Toby, how wicked of you! She's nothing of the sort." She went on to describe the beauties of Lady Meliora's ancestral home, which had just been turned into a holiday hostel for the Young Men's Agnostic Association, and her guests followed her remarks with rapt attention. They

33

obviously had not been invited by Toby: they were too prim. Toby liked genial and quick-witted listeners who would respond to his talk and exchange with him the sort of gossip he liked. He liked artists and dilettanti: he was by way of becoming a painter himself and had an extraordinary knowledge of the history and technique of painting. He liked actresses: there was something theatrical in his nature, as in his mother's; both could appreciate and could sometimes achieve the carefully studied brilliant effect that seems natural and gains immediate applause. And he liked exotics. In those days colored entertainers, singers, and dancers were much in vogue. Toby seemed to know them all. He had even spent some weeks in Harlem.

If his mother entered into the role of hostess like an actress, she always acted as what she was, a lady used to good company, a warm and somehow childlike woman, half naïve and less than half worldly-wise, who might by now have been a grandmother. How delighted she was at dinner one night, when among her, or rather Toby's, guests there were two highly successful and cheerful and at that time famous Negro entertainers called Crichton and Curzon, and when Curzon, or it may have been Crichton, turned to her suddenly, clasped her little white hand in his two great black ones, and said earnestly, in a rich stagey voice full of the deep South—a bay from the bayous, as it were:

"Why, mam, you sho' are jes' de breathing image of ma old mammy way back home. I'll say you two sho' are jes' twin sisters under de skin."

"That's one of the greatest compliments I've ever been paid," said Mrs. Mountfaucon gravely, pressing for a fleeting instant those great Congo fingers, "and I wish I could meet her."

The compliment had its funny side, but it was evidently sincere, even though Curzon's (if it wasn't Crichton's) natural expansiveness had been increased by champagne and the congenial atmosphere, and even though his plantation accent was put on.

FIVE

The innocence of Mrs. Mountfaucon, as I have suggested, went with an incapacity for what may be called business. Although she had grown up in no more luxury than could have been expected in the house of a country clergyman with a no more than moderate living, she had, like many young women of her class in the second half of the nineteenth century, been brought up with no more idea of the management of money than of the ins and outs of conjugal life; but whereas experience of two husbands had taught her something of the latter, she appeared still, in money matters, a trusting and docile virgin. However, her affairs were safely in the hands of a man she sometimes referred to as "my trustee" and sometimes as Mr. Basingfield.

This personage I saw from time to time at Duchess's Gate, a tallish old gentleman with the slenderness, straight back, and flat belly of a young man but with the unsupple movements of an old one. He had uncommon distinction and the most perfectly unaffected manner imaginable. It was a quiet manner, and he was not talkative, though he told interesting stories about people he had known, or known about, in his younger days. His anecdotes, which always had point, were usually about grand or eminent people or their servants. The middle classes, which had been expanding rapidly all through his life, until they had practically absorbed or squeezed out of existence the old upper and lower classes, had evidently either escaped his notice or failed to retain it. One felt therefore that he was living in a world of memory, that is to say, a world of fantasy.

Eustace Basingfield, a widower and childless, had been a friend, when a young man in a cavalry regiment, of Morven Mountfaucon's. This suggested to me a slightly rakish youth, but whatever he had done when young he seemed to have done nothing since, and to have no special interests of any kind, whether in politics, sport, travel, science, or literature. If any of these topics came up in conversation he was not at a loss for one of his pointed anecdotes, and one rarely heard them twice; they would more often be about such persons as Disraeli, the Lord Salisbury who was Prime Minister, Lord Ripon, Mrs. Langtry, Lady Dorothy Nevill, or the Empress Elizabeth of Austria, than about anybody still living. It was not difficult to discern that he was conscious of himself as something of an old beau and that his susceptibility to women was by no means extinct. More than once I saw him looking at my legs with an appraising eye.

Mr. Basingfield was such a good listener that people used to say, "Such a charming man! So very understanding and well-informed, such urbanity, such wonderful manners, so *right* about everything, don't you think?"

Anybody who talked to him was likely to feel more interesting and important than usual. He seemed to share or at least to understand one's prejudices and dear beliefs, and yet there was not the slightest soapiness in his manner. He remained grave and attentive, obviously the perfect trustee, and at suitable moments smiled responsively but discreetly in his neatly trimmed grey beard, while a kindly radiation of lines, like the delicate footprint of some rare and elegant bird, appeared at the corner of his mild blue eye.

In spite of all this, his appearances at Duchess's Gate often seemed to me somewhat phantasmal. One might catch sight of his straight back as he was going upstairs, and one felt that the house was haunted, his movement was so deliberate, so noiseless, so non-attached. Or one might come into the drawing-room and again catch sight of his back as he was looking, with seeming absentmindedness, out of the window, and then one felt that he might be merely one's idea of Mr. Basingfield, might not really be there at all, or might disappear as one approached.

Toby treated him with a respect which he usually reserved, so far as I could see, for persons of great accomplishment in the arts, and politely called him "sir"; but I thought it a little formal of Mrs. Mountfaucon to speak of him always as "Mr." Basingfield, since she had known him for at least a quarter of a century and he had been best man at her wedding to Morven Mountfaucon. Perhaps his quiet courtliness, like that of an old-fashioned diplomat, was a bar to intimacy; and the lack of intimacy helped to maintain what I thought the ghostliness of his presence.

I once had the opportunity of meeting him in a different environment. I went to stay for a few days at a country house in Dorset, and as I seemed, on the first evening, to be the first downstairs after dressing for dinner, I went for a stroll by myself in the garden. At the end of a grass walk, sunk between two tall black yew hedges which made it seem like the bed of a waterless canal, I saw the motionless figure of a man with his back to me. It looked vaguely familiar. He seemed to be surveying the view. For some unknown reason I hesitated to disturb him. Some atavistic instinct drove me to turn aside, and I was about to do so through a convenient archway in the hedge, when Mr. Basingfield, who was still some way off, turned, as if he had seen me with eyes in the back of his head. He at once recognized me and waved to me, and as I came near welcomed me with quiet affability, though, as it turned out, he had no idea that I was even acquainted with our host and hostess, let alone that we should be staying with them at the same time. He was evidently the sort of man who is not easily taken unawares.

"I hope I didn't make you jump," I said, "by suddenly and unexpectedly materializing."

"Not at all," he said. "I heard you coming. I heard your dress rustling." Then, I thought, you must have a supersonic ear, like a bat's, because it isn't made of a rustling kind of material. Inevitably, having alluded to the garment in question, he made some complimentary remark upon it.

He next inquired about how I was getting on with my work at Duchess's Gate.

"I'm sure there's no need to ask how Mrs. Mountfaucon is," he said. "She's so wonderfully equable in her health and temper."

I thought, perhaps mistakenly, that I detected a very faint undertone of irony. Possibly he regarded Susannah Mountfaucon's naïveté, her eagerness, her slightly flamboyant and actressy clothes, her relationship with her son, and so on, as a little absurd; possibly he was hinting to me, "Of course she's a dear, but you and I can't help seeing her little weaknesses and can't help being a little amused by them." Naturally he would have been incapable of *saying* anything like that, even if, as I half-imagined, he might think it and might unbecomingly allow me to guess that he thought it. Whether I was right or wrong, I took faintly against him, but I must say nothing occurred to confirm this tiny suspicion.

"Whom do I find here," I wrote in a letter to Toby, "but that distinguished ghost, Mr. Basingfield." This pleased Toby, and afterwards, whenever he spoke to me of Mr. Basingfield, he always referred to him as the Distinguished Ghost. He understood exactly what I meant by Mr. Basingfield's ghostliness and once admitted to me that he never felt absolutely at ease in his presence. He said he didn't really know why, unless it was because the old gentleman had been a friend of his stepfather's.

The presence of his dead stepfather continually made itself felt. One morning on the landing, as I was on my way to the "muniment room," Toby was on his way downstairs.

"Have you ever noticed *that*?" he asked, pointing to the portrait of Morven Mountfaucon in a blazer. "That's my stepfather."

"Oh, I know. Your mother showed it to me ages ago."

"I've no doubt she did."

"Was he really like that?" I asked, peering into the alcove.

"Not when *I* knew him. When *I* knew him he was just a faded soak, with the remains of one of those perfect profiles that the First Cause only bestows as a rule on perfect morons. That kid-glove complexion, if it ever existed, had gone and his face was as mottled as a fritillary.

Drink had disintegrated—I won't say his mind, for he had none; or his character—let's say his personality. He was irritable, he had delusions, he could no longer distinguish between right or wrong, truth or lies."

"Delusions, Toby? What kind of delusions?"

"Jealousy. Persecution. Everything, even of grandeur. If he had lived only a little longer I've no doubt he'd have seen nothing but lizards playing violins, and bees in sailor hats playing croquet on the ceiling."

"Poor man!"

"That's what *you* think."

"You've got a Hamlet streak in you, haven't you?"

He recoiled visibly, stared at me with large, approving eyes, and laughed rather abruptly.

"But, Jane, of course I have!"

He looked at me so intently that I felt myself blushing faintly, so I rather sharply said, "But we mustn't stand about analyzing you on the landing. I must go to my papers."

I was half-apprehensive that he would follow me, but he didn't. The whole proceeding with the papers bored him. It would only interest him, he had said, if any of them could be sold for some perceptible sum of money; and probably because his mother never tired of talking about them, he wouldn't talk about them at all.

A day or two later I was talking to her about a discovery of mild interest that I had made among the Mountfaucon papers.

"Oh don't tell Toby about them!" was her first thought. "I'm afraid he might make away with them. Poor Toby, he was dreadfully jealous of his stepfather. Once at Marsh, when Morven—my husband—had dined a little too well (his heart was not very strong, you know, I always thought he must have strained it when rowing at

Eton as a boy) he fell down in the drawing-room, with his head almost in the fire! I shrieked and rushed to rescue him, but Toby cried, 'For God's sake, mother, leave him! Let him burn!' "

She hid her face in her hands, and her shoulders quivered. I took out my handkerchief to dry her tears, but when she took her hands away I saw that she was laughing.

"Of course he didn't really mean it. I'm *sure* he would have helped me if it had been really necessary. I know he hates the smell of anything burning" (she said this quite gravely) "and he has an *unerring* way of doing the right thing in a real emergency, however naughty he may be over little things."

His naughtiness, I suppose, included his habit of snubbing his mother, which I found outrageous until I got used to it. His way of snapping at her was like that of a husband snapping at his wife, and sometimes I used to take her side.

"I think your mother's quite right," I said once quite early in our acquaintance, "and I think you're much too hard on her."

"Thank you," said his mother, "but I assure you I'm quite used to it. He can't help it, he's just like his father. And don't think he really *means* it."

"Of course I mean it, mother, I mean every word of it," he said, with a completely disarming smile.

If she had brought him up in too close an emotional relationship with herself, that may have been unwise; but it was not difficult, after a time, for me to understand how it had come about. Inured first to the caprices of "Daddy," her first husband, and then a good deal tried by the beau, her second, who decayed and was finally sodden, she had grown used to dealing with the foibles and vagaries of a man of her own, a man whom in each case she loved, in her own way, and was loved by. Widowed for the second time, she had probably little idea of the possibility of marrying again, and had transferred to her only son the habit of coping with a difficult man. From what she told me, Toby when still very small had shown traits like his father's, and she had dealt with him accordingly. Captain d'Arfey had had that kind of independence, that indifference to other people's opinions, which makes for eccentricity, and he had been obstinately impatient of anything like control.

"Poor Daddy," she said to me reminiscently, "there were only three ways to influence him. I learned them soon after we were married. If I pretended to yield to his wishes, I could sometimes bring him round to following mine. Or I could sometimes get him to do what I wanted by pretending that I wanted him to do the opposite. When everything else failed, as an extreme measure, I would let him think that my feelings were hurt. Of course they weren't *really*, he *couldn't* have hurt me, bless him. But I *had* to do that once or twice. . . ."

Marriage can be a wonderful training in diplomacy. The technique which she had so candidly explained had worked well enough with a man old enough to be her father, and whose character had been formed before she was born. When she applied it to her son, it worked again: but it may have had the effect of helping to form him more closely in the image of the father than would otherwise have been the case, so that by now the relationship between herself and Toby was evidently much like that formerly existing between herself and his father. Her deference to Toby's whims, her assiduous attention to his welfare, were very like those of a good young wife to an odd old husband. To say that she had spoiled her son would be superficial; what she had done was unconsciously to train him as a sort of substitute for his father.

What the woman who had uttered the parrot-phrase "mother-fixation" had failed to understand was that the relationship had not at all for Toby the limiting and absorbing singleness that it had for his mother. I should say that he understood it perfectly, accepted it as a *modus vivendi,* and allowed it to continue because he was very fond of his mother and respected her far more than his impatience with her seemed to indicate. He had no wish to deprive her of what had become almost her sole reason for existence, namely, her devotion to himself. Nor did he exploit it. It is possible that by some drastic step like marriage he could have freed himself to some extent from the weight of his mother's devotion, but what would have been the consequences to her?

SIX

Because she now perhaps had nobody to confide in apart from her son (who was apt, as she said, to "bite her head off" if she bored or irritated him), and Mr. Basingfield (with whom I suppose she mainly discussed matters of business), and perhaps Lady Meliora Sperrow (whom I had not yet met), Mrs. Mountfaucon sometimes took me into her confidence about money matters and other private anxieties, and asked my advice.

I had learned to allow for her exaggerations. When for example she said "I'm quite at my wits' end—" I knew that she was too solid a nature ever to be likely to come anywhere near that uncomfortable terminus, and when she added "—about Toby" I knew that she simply wanted to talk to me about her son's future, in the light of his past and present. Like other parents, she wanted her offspring to work, to be happy, to find his proper level in the world, but it was a level which she did not seem to have attempted to define. In his early twenties he had wished to become an opera singer, and his voice had been for a time trained "regardless of expense." An unnecessary diffidence, she explained, had caused him to stop. At present he was bent on painting, and she backed him just as strongly. Too loyal and fond a parent to say anything disparaging about him, she began to make it clear that she did think me capable of having a good influence upon him, and therefore that she thought him in need of such an influence.

"But," I protested, "I shouldn't really feel that I had any right to try and influence him, even if I wanted to. At his age his character must be formed, for better or worse. After all, he's just on thirty."

"Oh, I wish," she exclaimed, clasping and wringing her hands, "I do wish I knew what to do for the best."

Toby had already been through too much money. Even at Eton, it seemed, he had been allowed to run up debts which, for a boy, were too big. When he left Eton he lived at Oxford for a time and was privately tutored. He had refused to be entered at any college, because of some obscure but strong objection of his own to collegiate life. It was at Oxford that there occurred the incident of the motor-bicycle. It illustrates his character, and I have always remembered the way he told it.

"In those days," he said, "there was a make called the Indian. What bikes they were! Heavy, painted bright scarlet, and flashing with gadgets, they were then much used by wild young men dressed in belted trench-coats and gorblimey caps. *I* was a wild young man, and I felt I must have one too, so I wired to mother in London to order one for me and have it sent. And so it happened that one fine afternoon in Oxford I found myself all ready to get on to the thing. I had had it filled up with the usual fluids at a local garage, and in the presence of admiring bystanders I established myself in the saddle. Not only had I never ridden a motor-bike, except as a passenger, but I'm the least mechanical of men. The workings of the thing had been explained to me, but they might as well have been explained to a stone wall. All that interested me was the big new machine and my really furious appetite for power and speed.

"After a flying start, which caused some alarm and shrieking among the passers-by, I accelerated, forgot how to slacken speed, and accelerated more. If I'd been seated on a runaway stallion (and I felt I was) I could hardly have found the way clearer before me. The Israelites crossing the Red Sea can't have had a clearer passage. Cars, carts, pedestrians, dogs, telegraph boys, elderly cripples, all curled back from my approach in waves. I had the feeling of speed all right, but hardly of power, for I hadn't the faintest idea how to control the thing.

"Away I flew down the Woodstock road, clinging for dear life to the handlebars. In no time I was far from the dreaming spires, and suddenly, with horror, I saw racing toward me—a village school! The children, as village schoolchildren did in those days, were drifting into the road in twos and threes and little straggling groups as they came out of school. Hearing a thunderbolt approaching, they gaped, hesitated, scattered, and were about to make me the leading man in a second massacre of the innocents.

"Wondering whether to rush them with my eyes closed, or whether, with my eyes open, to rush the hedge, which would have been suicide, I saw at that instant a massive pair of trophied stone gateposts drawing near so rapidly that they were expanding in my face like toy balloons. The gates were open! The children were saved! I managed to swerve in through the gateway like a trapeze-artist going through a hoop, and in the smallest possible fraction of a second my brain photographed the amazed and terrified and outraged face of the lodge-keeper's wife. I found myself, with some feeling of relief, flying like a rocket up a vast and fortunately deserted avenue. But far more portentous than a village school, there now loomed up before me—a Vanbrugh palace! Loomed? No, it was charging me, façade on, full tilt—and, horror of horrors, a ducal tea-party was in progress out of doors in front of that grand, that enormous façade. 'Swerve, Toby, swerve!' I said to myself, and did so, but the sense of gate-crashing caused a rush of politeness to the head. My instinct was to take off my hat in passing and to bow the apologies which I couldn't possibly stop to make; but even before I'd left Oxford my hat had hurtled away from me in the wind of my own speed (Shelley, I think?) and in any case I didn't dare let go of the handlebars; so I bowed, forcing an apologetic smile that may have looked like a leer, and vanished beyond the end of the house.

"The noble tea-drinkers and their guests, of whom I had had an uncommonly fleeting impression, with cups half-way to mouths, with cucumber sandwiches poised unbitten, and looking at one another with a wild surmise, can hardly have had time to say 'An escaped lunatic, presumably,' when my scarlet Indian and I burst into sight again beyond the opposite end of the house, which I'd circumnavigated, I'm prepared to bet, more rapidly than anybody had ever done before. Again I bowed, again I leered, and in a flash I roared out of sight. It was only then that I began to gain some elementary notion of how to go quicker or slower, so I got back to Oxford at last with no more blood on the wheels than that of a hare that I'd overtaken."

"I wish I'd seen you bowing," I said. "How right your mother was when she told me that you always do the right thing in an emergency."

"Mother is so romantic," he said, but was evidently not displeased at having this chivalrous trait attributed to him.

Mrs. Mountfaucon told me that he had soon tired of the motor-bicycle, and of Oxford too. He had had none of the makings of a scholar, no wish to qualify for any profession or worldly career, and had been much less interested in undergraduates than in the great world outside, with its lavish and various promises of aesthetic and amorous adventure.

His first journey abroad, soon after the First World War, and apart from a short visit to Paris, had been a wild-goose chase to which Mr. Basingfield had given his perhaps necessary assent, Toby then not being yet of age, but not, I understand, much encouragement. This was an expedition to the Baltic States to buy jewelry from Tsarist refugees. According to Toby, these displaced persons were then supposed to have their pockets full of diamond tiaras, ropes of pearls, gem-studded ikons, and Fabergé Easter-eggs made of entire rubies and filled with emeralds, or vice versa, all of which they were supposed to be ready to sell for the bare needs of a few weeks. He had arrived in Riga in a prodigious beaver-lined coat with an astrakhan collar which his mother had bought for him, and there he gave wild parties which were attended by sharpers and adventuresses of various nationalities and in various stages of recklessness and adroit parasitism, parties lubricated with quantities of schnapps, vodka, and Danziger Goldwasser.

From this expedition, so Mrs. Mountfaucon told me, he came back in high spirits, without the fur coat, which he had given away, and bringing home a harvest consisting mainly of a rivière of sapphires that turned out to be false, a Byzantine chalice, an improper snuffbox of fine workmanship, and a malachite vase that stood five feet high on a porphyry base, and so could hardly have been brought out of Russia by a refugee.

"Lydia Delap, I'm afraid you must have heard of her, *begged* him for the snuffbox, and he gave it to her. I don't want to misjudge her, but oh, I *wished* he'd never met her! The chalice was *exquisite* and quite genuine, it was really clever of him to have got it, and the proceeds of the sale—for it was of course snapped up by Gundelfinger —the *superb* Gundelfinger collection which, as you know, has just been left to the V. and A.—it paid, I think, for nearly half the expense of his journey, which had turned out to be a good deal more than we'd expected, because of the entertaining he of course had to do."

"And the malachite vase?"

"Oh, Jane, it's still in his bedroom! He couldn't bear to part with it. You must ask him to show it to you. He hates me to go into his bedroom, but I must confess—oh, but don't tell him I told you!—that when it had been there a couple of years I looked inside and found he'd been using it as a waste-paper basket. It was nearly half full of unpaid bills, mostly from his tailors and the frame-makers, and mostly, oh dear, *unopened*!"

SEVEN

During the nineteen-twenties, which coincided with his own twenties, Toby had often traveled, especially in France, Spain, Italy, and Greece, also in North Africa, and once as far as Bali and Cambodia. His traveling, like his equally various reading, had been capricious, the expression of an insatiable and romantic appetite for experiences and impressions, not part of the carrying out of any ambitious purpose or methodical plan. His restlessness was evidently that of the neurotic who continually expects more of life than it is likely to give—or to give without exacting a heavy price.

The nineteen-twenties were not pre-eminent for restraint on the part of those who were young, independent in character and fortune, free of responsibility, and inclined to move in the new international Bohemia. To that sphere, I was interested to learn, Toby had been introduced by Lydia Delap, whom his mother still continued to wish he had never met.

Lydia was about ten years older than Toby. She was,

49

I suppose, typical of the twenties; but one can't isolate a decade, one must look back always to see what went to the making of it and of its typical representatives. What went to the making of Lydia is a matter of conjecture. She was brought up by the Arthur Delaps as their niece. It was variously alleged that she was an illegitimate daughter of Arthur Delap, of his wife, or his wife's sister. Lilac Evans had some bound volumes of a defunct illustrated paper, *My Ladye's Mirror,* and she once showed me a full-page photograph in the volume for 1907. In the background were a kind of loggia with a good deal of fancy white-enamelled trellis-work, an imitation Louis Quinze sofa, and two or three palms in *art nouveau* jardinières. In the foreground was a lily-pond, congested with lilies and with a punt afloat upon it. In the punt were Lydia and Mrs. Delap, their bare shoulders emerging from cloudy swathings of white tulle. They were sitting in a studied pose probably meant to display elegance and suggest mutual affection. What it did show was a falsely soulful unanimity of interest in a water-lily which seemed to be larger than the rest. In this photograph they looked like sisters. Not only were they dressed alike, not only did they have the same wasp-waists, not only was their hair equally abundant and piled up in the same way, but they had the same tipped-up impertinent noses, the same round and too prominent chins, the same hungry little mouths.

"And yet," said Lilac, "I know for a fact that they're not related to one another in any way. Just two period types reflecting one another, and the period."

Because they were looking downwards their eyes were hidden. Each wore an affectedly yearning expression, yearning and yet somehow aggressive, as if after fawning upon the water-lily they were going to devour it. At that time they were still on speaking terms. The final break, it seems, did not come until soon after 1914.

Delap was an Englishman and a gentleman, a Conservative full of radical ideas, extremely conventional in some ways but with a vein of cynicism. His outspokenness was said to have spoiled his career as a politician. His wife had inherited a fortune from her father, an Australian wool-millionaire. She was said to have had large social ambitions, and I noticed that *My Ladye's Mirror* had called her "one of the new leaders of Society." Apparently childless, she seems to have set herself to form Lydia in her own image. They had seemed much alike in character as well as in looks. Was it just because they were so much alike that Lydia had revolted? Whatever gentle or grateful feelings she had ever had toward Mrs. Delap had gradually turned, perhaps because of a sense of rivalry, to hatred, and this had produced in time a complete inversion in her of Mrs. Delap's conventionality.

Just before the 1914 war Mrs. Delap had maneuvered Lydia into an engagement to a highly "suitable" young man. At almost the last moment Lydia broke it off. She was of age, had come into money of her own, and now declared herself independent. Here is her subsequent development so far as I have been able to reconstruct it. During the 1914 war she was for a short time a nurse, not, as might have been expected, attending upon convalescent officers in a country house, but upon wounded Lascar seamen in a small improvised hospital in the East End. She was seen occasionally dancing at the Ritz with "foreigners," generally minor Latin American diplomats, and was much gossiped about by women who envied her looks, energies, and opportunities. Before the war was over she had hardened, or softened, into what was then still called a Bohemian, but she didn't know that in defy-

51

ing convention she had adopted a new convention: she wore her emancipation like a uniform.

By this time she was living openly with a consumptive sculptor, half-Chinese and half-Hungarian, of mediocre talent and small means. Art, or artiness, offered her just the kind of life she wanted, and she had soon surrounded herself with a raggle-taggle of "advanced" tyros or failures in the arts, would-be aesthetes, and half-baked intellectuals, for the most part male, or ostensibly male, rather than female, though she had for a time an ambiguously close friendship with a young woman of striking appearance, who died of taking drugs, said to have been obtained through one of Lydia's rehabilitated Lascars. In those days Lydia subsidized concerts of Burmese or Patagonian music, exhibitions of bad expressionist painting, and a coterie magazine. Then she published a novel, *Poisoned Milk,* which contained a ferocious sketch of Mrs. Delap, her strained relations with whom thereupon snapped apart for good.

Lydia's exotic tastes soon took her to Paris, where she entered with appetite into the feverish equivalent there of her life in London. She had a fatal attraction for the more effete of the younger American expatriates, to whom she became a sort of broody, fascinating, and corruptive elder sister. She was to be seen often at the Dôme or the Deux Magots, surrounded by a little court of pretentious noodles. There she sat, looking like an expelled schoolgirl, her abundant red hair now bobbed, a beehive hat clamped over her eyes, and her skirts above the knees in the fashion of the time. And she used to wear a longish necklace of parti-colored, irregularly shaped, and rough-hewn semi-precious stones, which looked, according to Lilac Evans, "exactly like a collection of half-sucked sweets." Elbows on the table, she displayed her plump arms and smoked a dark brown "Russian" cigarette in a long holder, sitting always with her head tilted back and her snub nose and big chin up, exposing her fat white throat, and talking in a purring, yearning voice. She would quote half a line from Baudelaire or Donne, and then pause for effect, as if she had said something original.

In her next novel, *Bones of Wonder*, Mrs. Delap, although only a minor character, was again whipped at the cart's tail. The style had become more oblique and affected, and a good deal of cosmetic prose was plastered on to suggest the ineffable. I suppose her books are forgotten now, but I happen to have a copy of *Bones of Wonder*. Here is a passage from it chosen almost at random. It is the beginning of a love scene, and the setting is an ancient and apparently disused china-clay pit somewhere in France:

Waited again in that airy amphitheater of wonder. Just waited. . . . *Mage ou ange,* Shelley would have recognized him. Yes, and the essential mystery of that glutinous soil, no longer used for the winged porringers and loving-cups which the Merovingian nobles, fabulous ancestors of his, saw and approved on their great tables of elm-wood. Sap once in wood, hearts now as ever of earth, the sword against the thigh. . . . *"Yet once more, gracious hope . . ."*

And so, by the mystery path, you wound towards him, brushed by myrtles. They were in the conspiracy too. Whispered for you against the old Madam. "That nurse of vipers," he had called her. You pressed on. The dew saluted you with its tiny heliographs. You smelt the aroma of history, pressed with eager feet the old potters' earth, Merovingians forgotten now. You remembered only the turn of his wrist, the tassel of hair lifted by the wind, his ear, Antinous-shell, the way it joined his head, the small lobes. *She* knew where you were going, a witch divining from afar. And was impotent. The pin of your hatred stuck in the clay model of her figure, overblown and beginning to wither. If joy could curse— ! He waited. And you climbed. And the morning gilded your way with its flutes and violoncellos of light. Nearer now. *Et ses secrets affolants pour chaque vice—et sa gaieté effrayante.* . . . Alone, fierce, visible in the potters' amphitheater in the gilt gay morning, the dew on the cistus, the sap rising . . . He had seen you. *Douceurs* . . .

Even from this affected twaddle it is easy to guess the identity of "the old Madam" or "witch divining from afar," but it is not so easy to say what the novel is really about. The setting is mostly a Roman ruin in Provence, from which various mystical influences emanate and act upon the lives of a troop of nebulous and precious young persons with no visible means of subsistence and with names like Cyprian, Liselinda, and Turlough. These influences are only understood by a vamp-like female seer, the Countess Pelda. This name is a transparent anagram of the name Delap. How like Lydia to represent herself as a countess, and how in that she made me think of Mrs. Mountfaucon's poor dotty maid, Laceman! Indeed there must have been a real streak of housemaidishness in Lydia, whose whole life seems to have been given to wrapping herself in a mostly spurious glamour. What was she, after all, but a "little Dolly Daydreams?"

This Countess Pelda in the novel is a narcissistic, much heightened version of Lydia as she would have liked to be. She takes opium; murmurs tags from Sappho or, as we have seen, from Rimbaud; devises magic rites to bring Cyprian and Company into rapport with the buried past and with one another; associates herself with an arty, glamorous, and housemaidishly imagined "great lover"— the very one who was awaiting her in the "potters' amphitheater"—and yearns and gushes and twaddles and yearns again. The reviewers treated *Bones of Wonder,* and indeed Lydia's other novels, with ludicrous respect, so that intelligent readers, who had dipped into them and dipped out again pretty quickly, began to wonder if perhaps they hadn't missed something, if perhaps Lydia Delap might not show a promise, an achievement even, that they had quite failed to perceive. That her novels were always quickly remaindered suggested, to such readers, that Lydia had perhaps "got something" after all.

I think it was in Paris that Lydia had first gained a hold over the young Toby. Having in my time heard him talk about her, and Mrs. Mountfaucon about the two of them, and having heard the views of various people who knew them both when they first got to know each other, I have a clear picture of Toby with a freshness and eagerness about him which Lydia set herself to sophisticate in her own way, even perhaps to smirch a little, not out of wickedness—since she was evidently not wicked but silly —but for the mischievous fun of it, if fun is the word. I doubt if she ever did anybody much harm. The persons who came under her influence, or rather stayed under it, were silly in the same sort of way as herself. They flocked together and enjoyed their games of make-believe, seeing themselves not as preciosities of small talent and great irresponsibility, but as an interestingly emancipated "lost generation," boasting, with an almost arrogant self-pity, of their alleged perdition as if it was something to be proud of. And now, even if it is obvious, let me declare it. I hated the thought of Lydia as much as Toby hated the thought of his stepfather. I was jealous of her hold over Toby. In a way I still am.

Toby had far more in him than most of her protégés and she was quite clever enough to recognize it. She saw him, I think, as a younger male counterpart of herself— as a young man with a solid English background, with money, without ties or any apparent responsibilities; full of appetite and unborn poetry and embryonic talent; eager for sensations, for knowledge, and for what she would have called freedom. (To judge from her books, especially the one called *Off Limits,* a "free soul," as she termed her idealized young men and women, was somebody with the leisure and inclination to devote himself or herself to self-dramatization and self-indulgence in that arty convention in which Lydia, as an enemy of "convention," had become absorbed.) At any rate, she purred and yearned at Toby, encouraged him to drink, introduced him to all her court of exotics and ineffectuals, many of whom were notably good-looking and some of whom were tending steadily to self-destruction by excesses of one kind or another and liked to involve others in their courses. But she also did him good, brought him out and gave him a new confidence, and put him in touch with some lively French brains and talents, with people who really loved, cultivated, and knew about the arts and who were fountains of the best gossip, past and present. When she saw him gravitating towards them and preferring them to her inferior intimates and, it sometimes seemed, to herself, she grew more possessive.

For a time Toby had been pleased and excited by her acceptance of him, her fawning affection, her real kindness and usefulness to him, by the trouble she took to amuse and interest and encourage him, and by her own personality, which after all was by no means without charm. But inside him was a bone, not "of wonder," but of hard common sense, derived perhaps from his mother and her sound North Country forebears, the Underhays. In those moments, more frequent as he grew older, when the lids of his eyes came half down over that cold, judging look of his (the very look that had been caught and held in the white-tie portrait at Duchess's Gate) the bone of common sense had, so to speak, made itself felt; and Toby began to see through everything and everybody that had been amusing him.

Lydia, I suppose, had quickly perceived what may be called the emotional cat's-cradle between Toby and his mother, whom she had never yet met. She probably judged it as an exact parallel with her own relationship to Mrs. Delap; certainly it had soon become her dearest wish to set him completely against and to detach him from Mrs. Mountfaucon. What Lydia failed to understand (for her air of subtlety was assumed, an adornment to her vanity, like her necklace of "half-sucked sweets") was that while Toby was tied to his mother by a network of love and hate, she, Lydia, was tied to the aunt or foster-mother she so much resembled by a love which had become hate.

Directly Toby saw what Lydia was after, he rebelled. He loved and admired his mother, and respected her even though he snubbed and snapped at her, and he was loyal to her; whereas whatever he felt for Lydia hardly, I think, included respect. When Lydia wanted to be thought wicked, he thought her rather likeably absurd; but when he saw that she wanted to dominate him he shook her gently off, like an insect. There was no open quarrel, he remained friendly with Lydia, fond of her in a way, and in a way grateful to her, but she had lost for ever any chance of keeping a hold over him, and nowadays they rarely met.

Mrs. Mountfaucon, who had thought it prudent never to question her son's apparent obsession with Lydia, of whom, not without reason, she was deeply suspicious and disapproving, not to say jealous, had been greatly worried by it. When she gathered that it had lapsed she was again prudent and did not rejoice openly for fear that he might, out of obstinacy, go back to her.

Though Lydia had lost Toby, she had made him free of a world where only ennui was taboo. He instinctively recognized the first-rate but could enjoy the society of people who were lively and not hopelessly ordinary. A lifelong flight from constrictive influences in his early life made him at times act recklessly and often enjoy what was flashy or shallow. Memories of the decayed, "baroque" puritanism (as he called it) of the Mountfaucons; oppressive early experiences of the wet-Sunday-afternoon side of English life; a sneering laugh from his housemaster's daughter at Eton when he had uttered some solecism about cricket—such things had driven him to rejoice in hard gaiety or spurious brilliance, in unusual ways of life, loose though they might be, in emancipated or outlandish people, in foreign places of which foreignness was sometimes the only outstanding quality. In painting and music he responded only to what was good of its kind, and in the long run he only loved people who were free from the intolerable burden of preoccupation with themselves.

I have admitted that jealousy of Lydia was a bond between Mrs. Mountfaucon and myself. That amounts to an admission that I had begun to take an interest in what happened to Toby. In those days I had not formed so full and detailed a picture of Lydia and her part in Toby's life as that I have just given, but if my view of her then was sketchier it was accurate as far as it went. Mrs. Mountfaucon knew, and I knew, that Lydia was still about, and we knew that Toby's loyalties and impulses were incalculable. His manner to me was such that I thought he might, shall I say, just care whether I was alive or dead. But in my heart of hearts I was damned if I was going to be a steadying influence or any kind of influence upon him at all. I liked being with him, partly because he showed no signs of making any "demands" upon me. I had had enough of "demands," for the time being at all events, in my still recent marriage.

EIGHT

Among other things that Mrs. Mountfaucon and I had in common was our interest in the past and our particular interest in the family papers. When I began to realize that she was rather a lonely woman I encouraged her to come into the muniment room from time to time, so that I could explain to her how I was getting on. She could not help me with the work itself, the sorting and deciphering and so on, but she could answer usefully questions about the pedigrees and possessions of the d'Arfey and Mount-faucon families, and she knew a good deal about English history and heraldry.

I used to get her sometimes to come and sit beside me at the big desk, and she seemed to be enjoying herself when I showed her some deed I had unearthed and read it to her, or some document with a little human touch that she herself would not have been able to read, because of its antiquity and her lack of training. Some things—manorial surveys, parish surveyors' presentments, details

59

of lawsuits about property—were often pretty dry, but as soon as we came upon anything of more direct social or personal interest, she kindled at once. Some item from, say, a mid-sixteenth-century petty constable's vagrancy return would interest her as much as it interested me, and when we came to estate accounts or household inventories of any period, she was enthralled. I was delighted that the past was so real to her, and her pleasure took away some of the depression that still clung to me as a result of my unlucky marriage.

"It's rather sad," I remarked, "that Toby is completely indifferent to all this."

"Don't blame him, Jane; he can't help it. He has in fact a tremendous sense of the past, but he says it's entirely what he calls aesthetic. He'll *dote* on some beautiful object from the past, especially if it has nothing to do with his own family—and oh, *far* more if it has nothing to do with his stepfather's family. Pictures, furniture, tapestry, china, jewelry, buildings, books, music—all *that* he loves, but a pedigree enrages him and I simply daren't allude to a coat of arms. It's as if he wants to forget and get away from it all, all the wonderful tradition of it. Oh why *is* it, I wonder? Perhaps if he were married and had children of his own he would have more of the sense of things handed on, all the precious memories of the past. Ah, but never mind, he's very like Daddy in many ways, he's a real d'Arfey, and I love him dearly. . . . But now tell me, Jane, as far as you've gone, do you think there's anything here we can *sell*? I should hate to part with a single scrap of paper, but I'm afraid that's all that interests Toby."

I said I did not think that any of the papers I had so far examined were of any market value. I said they seemed co me interesting as a collection of family archives and it would be a pity if they could not be preserved intact.

"My dear Jane, if I were dead Toby would give them to the dustman. . . . Of course there's always Mildred."

"?"

"Mildred Purbind. A kind of collateral on her mother's side. Toby can't bear her, but she's very proud of the d'Arfey connection."

"Has she got children?"

"Only a daughter, rather strangely named Gwinifred, which was certainly never a d'Arfey name. But I suppose one daughter's better than nothing. When you think of the enormous families the d'Arfeys and even more the Mountfaucons were having not so very long ago, it does seem odd that they should have tapered away as they have. Toby flies into a rage if he hears me say anything like that. He says there's nothing but trouble ahead, that there'll be another war quite soon, and that *he* wouldn't bring children into a world like this. . . . When I asked about the possibility of selling some of these deeds and things, I didn't want you to think that we're exactly needy. But Toby plans to travel and paint, and he loves entertaining, and I should hate him not to have what he needs, and there seems to be some kind of crash in America, where we have a good deal of our money in a factory for making some kind of stoppers for bottles, and Mr. Basingfield fears that it may take a hard knock—not that it's *his* fault, I'm sure; the money was invested there on the *best* advice. Fortunately there are signs of the Rembrandt coming shortly to the boil, and crash or no crash, the Americans, they say, will give *anything* for a Rembrandt."

I had not heard much lately about the Rembrandt, but from this time onwards it became one of the main topics of conversation at Duchess's Gate. Mrs. Mountfaucon was so much occupied with the various negotiations in connection with the picture that she paid no more visits to me upstairs for some time, and Toby was away in Paris.

The room where I sat had become heavily impregnated with that smell I love, the smell of old papers and parchments and boxes and cases, of old drynesses and dampnesses, old ink, old bones, old stones and dust, like the smell of an old church. With its tinge of mortality and its hint of secrets to be discovered and many more secrets never to be discovered, it had long been as exciting to me as the smell of hot sand must be to an Egyptologist; but now it seemed to me melancholy. I began to find it difficult to concentrate. Sometimes I would get up and go and look at my face in the glass over the chimneypiece. I asked it questions without words, and got the kind of answers such questions invite. Yet I cannot say I was altogether displeased with my appearance. Or my eye would range round the room and rest on a uniform-case which had belonged to Morven Mountfaucon and which I knew (for I had looked into it) was full of rubbishy letters and bills and advertisements hoarded by his parents and grandparents at Cheveley and Holderfield, together with frequent and elaborate prescriptions of medicines of a decidedly drastic kind; or on an obsolete hatbox which had accompanied Toby's father to the Crimea and now had an air of extreme antiquity. Or I would go to the window and stand between the red-and-white striped curtains and look out at the plane trees, and a mixture of sadness and restlessness seemed to be taking hold of me. I couldn't shake it off. The prosperous hum of traffic sounded futile. Time seemed to be slipping away. The future seemed full of vague menace. Was there something the matter with me, or with the world, or both? I don't think I am by nature moody or introspective, but at that time I was both. I told Mrs. Mountfaucon that I thought I had better go away to the country for a few weeks.

When I got back to London I felt much better, and on the first day that I returned to Duchess's Gate I lunched alone with Mrs. Mountfaucon and Toby. He was back from Paris in high spirits, even for him. He was in one of his sparkling, mischievous, and to me most engaging moods. I remember that day particularly. It was the day he described the dog, and the description put me in mind, not for the first time and God knows not for the last, of a remark of Voltaire's that my father was always quoting: *C'est le propre de l'esprit humain d'exagérer.*

At luncheon he held forth amusingly about people he had been seeing in Paris. I didn't at all mind the certainty that it was I who was his audience, and that if he had been alone with his mother he would have been far less expansive. We were just finishing coffee in the drawing-room when the Countess reappeared. Fixing her gaze upon some point above our heads, she announced, "Lady Meliora Sperrow is on the telephone." She wore a wry expression as if she found it distasteful to have to carry a message from someone over whom she felt she took precedence.

"Oh dear!" cried Mrs. Mountfaucon in panic. It cannot have been very rare for her to be rung up by Lady Meliora, but she was always stampeded by the telephone. She belonged to a generation for which it had once been a novelty, and seemed never to have got used to it. Although she must have used it every day for many years she still seemed to regard its ringing as an alarm, and whenever she took up the receiver she raised her voice unnaturally. "What *can* she want, I wonder?" she now asked. "Is it for me?"

To this quite unnecessary question the Countess gave a chilly assent.

"Meliora is a *dear*," Mrs. Mountfaucon declared with a sweeping gesture as she backed rapidly away from us, "but I'm afraid she may keep me some time. Do forgive me!" And she turned and sprinted, head down, out of the room.

"We shall be lucky," said Toby, "if we see mother again in the next half-hour."

"Does Lady Meliora often come here?" I asked inquisitively.

"Quite often, I dare say, as soon as my back's turned."

"Tell me about her," I said. "I think I've heard nothing about her since she had that mishap with a large dog."

"Ah, but she once had one of her own. It was called Elsie. It was years ago. Mother for some reason forced me to go by myself to see Meliora. She lived then in the region of Holland Park. The door was opened by a maid with a hare-lip and I was shown into a drawing-room furnished, I should think, in the nineties by Shoolbred's. One could hardly move, it was so crammed with photographs in silver frames, coffee-tables of Benares brass, man-sized vases full of bulrushes and pampas grass, standard lamps with flounced shades, footstools, beaded fire-screens, and watercolors of Malvern and Grindelwald. I remember also seeing *The High Churchman's Kalendar,* and a wooden plaque that hung by the fireplace. On it was written in poker-work:

> 'Just keep smiling,
> Let things rip,
> Only apples
> Should have the pip.'

64

"I was so shocked that I learned it by heart and I've never forgotten it.

"There was a frightful stink in the room, so I made for the window. It was like an obstacle race. Then I noticed in an armchair a dirty black bundle tied up in an old shawl with motheaten fringes. Ah, I thought, throw-outs from Meliora's wardrobe—or perhaps her weekly washing, waiting for the van from the laundry. Suddenly the bundle moved! I shrank back in alarm, and I saw that it was alive! It had a head, and it was training a pair of weary and reproachful eyes upon me—eyes of an impure gamboge. They had a look at once deeply resentful and falsely soulful, like the eyes of somebody pretending to listen to a Beethoven quartet but thinking about an assessment for income tax. The brown of the eyes seemed to have run into the whites, which were too much exposed; the inflamed lower lids had sagged. The same looseness had affected the monster's lower lip, a wet and piebald lip which hung inside out, and from which slowly descended two thin stalactites of saliva, like steel knitting-needles, into what might have been a bundle of unfinished knitting.

"The whole organism gave out a sound between a wheeze and a groan, heaved itself on to its feet, and lowered itself towards the carpet. From either side of the head fell two long ears, like strips of ravaged fur, revealing the creature to have once been a spaniel of some kind. Its ears were the first part of it to reach the floor, and the smell at once became much stronger, so I recoiled, so far as the exuberant fancy of Shoolbred's would allow me, into a corner. The rest of the dog, amorphous and obese, began to pour slowly down after its ears, but as its forelegs couldn't support the weight, it made a crash-landing, and lay for a second or two ignominiously out of control, with its behind swaying over its head. It then heaved itself up on four tufted feet from which protruded long earthy claws, like a bird's. It then began to scramble —slightly faster, I may say, than its aroma—in the direction of the door, holding out behind it a tail like a dirty and bedraggled feather, which looked as if it had been used as a pipe-cleaner."

"Poor old thing," I couldn't help saying.

"Poor old thing? The sound of its breathing was like the death-rattle of a tubercular hippopotamus. Its claws clicked and scraped on the parquet, the door opened, and in came Meliora. We had tea off one of the Benares tables, and it was then that I learned that the creature was called Elsie. Reeking to high heaven, and agitating her filthy tail, she heaved herself up on her hindquarters and put her forepaws on my thigh. In the shadow of the table I could see her eyes looking up at me—pleading, gluttonous, bloodshot, Landseer eyes—and I could feel her long claws slipping and clutching at my trousers, as if she was trying to dig out my thighbones. I tried to kick her in the belly, and failed. I looked my sharpest daggers at her, and she merely wagged her tail harder than ever."

"Dogs always know," I remarked, to tease him, "bitches particularly, when a man has a better nature that can be got round."

"You're telling me! . . . But beside Elsie, let me tell you, a skunk would have been attar of roses. 'Here!' I said sharply, 'don't you tear my new trousers!' Elsie made no attempt to get down, but looked deeply hurt. So did Meliora.

" 'Come, Elsie,' she said, 'you know you mustn't worry visitors. Soon be chocky time for a good little gel.'

"Emetic, don't you think? Elsie took no notice whatever. With my right hand I passed my cup for more tea; I put my left on Elsie's head and pressed hard. The forelegs began to slip, and with a flop and thud she collapsed on the floor. Then, stumbling over her ears, and trailing rattling fringes—she seemed to be caked underneath with dried mud like a sheep—she waddled over to the hearthrug, followed slowly by her effluvium.

" 'Elsie adores really *thin* bread-and-butter,' said Meliora, 'and really milky tea,' and she took a quantity of both over to the hearthrug. Elsie was a loud eater and polished off her victuals in no time. Then she rolled over on to her back, displaying a bald, distended stomach, mottled with patches of black and whitish pink, like some bad 'modernistic' pattern, and in texture like the skin of some dreadful cave-dwelling lizard. This posture, according to Meliora, meant that it was chocolate-time. She then gave Elsie two or three chocolates out of a box.

" 'I sometimes think,' she said, 'of all the poor dogs in Russia. It's dreadful, isn't it, but Elsie is so plucky, and I expect they are too.'

"I said that a friend of mine just back from Russia had been greatly struck by the care taken of stray dogs: they were put in convalescent kennels, centrally heated, and given special diets, sun-ray treatment, and massage. The word 'massage,' you know, generally kindles a spark in arthritic old ladies on whom there have been few, if any, to lay hands, at least for a good long time—or to fondle, for that matter, with a barge-pole.

" 'I only hope it's true,' said Meliora, 'but that's not at all what *I've* heard.'

"Later she condoled with mother for having a Bolshevik son and said she would pray for me. Mother told her that it was the first she'd heard of it and that I must have been pulling her leg. Then I told mother that if I had been looking for legs to pull I should have chosen one rather fresher and plumper and more elastic. And there the matter rested."

He looked beamingly at me to see what effect this story had had on me. I didn't say "I don't believe a word of it." I didn't say "C'est le propre de l'esprit humain d'exagérer." I didn't congratulate him on his virtuosity in description. I didn't say that I didn't know whether to be amused or horrified. Because he looked so eager and boyish I couldn't have carped at him. I laughed and said, "But you've told me a good deal more about Elsie than about Lady Meliora. I can't help wondering what your mother has in common with her. After all, your mother doesn't keep a dog, and I don't believe she's particularly fond of dogs."

"She's not particularly fond of women either, as a rule, but she loves Meliora. Mother's a country parson's daughter; Meliora is the daughter of a bishop. They go to the same church, and they get together over good works or something, but not when I'm about. One must draw the line somewhere."

"You seem to draw a good many lines round your poor mother."

"Oh, she likes it. She says my father did exactly the same. She's used to it. . . . But as she seems to be glued to the telephone come upstairs to the room I paint in— not that I've got anything worth showing you."

That was a moment of triumph for me: his mother had told me that he couldn't bear to show anybody his paintings. I followed him upstairs to a bare upper room.

He propped one of his own canvases on an easel. It was a landscape, a glade in a wood with a green glow. It looked like a copy of a Courbet.

"It might almost be a Courbet!" I said.

What was even more extraordinary was that he replaced it with a Manet-like still-life, again painted with much more than ordinary skill, and then with a picture of an old actress at a dressing-table, painted freely in the manner of Daumier.

"That's all I have to show you at the moment." He fidgeted nervously.

"I'd no idea," I said, "that you had such technical skill. You show me what might almost be a Courbet, then a near-Manet, then almost a Daumier, wonderfully well painted, all three of them. But what you haven't shown me is a picture really painted out of your own self. Perhaps you've never yet really lost yourself, so you haven't yet found yourself."

He looked at me intently for a moment with his head on one side.

"Probably true," he said.

"These pictures are real feats," I said, "but feats, it seems to me, of acting."

I couldn't judge whether he had it in him to be a painter, or whether he was perhaps too sociable and volatile. Perhaps the white-tie Toby of the portrait in the drawing-room was too strong, with its love of theaters and films and parties and smart women and smart gossip. Perhaps he needed the immediate response that he got in conversation, the electric contact between speaker and hearer over an elaborate dinner-table. Perhaps he was frightened of that silence which hollows out theaters and drawing-rooms when plays and parties are over. Perhaps to be alone in a bare upper room with a blank canvas and an unformulated impulse was a test he could not pass.

"Jane, my dear," he said, with a sudden and all too recognizable thickening of the voice, which at once put me on my guard, "I didn't know you knew so much about painting."

"I don't know much," I said airily, "but I had a cultivated father, and he tried to cultivate his children. He was very disappointed to see me taking to what he called a lot of grubby old parchments."

"And not only painting. You know far more about me than anybody else knows—"

"Oh nonsense, Toby."

"Far more than I know myself."

"Nonsense!"

"Jane—" He seized me by the hand, and his face suddenly loomed at mine, the eyes enormous and disquietingly intense. I had a moment of panic and snatched my hand away. It was a triumph I didn't want. Or did I? I didn't want it just then: that much I did know. It was on the tip of my tongue to make the cheaply obvious remark about not having come upstairs to see his etchings— how he would have hated me if I had.

The moment of panic passed; I didn't want to hurt his feelings; I didn't want to lose him.

"Toby! We must go down again—your mother will be wondering where we are."

He followed me out of the room and shut the door.

"A poor excuse," he said, "and it won't prevent me returning to the subject later."

NINE

"The only thing that interests me at the moment," Toby announced two days later, "is the Rembrandt, how soon it's going to be sold, and for how much. Then I can really settle down to paint. I need the money, to feel really free."

It is true that his mother was present, but I had imagined that there was something else in his mind. Since my visit to the painting room he had almost completely hidden from me the feelings which seemed to have driven him to make a pass at me. I say "almost," because although we had not since then been alone for a moment, he had followed me obsessively with his eyes. The extraordinary thing was that he had made no attempt to see me alone, or even to telephone to me. I tried to behave as if nothing had happened. I dare say he took this for a kind of coquettishness. I dare say it was.

And now I seemed to catch Mrs. Mountfaucon looking at me rather inquiringly. After all, she would probably have detected at once in another woman any flutterings of responsiveness to her son.

"At the moment, Toby dear," she said, "we can only wait and see. I've done all I can. I'm quite worn out with

all that has had to be done. You had better put the picture out of your mind for the next week or two. One never
knows, nothing may come of it at all."

"We *must* have the money, mother."

"Well, dear, if the worst comes to the worst, there
are always the cottages at Crotchester." She turned to me
with a sweet smile. "A little house-property," she politely
explained, "a sort of tiny nest-egg."

"Tiny indeed, mother. A sort of mare's-nest-egg. The
cottages must be worth quite twopence-farthing. Whereas
from *Susannah and the Elders,* if it hadn't been for this
dégringolade on Wall Street, we might have expected a
good round sum."

When he glanced at me, as if for support, I was aware
of his glance but didn't show it; I must have appeared to
be gazing absently out of the window. In fact I was far
from absent. My mind had gone skating away towards an
imaginary scene with two participants, Toby and myself—
a scene that was dreadfully hackneyed, the scene in which
a man makes love to a woman, whereupon she has the
delicate task of saying, and meaning, or thinking that she
means, that she "isn't having any." I found my lips moving as I began to compose an imaginary sentence something like this: "I can't tell you how touched I am, how
proud really and grateful. You know, Toby, that I'm very
fond of you—how could I *not* be? And I hope I shall
always be—but it's no good pretending that I feel about
you—well, you know, quite *that way.* . . . It's so much
better not to pretend, isn't it? I'm sure it would be such
a mistake if we just rushed into bed together, found it a
flop, and then found we'd upset the balance of our—well,
our liking for one another." I foresaw Toby taking this
with more resignation than ardent protest, and certainly
not planning at once whatever was the contemporary

equivalent of that safari in which frustrated young men of means sometimes eased their feelings by killing the fauna of tropical countries.

And I confess that I was disappointed at the prospect of his resignedly taking No for an answer. I'm only a woman after all. I had no intention of marrying Toby, or of going to bed with him, but I should have been interested to see him carried away, for at least a measurable distance, by the emotion I appeared to have aroused in him. . . .

At this point in my thoughts I started visibly as I heard Mrs. Mountfaucon say something she never said in my hearing before that moment, or after it:

"Jane! A penny for your thoughts!"

"You should bid higher, mother," said Toby dryly. "You don't flatter her by offering so little. Did you see her jump? It was evidently with shock at your parsimony."

"Not at all, dear," said Mrs. Mountfaucon, who seldom so flatly contradicted her son. "I'm sorry I made Jane jump. I think she jumped because her mind was far away from what we're discussing, far away in some delicious day-dream of her own, and I did what they say one should never do to people who walk in their sleep—I woke her suddenly. Jane, I *am* sorry."

"It's *I* who am sorry," I said, "for seeming so vague." I felt myself blushing, as if my thoughts had been discovered. "As a matter of fact," I lied, "I was wondering how the value of your Rembrandt—of any Rembrandt— could ever possibly be affected by some fluctuation in the stock-market caused, I suppose, by people who've never heard of Rembrandt."

I believe I should have been faced that very afternoon with a "show-down" with Toby, if it had not happened that a curious little train of events reached its climax, a

73

climax that had nothing to do with Rembrandt or the slump but a good deal to do with Toby and myself.

Some weeks before this, Toby had taken it into his head that he wanted to paint a picture of a bevy of stuffed humming-birds in a glass case. At Marsh, in his childhood, there had been just such a thing, and his awakening sensibilities had been strongly excited by the jewel-like little birds. They still haunted his memory, and had lately begun to haunt it insistently. He spent some time searching auction rooms, junk shops, and the Caledonian Market, but could not find what he wanted, so he told all his friends to look out for a case of really dazzling humming-birds and if they saw one to get it for him.

Mrs. Mountfaucon, ever eagerly maternal, had not been backward in spreading word of this desideratum, and among the persons to whom she had made it known was Mildred Purbind, that "kind of collateral" of whom I had heard her speak. Mrs. Purbind sounded quite harmless. She lived in Metroland with a husband who was employed, according to Toby, as "something" in an accountant's office, which Mrs. Mountfaucon referred to as "the Bank"—but then in her scheme of things a goose was automatically promoted to the rank of swan, and she probably had only a vague idea about the functions of an accountant. One of Mrs. Purbind's grandmothers, it seemed, had been an obscure offshoot of the d'Arfeys, and Mrs. Purbind made the most of the fact. It perhaps helped to sustain her in an environment of unchanging mediocrity to remember that the d'Arfeys had had, for nearly six centuries, the right to bear the royal lilies of France as part of their arms—a proceeding which, as I had heard Toby slightingly observe, would butter no parsnips whatsoever. Possibly the d'Arfey pedigree served as a stick to beat her husband with, when, like many quite equable women, she was in one of her oh-why-did-I-ever-marry-you moods.

Why had Mrs. Mountfaucon taken up Mildred Purbind? I think it can be said without unkindness that she liked having somebody to patronize: her upbringing, character, religious beliefs, and social experience had not been of a kind to prevent her assuming easily the role of a Lady Bountiful. Then she found Mildred a ready listener to the genealogical and heraldic lore about the d'Arfeys with which her head was stuffed. And then she was rather a lonely woman, and there were times, I dare say, when Mildred seemed to her almost like a kind of deserving niece, who was glad to be with her and looked up to her with a kind of affectionate respect. Yet Mildred, like other of Mrs. Mountfaucon's friends and acquaintances, had to be kept out of the way of Toby, and of the sarcasm or coldness he was liable to show them, presumably because of some kind of possessive jealousy. His father, Mrs. Mountfaucon told me, had been "just the same," and had wanted her all to himself.

It seemed that Toby had only once met Mildred and had not only shown complete indifference to the kinship of which she was ready to make so much, but had given her cold looks and bleak civility. Whatever effect his bad manners had had upon Mildred, they had not prevented her from seeing in his need of humming-birds a heaven-sent opportunity of advancing herself in the graces of Mrs. Mountfaucon, and perhaps incidentally of inducing in him some slight semblance of a move towards something more like tolerance, if not politeness. She had spent days in a humming-bird hunt, and seldom had leafy Bucks seen a keener bird-watcher, or would-be bird-watcher: she had at last been successful when attending the sale of the contents of a fusty cottage at Chalfont St. Swithin's.

75

Toby knew nothing of this, and when his mother, now with real or feigned timidity, told him that Mildred Purbind was coming to tea this very afternoon, he burst out with:

"For God's sake, mother, who is this dingy bore, and why do you have to have her here?"

"You forget, dear, that she's your kinswoman."

"I remember it all too clearly! Blood may be thicker than water, but must we *wallow* in it? What does she want, anyway?"

"If you must know, Toby, she has succeeded where everybody else had failed. She has found you some humming-birds!" The note of triumph was supported by a fine gesture, with a small, unpractical hand outflung.

"H'm."

"Now do be nice to her! Do show her that you're grateful for the trouble she has taken!"

"That depends on the humming-birds." He rolled his eyes mischievously, showing the whites, like a horse that means to kick.

"I shall be so pleased, Jane, if you'll stay to tea with us."

"But you should be warned," said Toby, "that for some reason best known to himself (if indeed reason entered into it) the Great Architect has seen fit to set Mrs. Purbind's teeth horizontally in her head instead of vertically, and she has done nothing to correct it. She spreads them out at one, like the sticks of a fan."

"Oh hush, Toby!"

On that note we dispersed, and when we reassembled there in the drawing-room two hours later, I could not help feeling how little enviable was this Mrs. Purbind. I envisaged her as a woman lacking assurance, and here she had to step into an environment not her own and to face in it one hostile and one strange being.

"Mrs. Purbind," said the Countess, appearing at the door, and I realized from the edge on her voice that the visitor's ordeal had begun at the front door: the Countess might almost have been naming something undesirable brought in by the cat.

In came Mildred Purbind, in a reddish beige coat and skirt, with a regrettable fur collar to the coat, and on her head a miscarried-looking hat, obviously quite new. In her arms she carried a domed glass case of stuffed humming-birds, at which I caught the Countess casting the kind of glance that is equivalent to a shrug. Mrs. Purbind was smiling, shy but triumphant, over the top of the glass dome: of course Toby had exaggerated again; her teeth were only a trifle rabbity.

"*There,* Toby!" cried Mrs. Mountfaucon. "Oh, how *clever* of Mildred to find them! Mildred, Toby has searched *everywhere,* we have *all* searched!"

Toby made a short and effusive speech of thanks, every word of which, to my ear, rang false; and having placed the case of humming-birds on a side-table, he took no further notice of it, but drew up a chair to the tea-table and pretended to take part in the conversation. This, soon turned by his mother to the past glories of her first husband's family, quickly reduced its sole living representative to an irritated silence. His legs were crossed and he showed his irritation by wagging up and down the foot which was in the air—and in a very well-cut shoe. He wore a forced and slightly intimidating smile, a sort of leer, and from where she sat Mildred Purbind could see looming above and behind him his full-length portrait in full evening dress and with its sceptical look.

From where I sat I could see over his shoulder the case

of humming-birds, which stood about eighteen inches high. I must say I failed to catch any of those ruby and emerald gleams that one naturally looks for. I thought perhaps the light was at fault, for the case stood on a table between two windows and somewhat in shadow. There was no sunshine that afternoon, and the sky looked like grey flannel: one was glad of the fire.

"In the fifteenth and sixteenth centuries," Mrs. Mountfaucon was saying (and Mildred Purbind was drinking it in), "we intermarried so often with the Beaumonts that we're as much Beaumonts as d'Arfeys, and the Beaumonts are quite as much d'Arfeys as Beaumonts. The great Beaumont himself, you know, was more than half a d'Arfey."

An immense bubble of laughter arose in my throat and nearly choked me. The proprietorial "we" from the somewhat obscure clergyman's daughter, the erstwhile Miss Underhay, was characteristic: Mrs. Mountfaucon hardly ever alluded to her own forebears, who, though neither aristocratic nor glamorous, had, according to Toby, been solid and by no means uninteresting people.

The tea-party was worse than not a success. Toby told an anecdote about a night-club, I don't know with what motive. It depended for its point upon a knowledge of current gossip about a world obviously outside Mildred Purbind's orbit. I think it only puzzled her. She wore that fixed smile of a person of goodwill out of her social depth and yet anxious to show appreciation. I found it pathetic and touching, and much nicer than any degree of self-assurance would have been. Presently Mrs. Mountfaucon asked after her daughter, the girl called Gwinifred, and expressed a hope that Gwinifred might be brought to Duchess's Gate one day.

"I should like to see her, and I think she might like to see some of the d'Arfey things."

At this, Toby's foot wagged like a metronome.

Still feeling sorry for Mildred, I offered her a cigarette, and she seemed pleased and took one. Toby then sprang up and offered her a light with an exaggerated courtly gesture. She was evidently both frightened of him and unused to smoking. She inhaled by mistake, coughed violently, was patted on the back by her hostess, and was watched by Toby with a look that would have withered a cactus. After she had recovered she made the tactical mistake of being overheard by Toby when she was asking his mother some polite question about his late stepfather; and when at last she got up to go, on the pretext of having to catch a train, he took her to the front door with an ominously false smile.

"Oh dear," said Mrs. Mountfaucon, wringing her hands, "I'm afraid Toby doesn't like Mildred at all!"

"And shows it," I said with some asperity.

He was back almost at once.

"Mother!" he cried, bursting into the room with flashing eyes, "why *must* you have that woman here!"

"Oh, Toby, she means *so* well. She said she looked *everywhere* until she found you the humming-birds."

"Well, she should have looked further. Humming-birds, indeed! Look at them!"

He rushed to the table and lifted the glass dome, revealing the conventionally mounted but too soberly colored flock of little birds perched with outspread wings on a little tree encrusted with imitation lichen and rising out of tufts of dyed grass and a papier-mâché rock.

"Look! They're nothing but a gaggle of moth-eaten sparrows!"

"They're nothing of the kind, dear! Of course they're

79

humming-birds, aren't they, Jane?" I nodded assent. "You must remember, Toby, there are many, many varieties."

"There may be. I just don't happen to like the dun and drab varieties."

"Oh, but look at this one!" Mrs. Mountfaucon was stooping and peering through a lorgnon. "It has an *exquisite* touch of peacock-blue near its tail."

"The rest of it has probably faded," said Toby coldly, "and small wonder. Let me lay hands on that woman, and I'll give *her* an exquisite touch of peacock-blue near the tail. And that goes for Gwinifred too. Why do we waste time gaping at these abortive hedge-sparrows? Caught, I should think, with birdlime at—what was the place?— Chalfont St. Swithin's."

"Not *very* far from Milton's cottage at Chalfont St. Giles," said his mother irrelevantly, perhaps hoping to distract his attention.

Without another word Toby took up the stand and the bird-laden tree, strode across the room, and placed the whole construction firmly on the fire.

"Toby!" Mrs. Mountfaucon almost shrieked, and then began to shake with laughter. I thought this laughter disconcerting: it seemed too like that of a woman who, secure in a man's affections, triumphs over the failure of another to obtain them. And I was uneasy, not over the holocaust of the drab humming-birds, but because Toby had distorted a plain, harmless, well-meaning woman into an ogress, and had been hardly polite to her "under his own roof," as they say.

There was a brisk crackle as the trophy took fire. The grasses vanished in a puff of flame, the tree became red-hot, the birds featherless. They now really did look abortive, and mummified as well. One by one they popped like roasting chestnuts, but did not leave their now glowing perches, to which their tiny feet had been attached by fine wires. The wires became incandescent and the charred birds careened slowly over and hung for a few seconds upside down. Then the twigs gave way and were consumed, and there was nothing left but a charred stick.

I was worried about the whole incident, just as I was worried by Toby's attitude to Lady Meliora Sperrow and by his grotesque account of her dog. I could hardly believe that jealousy was the sole explanation for his open hostility to his mother's friends. I had long since discovered that the people we hate are not those who are most unlike ourselves. They are rather those who profit by, or at least display, qualities which lurk in ourselves, but which we have repressed or failed to develop. If a conservative hates a revolutionary, or a revolutionary a conservative, it is because each contains the other. If we despise or condemn other people, we may be despising or condemning what we ourselves might have been.

I could hardly suppose that Toby could envy or fear a woman like Mildred Purbind, or that even unconsciously he could regard her or Lady Meliora as successors in a small way to his stepfather—that is to say, as potential alienators of his mother's love for himself. His character, it seemed to me, could be called aristocratic. He had something of the feudal selfishness and arrogance which may make an aristocrat behave as if it is the duty of the rest of mankind to recognize or minister to his superiority and serve his pleasure. He had an aristocratic indifference to what other people might think of him, and he had what might be called an aristocratic generosity and carelessness about money. But just as very rich people sometimes have little meannesses, and hate for instance to see a match or a halfpenny stamp or a piece of string or a crust of bread wasted, so the aristocratic Toby had in him a subdued or embryonic other self which believed in thrift, prudence, conformity, duty, solid decency, and inconspicuous worthiness. In Mildred Purbind this hidden other self was embodied. She was more than a symbol of a commonplace, conventional, domesticated existence. A suburban housewife, unselfish, leading a settled life, and no doubt resigned to her want of opportunity, she was evidently living a kind of life which Toby could never live and which part of him understood, and perhaps almost needed. It was as if he had been evolved beyond the confines of ordinary habits and responsibilities and was like a climbing plant which aspires to the sun and gropes for something—or somebody—to hold on to.

I was now quite clear, as I had not been before, that that somebody could not be me. It seemed to me that Toby's hostility to Mildred Purbind was somehow feminine: it seemed to resemble the dislike of one woman for another. When I saw the frantic waggling of his foot at tea-time that afternoon, it was like a sign of potential violence; and the burning of the humming-birds, which had its ludicrous side, grew to enormous dimensions in my mind and seemed a kind of witchcraft, as it were a symbolic murder of Mildred. He had displayed a complexity with which I could not wish to become too closely involved. I certainly felt no inclination to save him from it. And his behavior to Mildred was to me so much the reverse of attractive that I had to restrain myself from arriving at a moral judgment. In spite of it, I was not less fond of him, but I was further than I had been from the possibility of loving him—or pitying him, which might have come to much the same thing. Feminine ruthlessness is not one of the qualities I like in a man, though I must say I don't fall automatically for masculine ruthlessness: so I suppose ruthlessness (at least in others) is just something I don't like at all.

TEN

The show-down occurred the next day. No telephone call from Toby had disturbed me at Tregunter Road, though I had half-expected it, and indeed would have preferred it; nor had there been any invasion of my peace and privacy there by Toby in person. A knock on the door of the muniment room was the signal for action. Before I could answer it Toby was inside the room with a look of brilliant animation.

"Jane! I hope I'm disturbing you?"

"In a way, yes," I said. "But not, I'm afraid, in the way I think you hope."

"I can't stand seeing you grubbing about in all this rubbish." He waved a disdainful hand at his family papers. "I should like to rush it all off to the incinerator on one of the days when you aren't here."

"It isn't rubbish," I said. "Even the prescriptions that one of George III's doctors wrote out for your great-great-grandfather are interesting, though they rather overdo the use of mercury. And I've just come across a wonderful little batch of seventeenth-century recipes—"

83

"Well, let me be your twentieth-century recipe." He caught hold of my hand and scrabbled at the palm.

"Don't!" I said sharply, snatching it away. "That tickles."

"It was meant to," he said, with a disquieting seriousness.

"You know your mother made a rule that I was *not* to be disturbed in here."

"If I could only be really sure of thoroughly disturbing you, I wouldn't mind *what* room you were in. . . . Don't you hate living alone?"

"Not at all. I like it. It's restful."

"Restful! What do *you* want with rest? Only the aged ought to want rest."

"You didn't know my husband," I said.

"No, but I want to be his successor." His voice had grown suddenly tender, his eyes glistened, and everything pointed to a difficult emotional scene.

I was sitting down. I didn't want to get up and so invite pursuit and perhaps incur an embrace. At the same time I didn't want either to give him the slightest encouragement or to hurt his feelings. He had got hold of my hand again.

"Oh, Toby," I said, "why on earth should you suppose that I've got the slightest intention of marrying again?"

"Oh, if you don't want to *marry*—I simply thought it was more of a compliment to put it like that, and I know we should hit it off together, I'm absolutely certain. But if you'd rather feel free—"

"Oh, it's not that!"

"You don't dislike me, do you?"

"You know, Toby, I'm very fond of you. How could I *not* be?"

84

"Don't say it, Jane! I know exactly what you're going to say!"

"I was going to say that I can't tell you how touched I am, how proud, yes, and grateful. I think you're unique, and I take it as a tremendous compliment to be asked by you—"

"I know, I know! But I don't feel about you the way you feel about me. Don't say it!"

"Toby. It's better not to pretend, isn't it? It would be such a mistake if we just rushed into bed together, found it a flop, and then found we'd just upset the balance of our—well, our affection for one another."

Where on earth had I heard all this before? I had a feeling that I was reliving an experience I had already been through.

"Jane! If you knew how I long for you to be an absolute part of my life. After all, I've sown some quite pleasant wild oats, but it's time I sowed something better. It's not that I want to 'settle down,' as it's called—God forbid. But I want somebody to work for, to go about with, to quarrel with, to *cherish*."

His voice had risen to a kind of gulp, and I was never nearer to yielding. And now the embrace was upon me; he had slipped round behind my chair; his arms were round me; he was kissing me—and my one idea was to free myself. I won't say I was annoyed: I will say that I felt instinctively the truth of what I already suspected, that this was a show of affection rather than of passion.

"Don't, Toby, don't!" I said, wriggling desperately. "The Countess might come in at any moment!"

As soon as I could free myself I stepped across to the fireplace and hurriedly tidied my hair in the looking-glass above it. I could see the reflection of his big eyes mournfully watching me, and they wrung my heart: after all, it was perfectly true that I was very fond of him. That stricken-deer look was too much for me.

"After all, Toby," I said, in what was meant to be a sensible, practical tone of voice, "life opens out before you like a flower. You're young and healthy. You've got talent and opportunity. You're free to do what you like, or you will be, I suppose, as soon as the Rembrandt's sold. And if you want to marry, you ought to find somebody smarter, grander, more dashing than a dim palaeographical widow like me—somebody like Lilac Evans, for instance—"

"Oh my God, I don't want to live with a fashion-plate!"

At that moment there was a knock on the door. I said "Come in," and the Countess entered with a glass of champagne on a salver. She was visibly surprised to find Toby with me.

"Oh, Laceman," he said, "you might bring another glass."

"No," I said, as she turned to go. I thought it very inconsiderate of him to require her to go all the way downstairs and up again to fetch him a glass. "No, Laceman, don't bother, please. Mr. d'Arfey shall have this. I think perhaps I'm better without it this morning."

"Very well," said the Countess, throwing me a grateful glance, "but it would be no trouble at all."

"No, no really," I said. I felt like Sir Philip Sidney: I'd have given anything for a drink just then.

"Are you sure?" said Toby, already putting out his hand for the sparkling glass.

"Quite sure," I said. The selfishness and obtuseness of men, even intelligent men, often passes belief.

"Perhaps I ought to say, sir," said the Countess, "that

86

Mrs. Mountfaucon has been looking for you everywhere. She thought you had gone out."

"Have you any idea what she wants me for?"

"I couldn't say, sir, I'm sure, but she had a telegram in her hand."

"All right, Laceman. Tell her I'm coming."

The Countess withdrew, and Toby tipped the champagne down his gullet.

"I suppose I'd better go," he said. "I won't say I asked for bread and you gave me a stone: I asked for your heart and you gave me a glass of champagne. How like life! Darling Jane, I leave you, and how unwillingly, with my ancestors."

And he was gone.

Let it not be thought that I have described this little incident of the glass of champagne merely to show that I was more considerate than Toby towards servants. I *was*, but that is not the point. I did want to save the Countess, who was no longer young or strong, the trouble of going downstairs and up again, but I honestly believe that I wanted, that I often wanted, to save Toby from himself. To have married him would have been to undertake a life-long salvage operation, and I did not love him enough for that. In any case I'm not a reformer by disposition and am inclined to be lazy.

When I went down to the drawing-room before luncheon Toby was arguing with his mother, or rather preaching at her. He rolled a sidelong glance at me but did not break off his discourse. I don't know from what it had arisen.

"The trouble with us, my dear mother," he was saying, "is that we're museum pieces. You're a museum piece; both your husbands were museum pieces, particularly your unaccountable second choice; *I'm* a museum piece. I don't

87

boast of it; I accept it. I can even say I try to make the best of it."

"I don't admit any of it for a moment," said Mrs. Mountfaucon.

"It doesn't matter, mother, whether you admit it or not. We're survivors, or survivals, from the past. We're here by a lucky fluke or freak. Don't let's pretend that we're adaptable to an age of community-singing, by-pass roads, bed-sitting-rooms, plastic dinner-plates, and (very soon now, I suppose) television and prefabricated houses."

"But surely, Toby dear, those things may be very convenient."

"And since when, mother, was convenience a virtue? I prefer *style*."

"I can't see why one shouldn't have both."

"Whether you have both or not, don't forget that many people today would already regard us as prehistoric monsters—harmless, perhaps, but quite useless and unnecessary. I may be a dinosaur, but I mean to have my fling before the next lot of monsters crowds me out."

"It does rather look, dear," she said, "as if you may be able to have a fling after all. Oh my dear Jane, it's wildly exciting! Where is that telegram? Where are my spectacles?" She pounced wildly on both and waved them above her head. "It's about the Rembrandt."

"Which is not yet in the bag, mother," said Toby severely.

"Oh but, Jane, Sir Fortescue Higgin and Mr. Calzoni have removed all possible doubt. They've been quite wonderful and of course *wildly* excited about it. It was Sir Fortescue who traced the whole history of the picture. It had simply been lost sight of, and oh, it might have been lost sight of for *ever*. But the overpainting! How anybody could have had the *insolence*—"

"It was prudishness, mother, puritanism. One must admit that *Susannah and the Elders* is a subject simply made for a prurient censor."

"But it's *Scripture,* dear."

"Sexy Jewish mythology."

"Toby, don't! . . . Where was I? Mr. Calzoni thinks there is not likely to be the slightest difficulty in getting at least fifty thousand. A conservative estimate, he calls it. What can he mean? I can't see how politics come into it."

"Nor can anybody else, mother," said Toby. "Conservative estimates have no more to do with politics than astronomical figures have to do with the stars. But pray continue jerry-building your castle in Spain."

"Toby," I protested, "you're *too* unkind."

"I'm not in the least unkind. I'm chivalrous. It is one of my missions in life to protect the female sex from its own illusions. I get little thanks for it, of course."

"You speak of illusions, dear, but Mr. Calzoni says the Americans are quite *ravenous* for Rembrandt. I'd far rather the National Gallery bought it, but it doesn't look as if they will. Of course our expenses will be enormous. We're getting the best restorer and Rembrandt-expert in the world over—Dr. Saas-Fee from Zürich. And that reminds me, Jane, I should be so happy if you could come and dine and meet him on Thursday. You *must*."

An unattached woman of presentable appearance and with hospitable friends must expect to be called upon at times to fill a gap, and she should take it as a compliment. I said I should be delighted.

"I've already had to find I don't know what for the insurance. Then we thought it best to promise a commission, a little rake-off, you know, to Sir Fortescue and Mr. Calzoni. Toby rightly thought it important to have them *entirely* on our side. I tremble to think what will happen if anything goes wrong, but Dr. Saas-Fee, they say, is quite infallible. I'm so thankful, for Toby's sake. It will mean that he can do whatever he wants to, with his painting and so on."

I felt doubtful whether a sudden access of fortune was quite what was needed to develop whatever possibilities Toby might have as a painter, but I hoped the picture would be sold quickly and that he would enjoy spending the money.

A couple of days later the evening papers got hold of the story of the discovery of the picture. It was useful for them, as there was a lull between murders. NEW REMBRANDT SENSATION, said the placards, and MISSING MASTERPIECE THRILL. The next morning an illustrated daily said PRUDE WITH A PALETTE—an allusion to the overpainting of Susannah's nakedness with a good deal of drapery. Mrs. Mountfaucon was agitated: she thought these vulgarities might weaken the resolution of prospective buyers. Toby assured her that they were an excellent advertisement.

On the Thursday I duly went to fill the evening gap at Mrs. Mountfaucon's table, and I met Dr. Saas-Fee, which was all very well for me but could not be of much interest to him, as I knew nothing about the restoration of pictures and nothing very much about Rembrandt. I led him on effectively, however, by talking about the little picture of *Jacob's Dream* at the Dulwich gallery, which my father had first taken me to see when I was a little girl.

Dr. Saas-Fee was a small, twinkling man whose English was fluent and incorrect. Also present were Sir Fortescue Higgin and his wife. He was a man of taste and learning with a correct and rather formal manner and a correct and rather dull wife. They both thawed a little under the influence of the slap-up dinner produced by Mrs. Crumpsey, the excellent wines chosen by Toby, and the vivacious efforts of Mrs. Mountfaucon to please. There was a good deal of talk about the history of the Rembrandt and of its various owners, especially the Golightlys. Mrs. Mountfaucon enlarged quite entertainingly on the past of that family and the pictures it had owned. Toby, who had begun to show some restlessness, then enlarged upon Cousin Harriet herself and her female friend, and with laughable exaggeration produced a characteristically scandalous legend about them, which seemed rather to startle the Higgins.

To me the evening is chiefly memorable for a remark of Mrs. Mountfaucon's. The weather had suddenly turned very warm, the room was too hot, and we were heated by wine.

"The room's like a furnace, mother," said Toby. "Do you think we could have another window open?"

"Oh yes, by all means, if nobody minds?" She looked sweetly round at her guests and was met with a chorus of approval. "Do you know," she then said gravely, as if making a conversational opening, "when I perspire, *it smells like lilies of the valley.*"

This staggering pronouncement was made with an ineffable coyness, as if by a little girl unable to avoid alluding to some advantage which might cause her to be singled out from other little girls and admired and envied. We had had several cocktails before dinner, of a pleasing potency, and had drunk what seemed much since then, particularly champagne, but I knew that Mrs. Mountfaucon, like her son, had a wonderful head, and that drink had a quickening but apparently not in the least intoxicant effect on them both, or I might have thought that the impulse to make such a remark had come from an alcoholic boldness.

For a moment nobody spoke. It seemed quite a long moment. I think we were all petrified with astonishment. The first reaction I noticed was a sort of swallowing movement in the upright and ageing throat of Lady Higgin, which caused a sympathetic movement of the narrow band of black velvet, with a diamond clasp, which she wore round her neck. This slight spasm suggested the strongest resentment on the part of one little girl towards another for drawing attention to herself, and even perhaps exciting admiration and envy, by telling a thumping lie—which would still be outrageous if it were not a lie.

Toby was the first to speak.

"Well, well," he said dryly, his eyes shining with mischievous excitement. "How enviable you are, mother! Some of us are less fortunate. I must say I've noticed no signs of inheriting this uncommon gift. I think it a little selfish of you not to have handed it on."

"*Mit* such a gift," said Dr. Saas-Fee, "*mit* alone a such gift," and he bowed towards Mrs. Mountfaucon, "a lady could become a *great* courtesan."

This was a little too much even for Mrs. Mountfaucon. She gave him a brief but winning smile and presently rose to lead Lady Higgin and me into the drawing-room.

The rest of the evening went perfectly. Mrs. Mountfaucon displayed some of her treasures, did what Toby called her "Pope turn," and did not altogether avoid reference to the past glories of the d'Arfeys. Seeing her son's cold eye upon her made her nervous and caused her oddly to pronounce the name of Leonardo da Vinci with a hard *c*, but apart from this little slip, nothing went wrong. Lady Higgin had no further occasion for throat exercise, and was quite forthcoming. Toby, I could see, was impressing her husband by showing, without showing off, his knowledge of painting. And I found it easy to be a good listener to Dr. Saas-Fee.

I felt that if a pleasant mood and a mellow atmosphere could stimulate the sale of rediscovered masterpieces, *Susannah and the Elders* need cause no more qualms. But in that drawing-room, all through the evening, I was strangely conscious of the two portraits. The portrait of Mrs. Mountfaucon, so sweet and summery, and Toby's, so lordly yet playful, so detached and ironical, seemed at moments to be more real than the originals. The painter had caught and fixed two attitudes to life, and I felt that I ought to be able to read the future of these two lives, since it could only be some obvious projection of the two characters I knew and by now had come to love. I use the word "love" here to mean a warm affection, the sort of love that I think Toby felt for me. I remember thinking, as I went to bed alone that night in Tregunter Road, how appalling the consequences would have been if I had encouraged him to think that his feeling for me was anything more electric than that.

ELEVEN

While Dr. Saas-Fee was beginning the restoration of the picture—a process that meant more than skilfully undressing Susannah, since there were other passages of overpainting—I was away for several weeks abroad. Before I got back I heard from Toby, who said he had developed such an intense admiration for the picture that he resented the necessity of parting with it. He also told me that the picture was to be exhibited for a short time at a gallery in Bond Street. I forget at whose insistence this was done. Perhaps it was hoped to raise a useful sum with the fees paid for admission. But the showing was evidently a mistake. On the private view day there were peerings and mutterings about the way in which the cleaning had been or appeared to have been done, and I arrived back in London in time to follow one of those recurrent controversies which break out in the correspondence columns of *The Times*.

A successful painter of animals tried breezily to expose a pundit to ridicule: if Rembrandt had been a quadruped, this correspondent's opinion might, or might not, have carried more weight. The director of a provincial artgallery fell foul of an analytical chemist who had specialized in ancient pigments. An art-critic of great learning and repute said that the picture was not only now as Rembrandt had left it, but was one of the most notable pictures Rembrandt had ever painted. An old enemy and rival of this art-critic insisted that whatever the picture had been like before restoration it was now a travesty of Rembrandt and an exposure of the vandalism of "Continental" methods of restoration. This brought a bland retort from the curator of one of the national collections that in matters of art and artistic knowledge England had not, for nearly two thousand years, been wholly isolated from Europe. And then an old gentleman, whom almost everybody but his housekeeper had thought dead, piped up to say what, in his opinion, would have been Holman Hunt's opinion of the whole proceeding. He was supported by a brace of faded Academicians, stingless, grounded hornets on the last of their legs.

"Rembrandt can hardly have foreseen," Toby remarked, "that his Susannah would excite *quite* so many elders."

In fact he and his mother were worried. They were kept busy rounding up support for Dr. Saas-Fee and his work. I remember forceful letters from Higgin and Calzoni, whose reputations were involved, to say nothing of their pockets; but I think the correspondence dwindled inconclusively, or was guillotined by an impatient editor. My friends had by now had it borne in upon them that the discovery and ownership of the picture was not an unmixed blessing: it was as innocents that they had strayed into the powerful, self-contained world of art-dealing. If the picture was to be sold in America, it seemed that that would almost certainly have to be with the approval of X., the dealer with the strongest international connection, or through his or his agents' mediation—and

X. was known to have expressed doubts about the way the picture had been restored, and was thought to have been annoyed because he had not been consulted in the first place. Faint suggestions of conspiracy might have induced a touch of persecution mania in a bosom less robust than Mrs. Mountfaucon's, but she continued, at least outside her small immediate circle, to radiate a charming optimism that looked as good as spontaneous (the actress in her was certainly not "resting"), while Toby, increasingly cynical in private about the picture's chances, backed her up in public with a less well-acted air of confidence.

The papers were meddling too much. Illustrated weeklies printed photographs of the picture before and after cleaning, and one of them asked in a headline, IS THIS A REMBRANDT? Mrs. Mountfaucon consulted Mr. Basingfield, and they went together to see a lawyer, with a view to bringing an action against the propagators of such a doubt. Begging and anonymous letters arrived in large numbers at Duchess's Gate, and a Mrs. Y., whom one knew vaguely by name, wrote from Clavicle's Hotel, on slightly scented paper, to offer her services in disposing of the picture. Inquiry showed that Mrs. Y. made a good living by exploiting her social connections in Europe and America to sell works of art privately on commission. She moved continually between Paris, London, and New York, was said to be a friend of Lilac Evans and to be an agent of X., whom Mrs. Mountfaucon wished to propitiate. So Mrs. Mountfaucon, supported by her son and Mr. Basingfield, invited the lady to luncheon at Duchess's Gate.

Nothing was settled. Mrs. Mountfaucon told me afterwards that Mrs. Y. had looked round at everything in the dining-room and the drawing-room with a calculating eye, like a valuer making an inventory. Toby had been observant of her appearance and manner, and said she was exactly his idea of a beautiful spy. The Distinguished Ghost said his information was that she was acting not for X., but for a French financier whose name "ended in whisky or viski" and who was said to be riding "for a fall," and that he, Mr. Basingfield, wouldn't trust her as far as he could see her and wouldn't care to know how she had obtained the jewels she wore, but he presumed, if his bluntness might be excused, that she had earned them not by art-dealing but by practicing arts of her own.

Sir Fortescue Higgin now had a stroke and lost the power of speech, and even that of writing to *The Times*. Dr. Saas-Fee, back in Zürich, lost his temper and wouldn't answer letters. Calzoni was asking for an advance on his commission. Expenses mounted up. Dr. Saas-Fee had to be paid, and as he was rated about the best picture-restorer in the world and had restored the d'Arfey *Susannah,* which one newspaper had described as "the world's most valuable picture," his charges were not small. There were fees for publicity and counter-publicity, for transport and insurance; and a certain Z., a confidant of Mr. Basingfield's, had been sent to America, at Mrs. Mountfaucon's expense, to do what Mrs. Y. had wanted to do, and try and negotiate the sale of the picture there, which meant that he had to keep up appearances and entertain, it seemed, on a handsome scale.

With Mr. Basingfield's help Mrs. Mountfaucon had been able to get a large advance from her bank, but the money was melting away, and she was beginning to be anxious, naturally enough, about the delay in selling the picture. She asked me if there was anything at all among the family papers that could be turned into money. I said there were some letters written at the end of the eighteenth century which might fetch twenty or thirty pounds, so we changed the subject.

In spite of all the fuss there seemed no doubt that the picture was still a formidable asset and that it would be sold. The question was when, and for how much. Toby, who was obviously feeling some nervous strain from the delay, said he would seek relief, during the time of uncertainty, in painting. He would paint some still-lifes. I should see, he told me, the beginnings, or so he hoped, of a style of his own.

"None of your crumpled dinner-napkins for me," he said, "with a newspaper, a coffee-pot, and a pound of sour apples. No. Opulence is what I'm after."

The trouble was that he now elected to paint in his mother's drawing-room. He could have used that upper room from which I had once fled, or he could have hired a studio, but he liked painting at home, and he liked the light in the drawing-room, so a round Empire table, inlaid with lapis lazuli, was heaped up with a fantastically lavish display of things, many of which in former years not long past the d'Arfeys or the Mountfaucons would have produced on their own estates, but which now, so times had changed, had to be ordered at much expense from the florist's, the poulterer's, and the fishmonger's. In the middle of the table, an immense urn held a sheaf of arum lilies and kniphofias, with huge roses and the big scabious whose flowers look like dark red pincushions stuck with white pins, with branches of magnolia and white buddleia, heads of crown imperial, sprays of love-lies-bleeding, and specimens of a new white iris with petals like very fine silk handkerchiefs, or like delicate membranes scribbled over with a fine puce network—all these intermingled with trails of a showy creeper with tubular crimson flowers. Heaped up round the urn were melons with figured rinds, bunches of monstrously big black and white grapes, a pineapple, clusters of lichees, some peaches, nectarines, and avocado pears, together with a fresh and tasselled ear or two of maize, the husks partly open and revealing what looked like perfect rows of grinning pearly teeth. A seventeenth-century clock of crystal and silver (now in the British Museum) was slightly flushed with the ripeness and efflorescence that overhung it, and just touching it were the relaxed-looking claws of one of a brace of guinea-fowl that lay prone, with lolling heads, like two neatly dressed but flighty matrons who had "passed out" as a result of drinking too much. The head and forequarters of a hare dangled over the edge of the table, and beneath it, on the carpet, a Meissen sauceboat—part of a dinner service which the King of Saxony had given to Morven Mountfaucon's father—had been carefully placed by Toby to catch any blood that might drip from the hare's nose. In the foreground of the whole composition, in itself a work of talent, were a heavyweight lobster and a bouquet of gardenias tied with a bow of crimson velvet ribbon.

Round this tremendous spectacle hovered Mrs. Mountfaucon, a tremendous spectacle herself in a gauzy and expansive summer frock which Butterball Evans had encouraged her to buy from a famous new dressmaker. She was a prey to conflicting emotions which made her prance about restlessly, like a colossal butterfly uncertain where to settle.

"For God's sake, mother, keep still!" cried Toby, tapping his foot irritably on the carpet.

Poor Mrs. Mountfaucon clasped her hands together as if trying an exercise in self-control. She knew that, whatever she said, her "head would be bitten off," but putting on a sweet and childlike look she said with a sigh,

"Oh, what a marvellous arrangement!" She was right, and it would have been difficult not to admire the skill and boldness and prevailing red and white of the arrangement, especially if one's own child had made it.

"Now for God's sake, mother, do tell that crackpot maid not to come near this table, or I'll tear the pants off her."

"My dear Toby," Mrs. Mountfaucon unclasped her hands and spread them out in a large and confident gesture full of warmth and humanity, "if you mean our poor Countess, I'm afraid there's nothing she'd like better."

"Yes, I forgot that for a moment. Well, then, tell her simply that if I catch her in here with a duster I'll ram it down her throat."

"Toby dear," his mother became suddenly grave, "you'll have to be very quick with your painting. In this weather, I mean."

"I know, mother, I know," he said petulantly; and then, rolling a naughty eye, "but after all it won't matter if the drawing-room smells a bit *faisandé*. We're a bit *faisandé* as a family, aren't we? Our whole civilization is a bit *faisandé*—so another little aroma won't do us any harm."

"Oh, Toby!" She ducked her head and smilingly looked up at me as if to say, "Isn't he a caution?" Then she turned to him and said solemnly, "You might get diphtheria."

"Why diphtheria?" Toby was adjusting his easel. "What an extraordinary idea! Why not typhus, leprosy, bilharzia, botulism, psittacosis, or yaws? And now," he propped a large clean canvas on the easel and began to fix it in place, "you'd better leave me, or I shall never get this thing started."

"Very well, dear. . . . Oh, it's going to be a *wonderful* picture!"

"That'll *do*, mother."

With her gauzes flying and her head down, Mrs. Mountfaucon almost ran out of the room, and I followed less precipitately.

The next day the sky was overcast and the light in the drawing-room was "all wrong," so Toby said, but he worked undisturbed all the morning. I came down a little before luncheon and tactfully paid no attention to what he was doing. I may have fancied it, but the air seemed to me already slightly gamy. Presently Mrs. Mountfaucon came in.

"Can't you do something about this damned thing, mother?" said Toby, without looking up from his palette. "It won't keep still."

"What thing, dear?"

"This abominable lobster, of course. It can't possibly be dead. How can I paint a thing that keeps waving its antennae at me? It's no more a still-life than you are. Can't you kill it, or do *something*?"

"Very well, dear, I'll see. But it will have to be moved."

"Oh, all right then, let it be moved, so long as nothing else is touched."

"You're going out to luncheon, you said?"

"Yes, but I shall come back later and go straight on painting."

I was remaining to eat with Mrs. Mountfaucon. As soon as Toby had gone out she came back to deal with the lobster. She had put on a large pale-grey hat trimmed with a spray of realistic artificial ivy, and was carrying a very small basket and a handkerchief embroidered with forget-me-nots. I asked if I could help, and she said she would be delighted if I came with her, though "it" would only take a minute or two. I went to put on my hat, and when I came back she had got the lobster on to the basket rather than into it and had spread the handkerchief over its back; the creature protruded a good way beyond the edge of the basket at both ends. She slipped the handle of the basket over her arm, in the style of Little Red Riding Hood going to visit her grandmother, and then she tripped along the hall and I followed her out into the street. I supposed we were going to the fishmonger's.

Two women were gossiping on the pavement. One of them, as soon as she caught sight of Mrs. Mountfaucon's hat, nudged the other. When she saw the little basket and the lobster sticking out of it, she gave her a second and more violent nudge. Serenely unconscious and full of maternal solicitude, Mrs. Mountfaucon pranced round the corner, but not in the direction of the fishmonger's. She made straight for the chemist's, a somewhat imposing shop, old-established and with an air of luxury. As I followed her in, a severe-looking, very clean, youngish man, rather like a solicitor, materialized behind the counter. Mrs. Mountfaucon paused in the middle of the shop.

"Good afternoon," she said, with her sweetest smile, the midday sunshine glinting in her very golden curls as she waved a white-gloved hand towards the little basket. "I have a lobster here."

The chemist could hardly believe his ears or eyes.

"Pardon?" he said.

"A *lobster*," said Mrs. Mountfaucon in her most winsome manner. She withdrew the forget-me-not handkerchief as if she were unveiling a memorial. The lobster waved a deprecatory feeler.

"You see," she explained, "my son is painting it. A

still-life, you know." She smiled sweetly. "But unfortunately it simply *won't* keep still."

The chemist shrank behind his glassy barricade of bath salts and laxatives, and Mrs. Mountfaucon glanced at me with a look of puzzled inquiry. "Perhaps I'd better buy something," she murmured to me. Then aloud to him she said, "Oh, and I want some scent. Have you got a bottle of *Mon Béguin*? If not, I'll take *Folie Lunaire*."

As the man hesitated, apparently hypnotized by the lobster, she said ingratiatingly, "I was wondering if you couldn't do something to it—some drug, perhaps, just a mere whiff of something, something *humane,* like veronal perhaps? To make it keep still, poor thing, and gently put it out of its misery."

The chemist recovered himself.

"I'm sorry, madam," he said coldly. "I couldn't undertake to do that. You'd better take it back to the fishmonger."

"Oh, how right you are! Now why didn't I think of that at first? *Good* afternoon!" she said, restored the handkerchief to its place, and turned to go. As the door was about to close behind us, the snooty expression which the man had assumed instantly faded. "Blimey!" I heard him say, as he hurried to the back of the shop, no doubt to tell the dispenser what he had just heard and seen.

Before Toby returned, the lobster was back in its place: it had been given its quietus by the fishmonger. But that generously planned still-life was never finished. Petals and pollen fell from the flowers on to the clock, the fruit, and the game. The ripest of the fruit grew soft, discolored, and then rotten. The two guinea-fowls and the hare began to assail the nose. And at last the Countess, wearing an expression of distaste, was allowed to clear away the whole arrangement.

On Toby's canvas everything had been drawn in outline, and two roses, a guinea-fowl, and half a melon had been skilfully painted in. The canvas was now discarded; it vanished into the limbo which had already, as I had now begun to understand, swallowed a great deal of money. Gloomy reflections on that subject were, however, at once dispersed by news of the arrival of an offer for the *Susannah,* an offer of sixty-five thousand pounds. It had a tonic effect at Duchess's Gate, but after the briefest of hesitations was turned down, because Z., cabling from New York, was confident that a much higher offer would be forthcoming from another quarter, and he strongly urged delay. Toby ordered half a dozen new suits. That was his only fresh extravagance. He retired to the upper room, went on painting, and finished several pictures, but he wasn't satisfied with them. I think he knew that there was some reservoir of power in him not yet unlocked.

TWELVE

As I had got to know Toby, it was his restlessness that impressed me as much as anything. No doubt the suspense about the selling of the *Susannah* had made him more fidgety than usual, but his lack of repose, besides being a sign of vitality, seemed to me that of a man not tethered by the need to earn a living or to support other people, a man, it seemed, not fulfilled, balanced, or comforted, at least at this time, by any steady sexual relationship. That is only guesswork, because although he treated me like an intimate, he continued to keep his close friends apart, as if fearing they might prefer one another to him. To this day there are two persons I have never met whom he saw often at that time, and I believe they have never met one another. I know that each of them was asked sometimes to Duchess's Gate, but never when I was there. It was true I was only there for a small part of each week, because I was engaged on other work.

Even when I was working at Duchess's Gate, I was often interrupted by Toby. Not that he would bother me with any more "intentions," but he seemed to enjoy talking to me. He was more inclined to entertain than to confide in me, and his pointed evasion of any allusion to his closer friends made me think often how hard a lesson he must have learned, early in his life, that affections can be obtruded upon or alienated. His talk did not grow less sardonic, and much of it went to the creation of his personal myth of the society in which he lived, a myth with a strong element of caricature. Then he was continually putting forth fresh schemes for traveling and painting. If he heard anybody else making plans for the future, he at once began talking about the coming war, which he took for granted. To do so in those far-off days was uncommon and even eccentric: in England Hitler had hardly yet been heard of, except by alert specialists in politics, of whom Toby was certainly not one. He was quite free from the false, shallow, unthinking optimism then so common among the well-to-do.

Sometimes his lack of harmony with the society in which he lived would express itself in grumbles about

English life, the English climate, and so on—as if perfection could be grasped by merely crossing the Channel: but I think it did not escape him that as much might be wrong with himself as with his country. He made it plain that he lacked faith in the future of England and Europe, or, to be more precise, of English and European civilization as he understood them. This was not so much a mark of what would later have been called defeatism as of self-knowledge: with a strong intuition he knew that he would hardly be able to adapt himself to whatever new form civilization might take after the impending war. He really felt himself to be what he had called a "museum piece." It was as if there was some close biological correspondence between himself and the era to which he belonged—or so I fancied; and I wondered if it was because he was an old man's child, an only child at that, and possibly the final offshoot of his family.

His self-knowledge may not have been complete or carefully thought out, but as far as it went—and it went a long way—it was deep and true. Naturally enough, his temperament, or attitude of mind, tended to make him fiddle, rather than join the fire brigade, while waiting for Rome to burn. His was not the pacifism of those who lived easily and opposed war because they feared that it might stop them living easily, and who were perfectly ignorant about what the Italian, German, and Japanese militarists were after, and why. No, it was the old-fashioned pacifism of the detached, humane, liberal aesthete who regards violence, organized murder and destruction, cruelty, and famine as unnecessary, senseless, and disgusting, and who at the same time has no belief that mankind has grown or is likely to grow more sensible, except here and there for a short time by luck or by chance. I think he would have been inclined to the theory that war, not peace, is the natural condition of mankind; that life is not peace often disturbed by war, but war interrupted at times, luckily for those whom he would have called civilized, by spells of peace. He would probably have agreed with Flaubert, who recognized that savagery is man's natural condition, and that war contains a mystical element that excites the rabble. At the same time Toby's strong, if vaguely formulated, conviction of impending doom reminded me of those religious fanatics whose conviction that the Day of Judgment, or the Second Coming, or the end of the world is at hand presumably derives from some strong unconscious personal anxiety.

He had been talking of going off, once the picture was sold, to Brazil or the West Indies, or of revisiting Italy or Greece. He felt, he said, that his power to paint could only expand in the sun. It seemed that all that was needed was a straight invitation, or sudden impetus, and off he would go.

Even before the picture was sold, his impetus, as it happened, was provided. But it did not send him sunward, and it came, most unexpectedly, from his old friend Lydia Delap. Whether, having heard about the Rembrandt, she wished to help Toby to squander the fortune it was about to bring him, or whether, as it would be more charitable to think, she felt a real affection for him and wanted to try and renew their earlier relationship, they had certainly been seeing each other again lately, and she seemed to suit his prevailing mood.

She had now told him that she wanted to write a novel about life in Berlin, and she wanted him to go there with her. She had excited his curiosity about it. Berlin had the reputation at that time of being "gay" with a freedom elsewhere unknown and in some ways unprecedented. Of course he knew, as every thoughtful person knew, that it was a gaiety and freedom of a kind that could not last, because it was morbid, desperate, and precarious; but the very precariousness and perversity of the "life" it notoriously offered to the moneyed and enterprising visitor was an attraction to one who, like Toby, had at once a rage for life and a foreboding of finality.

Of his decision to go to Berlin with Lydia I first heard from his mother. I had brought back from a visit to the country a bouquet of uncommon flowers from a hot-house. I thought she would like them, and took them round to Duchess's Gate. They worked like a charm, and not only upon Mrs. Mountfaucon. Toby was out, and in his absence the womenfolk at Duchess's Gate seemed to breathe more freely, and to expand. When the Countess opened the door to me, the flowers naturally caught her eye.

"Good morning, Laceman," I said, "aren't these pretty?"

"Oh, madam, they're much more than pretty—I should call them unique."

I was pleased by her responsiveness and by her using this word.

"Have they any scent?" she asked.

"Smell them," I said, holding out the bunch.

She bent to smell them, and there was something pathetic in her foreshortened face inclined for a moment against the showy flowers, in the bleached and anxious forehead that looked at close quarters as vulnerable as an eggshell, in the well-shaped but bloodless, sexless-looking ear, and in the pointed nose with its rather pinched-in but now slightly quivering nostrils. She stood up with a radiant expression on her face that I had never seen before.

"Oh, what a sweet smell! It exactly suits them." I thought this a good remark. "And how pleased Mrs. Mountfaucon will be, she so loves flowers."

This was not the freakish Countess of legend, but a thawed and friendly and interested woman. Yet by the time we reached the drawing-room door her spine had stiffened into its usual rigidity, and across her back the St. Andrew's cross of her starched apronstraps had its usual hard, heraldic look.

"Oh, Jane!" cried Mrs. Mountfaucon, rising from a chair. I saw she was not alone. "Oh, *pilkingtonias*! They take me back in a flash to Marsh, I haven't seen one for years. Daddy loved them so! Where *did* you find them? Are they for me? Oh, thank you, thank you, I shall put them in the big blue Sèvres boat-shaped bowl—if only I can *find* it. Look, Meliora, aren't they exquisite? But I think you've never met Jane. Lady Meliora Sperrow."

Lady Meliora made so quiet an impression on me, she was so little like what Toby's fantasies had led me to imagine, that I felt as if, going downstairs, I had suddenly missed a step.

"I've heard so much about you," she said.

That is always difficult to answer. One can reply, "And so have I about you," or "I hope it was favorable." I said instead, "Not from Toby, I hope?"

This might have been challenged by Mrs. Mountfaucon, but she had just charged out of the room, no doubt in search of the Sèvres bowl.

"Oh no, not from Toby. I never see him. He's so emphatic, isn't he? I think he likes to try and shock one a little. I'm afraid he doesn't approve of me."

"Oh, surely—"

"But never mind," she said, "we can't all dote on one another, can we? How cross he would be if he knew that I feel sorry for him. Don't you?"

"Feel sorry for him?" I said. "Oh, not more, I think, than for most people."

"Then you feel we're all to be pitied?"

"Well, aren't we?"

"But would it be good for us? So softening. . . . It might make us sorry for ourselves. And that would be rather fatal, don't you think?"

This was not at all the sort of conversation I should have expected, nor was I prepared for the soft voice and the fleeting, rather engaging smile, nor even for Lady Meliora's general appearance. I am not sure what I had expected—a grotesque, I think, someone dowdy, stupid, Philistine; and she was none of these things. The most one could say, at a first impression, was that she had an air of belonging to a dream of her own rather than to the rough-and-tumble everyday world. That would have applied equally to Mrs. Mountfaucon and her son, or for that matter to the Countess or even Mrs. Crumpsey.

The pilkingtonias came back into the room, duly arranged in the boat-shaped vase and almost hiding Mrs. Mountfaucon, who was carrying it.

"There!" she said, putting it down on a table and rearranging one or two of the flowers. "Of course my wicked Toby had it in his painting room. It was full of cigarette ends (I do hope he won't get nicotine poisoning), and what he'll say when he finds it in here I can't imagine. . . . Oh but I wish, I do wish, he had found somebody, anybody, but Lydia to go abroad with!"

"They're going together, then?" said Lady Meliora.

"Alas, yes, and to, of all places, Berlin! Jane, don't you think it a strange choice?"

"It's rather unexpected. He had been talking lately of the Mediterranean or South America."

"Berlin's much nearer, that's one thing. And of course I never *dream* of trying to influence him. But oh, with *Lydia*! I had so hoped all that was past and done with."

"Never mind, Susannah," said Lady Meliora, "he'll soon tire of her. She's no longer a novelty."

"Oh, but Toby isn't fickle. He's intensely loyal to his old friends."

"Yes, but he has seen through her long ago, from what you told me. He's no longer a boy, and she can't have cast a fresh spell. Why, I hear she has quite lost her looks and has a figure now like a sack of potatoes. Where Toby's concerned, she must have shot her bolt."

"Then all I can say is, my dear, I wish she had shot it a bit further. What is a bolt, I wonder? Can it be an arrow? Arrow or no, she's whisking him off to Berlin, and it's bound to be terribly expensive."

After this encounter I took the first chance of telling Toby how different Lady Meliora seemed to me from what he had led me to imagine. His eyes grew large, innocent, and childlike, as if I had accused him of falsehood.

"In what way?" he asked.

"Oh, I expected her to be a frump, dog-mad, and a bore."

"And?"

"And she never spoke of dogs at all. She seemed sensible and amiable and so understanding."

"Oh, and what did she understand?"

"Well, she understands how to dress herself."

His eyes opened very wide.

"I expected," I went on, "to see a sort of scarecrow in dirty lace with soup-stains down the front. What I saw in fact was a decent noblewoman, so quietly dressed that I haven't the faintest idea in what—except that her hat was, as they say, a darkness that might have been felt, and she had a very small cross of red stones on a chain round her neck."

"H'm. Making a parade of her Anglo-Catholicism as

usual. . . . I know that cross, and they're rubies. . . . You haven't seen her in her setting or with her dog. I shall get mother to take you, and then perhaps you'll sing a different tune."

"Well, you won't hear me if I do. I gather you'll be in Berlin with Lydia Delap."

He fidgeted a little.

"Only for a few days," he said, with the slight haughtiness he sometimes assumed when unwilling to explain or excuse himself. "Then I shall probably go to Spain. I want to see a great many Goyas and lie flat on my back in an arid landcape with only a few goats and grasshoppers and a few clumps of rosemary and cistus under a vertical sun."

"To recover from Berlin? I shall expect postcards from wherever you go, saying 'Having wonderful time.' "

"When the Rembrandt is sold I shall probably take a villa in Tangier or Cintra or somewhere, and you must come and live there for as long as you like and forget all about your life among the waste paper."

I smiled, and made no reply.

THIRTEEN

After Toby had left for Berlin, Mrs. Mountfaucon had disquieting news about the prospects of selling the picture.

So little were she and her son conversant with financial news, and so imperturbable was Mr. Basingfield, and so ignorant was I, that we had none of us perceived that the slump in the United States had been something more than a weak phase on Wall Street.

The rude awakening came in the form of a long letter from Z., who was still living in style at Mrs. Mountfaucon's expense. He had spent some weeks at Miami, ostensibly to cozen a prospective buyer, and had returned to New York. His report was not merely gloomy; it knocked poor Mrs. Mountfaucon sideways, clean out of her modest but confidently expectant attitude; it made of her a superannuated Danaë surprised by a shower of ashes.

According to Z., there was no longer any prospect of the picture fetching sixty-five thousand pounds or even a quarter of that sum. Some prospective buyers had been ruined "overnight," others had been badly hit; there was a general panic. In the circumstances there seemed no point in his remaining in New York. There was nothing more that he could do, and he would be returning to England at once, as urgent affairs there now required his presence. He had been putting them off as long as possible, as he had hoped to be of service to Mrs. Mountfaucon and to get the picture sold at a record figure. He much regretted that she had been put to so much expense and feared she would be greatly disappointed, but he had done his best, and the slump had been sudden, disastrous, and quite unforeseen. He felt that the best thing would be to store the picture against better times, as it was a great asset and things must improve in due course. The only alternative would be to sell it now "for a song." Would she please cable instructions?

She read this letter aloud in the presence of Mr. Basingfield and myself. She had sent for us both on purpose. While she was reading it the Distinguished Ghost fingered his neatly trimmed beard, as if to make sure that that, too, had not been affected by the slump. When she had finished she put the letter down in her lap and extended her arms in appeal to us both.

"Whatever happens," she said, "Toby must hear nothing of this—yet. It would quite spoil the pleasure of his tour. . . . Oh dear, 'slump' is such an ugly word. As far as we're concerned, I'm afraid it means that we've fallen out of the frying-pan into an empty grate. Of course it's quite out of the question," she looked at Mr. Basingfield, "to store the picture or bring it back here. Think of the insurance alone. It has put us deeply in debt already. It must be sold for what it will fetch. Z. must arrange that before he leaves, and then come back at once. He will have to have his commission and the passage-money, and then not another penny. . . . I'm quite at my wits' end," she explained.

"On the contrary," said Mr. Basingfield, who had heard her in silence, in his grave and gracious way, "you have a perfect grasp of the situation. I'm afraid there's nothing for it but to sell the picture for what it will fetch, and we can only hope that the price will cover the large sums that have already been spent to promote the sale of it."

"Oh, it *must*! Oh, my poor Toby, he will be grievously disappointed!"

"Perhaps," I suggested, "instead of telling him outright, it might be a good thing to hint to him that hopes of a high price have declined, and that he ought to economize a little while he's abroad."

"It would be a very good thing, Mrs. Valance," said Mr. Basingfield.

"Oh, you're both *true* friends! And now let us draft a cable, I'm so terribly anxious, to Z. But oh, suppose *nobody* will buy the picture? I simply daren't think of it. . . . And when we've composed the cable, let's put the whole thing out of our minds as much as possible until we hear more news, for better or worse. And then—oh, how late it is!—I must fly to the rector of St. Jude's. He's *counting* on me for a committee meeting for his holiday camp for deaf-mutes. It's near Clacton, you know, the swimming-bath is really *superb,* they built it all themselves, and it was designed by one of them too, a *most brilliant* engineer who seems to have quite triumphed over his handicap—he writes everything down like lightning on a little pad, and yet perfectly legible, and in quite a gentlemanly hand. . . ."

When the cable had been drafted and Mrs. Mountfaucon was about to depart on her charitable errand (and I thought it showed strength of mind on her part not to cancel it), Mr. Basingfield said he was walking across the Park to his club, and hoped I might be going in the same direction. I went with him part of the way. Out of doors he attracted some attention by his dignified bearing, his upright figure, his leisurely gait, and his long, tight-waisted overcoat, beautifully cut in the style of the nineties and almost reaching to his ankles. Dandified but not foppish, he looked like one of those few elderly grandees surviving from the last century, of whom the ordinary man or woman in the street seldom any longer caught a glimpse.

"A bad business, I'm afraid," he said. "A great deal depended on getting a good price for that picture. As you're a friend of the family, I don't mind telling you that a good deal of retrenchment will be necessary."

"I hope you don't mean that they're ruined?"

"Good God, no. But they'll have to live, I expect, rather more simply."

"Toby won't like that."

"I'm afraid not."

"Supposing the picture had never been discovered—?"

"They'd have had to retrench soon, in any case."

I couldn't help wondering why, as their trustee, he had not already made this clear to them. Perhaps he had, and I had heard nothing of it.

"It's a matter of adaptation," he said. "I've seen it often. When people have had money for centuries they're apt to take it for granted—just as they know, if they turn on a tap, that water will come out of it. Then one day there's no water, and sometimes they're quite incapable of going to the well for more—why, they don't even know what a well is! Can you imagine Toby *earning* money, or doing anything with it but spend it? He's a dear feller, but I can't see him as a breadwinner, can you? Plenty of backbone, of course, plenty of brains. But that's not the thing. It's *adaptation* that's needed."

He seemed pleased with this word, and I couldn't help agreeing with what he had said, though Mr. Basingfield himself did not appear to have felt any need to adapt himself to changing times. We parted in St. James's Street. I glanced back at his stately figure sauntering into the middle distance as if in search of a hansom, and as if quite oblivious of the thronging motor traffic beside him, and I wondered idly, as one does, what he was really like, what went on in his head, what he lived for, what he still looked forward to, what were his most cherished memories and secrets.

The next time I saw Mrs. Mountfaucon I at once asked if she had any news. She had none, and again expressed a good deal of anxiety about money matters.

"Can't Mr. Basingfield help?" I asked.

"Dear, good Mr. Basingfield! No, I don't think he can."

"But he's your trustee, isn't he? I don't want to butt in, but supposing you don't sell the picture, or can only sell it for a sum which won't cover what you've already had to spend on it, I hope he has allowed for that?"

"Oh, I'm sure he has! My dear Jane, it's more than good of you to show such sympathy, but we're not ruined! Why, the picture was only a chance discovery. We might never have known what it was, and we should have had to go on living as usual on, or rather beyond, our income."

This did not quite tally with Mr. Basingfield's talk of "retrenchment" and "adaptation," which it was certainly not for me to repeat to her. I concluded that she had probably not understood how large her overdraft had become, or how many sprats she had had to throw to catch a mackerel that now looked like not being caught at all.

A few days later I had a letter and two preposterous photographs from Toby in Berlin. He wrote from the Hotel am Zoo:

. . . Was ever a hotel more oddly named? Lydia is still at the Adlon, but I moved here because mother, for some strange reason, urges me to economize, and this is a bit cheaper. It's not *in* the Zoo. What is in the Zoo is a dreadful enclosure for crocodiles. There are supposed to be a thousand of them. The enclosure isn't large enough, and they lie piled on top of one another and crawling over one another round a fetid green pool. The whole place stinks. I'm no champion of kindness to crocodiles, but if this is how the Germans treat animals, how will they treat human beings in the next war? Or perhaps sooner.

We hear of nasty attacks by gangs of political yahoos on one another, some calling themselves Communists and some National Socialists—whatever that may mean. If this ripens into a civil war, that may divert the Germans from attacking France as usual. But with the world as it is, how can a civil war in any major European country be that country's concern alone? Ugh, enough of politics!

Lydia has developed a passion for the fantastic night-life of this town. She finds romantic what some people would find absurd or repulsive or merely pointless. She has discovered a Lesbian League. She isn't one herself, of course. It's organized like a sort of Y.W.C.A., with hostels, a magazine of its own, and so on. She is more interested in the male counterpart of all that, which is very much in evidence. She took it into her head that I must go with her and see from the inside a Lesbian *lokal,* and that I must then take her to see the other sort. The only way to do this was for me first to disguise myself as a woman, and then for her to disguise herself as a man— which we did. What a lark!

I enclose our photographs *en travesti.* I would have defied anyone to guess that that smartly bobbed hair was not my own. My breasts came from a shop that supplies false ones to women who have had theirs amputated. My make-up was put on at a theater—it took nearly an hour. My mannish coat and skirt was a rush job from a "little" Polish dressmaker. No trouble about shoes, as I could wear my own —high heels would have been out of keeping with my role as the dominant partner. My voice was the main problem—as you know, I did once train for a time as a would-be operatic tenor. After a little practice I managed to cultivate a sort of husky whisper. I was afraid it might have a fatal allure and that I might find myself compromised, but Lydia agreed to explain that I couldn't speak German and had a cold.

I must say I had terrific stage-fright. I was afraid of being found out and torn limb from limb, and I was also afraid of being made love to, but we arranged to be very much in love with one another in order to discourage casual advances. It was a great success. We danced together, I of course as "the man." Such an extraordinary assembly of women you can't imagine—all shapes and sizes and classes and nationalities, one might almost add "and all sexes"—some beautiful, others monstrous, everything from a Peruvian mannequin in white satin and amethysts to a hunchback Hungarian countess in jodhpurs *and spurs*. On the whole their behavior was decorous, even prim. The atmosphere seemed to me sad and somehow terribly respectable. I felt what I imagine I should feel at a party of christianized Central African Negresses sitting in frock coats and listening to a recital on the harmonium. It was as if those women were all playing at a life they could not share. But perhaps that's a false view of them. They were like actresses determined to go through with roles they hadn't chosen. Some of them were obviously enjoying themselves, while even the sad ones had a sort of dedicated look. I wouldn't have missed the occasion for anything, but I had an awkward moment or two when Lydia went to "powder her nose" (she told me afterwards that she was nearly abducted, in the process, by a woman who said she was a sculptress), and a girl came and sat in her place and began paying me compliments about my *Augen*.

The next night it was Lydia's turn, and I took her to a notorious place called the *Jugendquelle*. As you'll see from the photograph, she made a decidedly queer man, but as we were going to a resort of queer men, that didn't matter much. She has quite lost the boyish figure she used to have, and is getting a bit flabby and shapeless. This was an advantage in a way, as it aided the camouflaging of her upper works. As she has had an Eton crop for some time, there was no difficulty about her hair, except that the back of a woman's neck, when close-clipped, is apt to look quite un-male. The double-breasted suit (see photograph) was supposed to disguise her hips and big behind. "Your friend looks like a boxer," a saucy waiter said to me, "but he's a bit out of training, isn't he?" It's going to take Lydia a good many years to live *that* down.

There were several English present. I was introduced to a man who lives in Berlin and is writing a book. If it's as good as his conversation, it ought to be very good. He looked very quizzically at

Lydia, who hardly spoke, and then at me. I feel deeply compromised. Lydia is also going to write a book. These aspects of life in Berlin send her into her tiresome romantic raptures, and she plans to call it *Youthfountain,* all in one word like that.

After all this it was quite restful to go, the next night, to an honest-to-God night-club—or it would have been restful if there hadn't been in a floor-show a dashing mulatress who singled me out for attention and playfully knocked my cigarette out of my mouth with a high kick. I asked her to come and sit at our table, which she did, and she proved to be *English*. I've made a date to take her out to supper one night. She calls herself Bella Mestiza.

I wish that blasted picture were sold. Perhaps it's too late—I hear a lot of rich Americans have been ruined by the slump. I'm staying in Berlin for the present. Lydia and I have been offered a roomy flat in the Tauentzienstrasse, and may take it for three months. . . .

Only a few days after I had received this letter Mrs. Mountfaucon rang me up to say that Toby had left Berlin for Greece, but not, she was thankful to say, with Lydia.

"Why Greece?" I asked.

"Oh, he has been there before, you know, and he liked it very much. He does so love the sun and he finds it important for his painting. Of course he must do what he thinks best. . . . No, he didn't say for how long. Of course I'm dreadfully worried about the Rembrandt, but I do so want to spare *him* any needless anxiety, so you won't say anything to him about it when you write, will you?"

Very soon I received the first of a series of letters from Athens. It was from the Grande Bretagne, the best hotel.

I told Mother [Toby wrote] that I was coming to Greece to paint, which is true, but only half the truth. The fact is that Bella M., whom I told you about, has an engagement at the best cabaret here, and as we get on well together, I traveled to Athens with her. We don't get as much time together as I should like, as she is so tied by her engagement. She is a *succès fou* with what passes for the *beau monde* here. As she sleeps until lunch-time, I do some painting in the dry, white light, but we have both been taken up in a big way by a Madame Potter-Spanakis, whom I'll describe next time I write.

Lydia went off to Lapland with a Chilean who said he was an anthroposophist. I should think gynecophilist would be nearer the mark. She writes from the Arctic Circle that she has spent a whole night with him, but, owing to the midnight sun, the night only lasted three and a half minutes. I hope Mother isn't worrying too much about the picture.

The next letter was from a different hotel, the Xenias Melathron:

I've moved here, as I've not been able to get as much money as I hoped from England. It's a nice modern hotel, a shade less central than the G.B. I'm hoping to sell a landscape to Madame Potter-Spanakis. Half-Portuguese and half-Italian, she married an American who died and left her a lot of money. She settled at Kephissia, lives in some style in a big *art nouveau* villa, and has all the airs and the clothes of an Edwardian hostess. She boldly married her gardener, Spanakis, who is young enough to be her son, much handsomer than Valentino and obviously much brighter. He seems to enjoy every moment of his life, though his appearance is really *un peu trop rasta* even for the part he plays. They took Bella and me in a closed car to a picnic at Marathon, of which we saw little, as the blue-lace blinds were kept lowered to protect our hostess's complexion. She wore a feather boa and pearls. . . .

"Have you heard from Toby?" Mrs. Mountfaucon asked me.

"He sounds very happy," I said cautiously, "and he

seems to be economizing a little. He has moved to a cheaper hotel."

"Oh, bless him. He *knows* there's all this bother about money. Mr. Basingfield is going to explain to me exactly where we stand, and really without him I should be perfectly lost. The great thing is that Toby shouldn't be needlessly worried."

I had another letter from him, this time with the heading "Hotel Neo-Tourist."

. . . This hotel is very central, with high, old-fashioned rooms, so I can spread out my painting things, and a nice flat roof, from which I'm painting the Acropolis. Coming up in the lift one sees the Parthenon rising with one, floor by floor. One goes out for meals, which is a pleasure in this arid, brilliant warmth.

Bella and I motor out to Vouliagmeni for a swim every afternoon, then we drink retsina under the pine-trees, then come back and dine *en ville,* generally at the Averoff. Madame P.-S. is apparently not going to buy a picture after all. I dare say her husband wants the money for a new suit. He's such a natty dresser. . . .

The progressive grading-down of the hotels seemed a clear indication, not of economy (of which Toby was hardly capable) but of a diminution of income. Possibly, I thought, he was much overdrawn. Perhaps the Distinguished Ghost had put the screw on. More probably he was being generous and extravagant for the benefit of the mulatress. There seemed no doubt that he was enjoying something like a honeymoon.

At Tregunter Road the telephone rang, and as soon as I heard Mrs. Mountfaucon's voice I expected her to be needing from me some assurance that Toby's excursion was doing him good. But no; she had something quite different to say, something momentous.

"Oh, my dear Jane, it's always such a pleasure to me to hear your voice. I think you'll be interested to hear what I have to tell you. Our Rembrandt is sold!"

The tone of her voice, which was by no means exultant, checked my impulse to congratulate her.

"Oh, Jane, I do hope it was for the best," she almost wailed, before I could say anything at all. I knew that if she had not had the receiver in one hand she would have been clasping both hands together in the agonized gesture that went with that voice. "But we have had to part with it for a mere *song*—oh no, not a song—let me say, rather, for a *dirge*! It has been bought by one of the *very best* collections in America, so at least it will have a good home. But oh, what we're getting for it won't at all cover what it has cost us. After so much expense and worry, I could almost wish that poor Cousin Harriet had never left it to us, or even that my darling Toby had never spotted what it was—but oh, I mustn't say that, for after all it was *sacrilege* to overpaint a Rembrandt. And at least the sin has been expiated. Mr. Basingfield thinks we were lucky to get rid of it even at this price. He says the bottom has fallen right out of the American market, and he fears this may affect us other ways. Oh, what worries me most is breaking the news to my poor Toby. He'll be so grievously disappointed."

"Yes, he'll be disappointed," I said, a little irritated by her determination to cushion him against the shocks of reality, "but, you know, he's really very tough."

"He's what, dear?"

"I say he's *tough*. I've never yet seen him crying over spilt milk. And as you yourself have said, when things go wrong he can be counted upon to do the right thing. I expect he'll be thankful that you haven't got to worry over the picture any longer. He knows what an immense amount of work and worry it has given you. And so do I."

"Bless your heart," she said.

So that was that.

I felt that the air was full of Mrs. Mountfaucon's and Toby's castles, or exotic villas, dissolving like summer clouds. This disappointment was not all that he would have to face: it looked as though his dwindled fortune might in his absence have dwindled further—not that his presence would have made much difference, because he was completely ignorant about investments and the management of money and quite disinclined to learn about them.

I received another letter from him. He was still in Athens, staying now with an English archaeologist, who had been a friend of his at Eton. This suggested that even a modest hotel was now beyond his means, but he made no allusion to money. He gave me a glowing description of how he and Bella Mestiza had been on a Sunday to the crowded *plage* at Glyphada. While they were strolling along, she in a scanty, open-meshed bathing-suit, daring at that time for the Aegean, he in a batik loincloth and a Cambodian fisherman's hat, they received an ovation, all the bathers and sun-bathers clapping and smiling and cheering. "We bowed to right and left," he wrote, "and like the royal family in *The Flower Beneath the Foot* gave them 'the Smile Extending.'" He did not know whether their welcome was due to Bella's having been recognized, or simply to their striking appearance. It was just the sort of incident to appeal to the actor in him, and I could imagine how much he had enjoyed it. I guessed that this little incident at Glyphada was a peak of pleasure, a sort of public admiration of his liaison with this Bella of his, a sort of salute to their liveliness and well-being. He said nothing about when he was coming home.

FOURTEEN

My work on the family papers was nearly finished. It would have been finished sooner if I had not become so involved with their owners and so often interrupted. I had made an inventory of all that was worth keeping, and I had shown Mrs. Mountfaucon the more interesting items. Certain points of heraldry, and a couple of title-deeds, and some letters written by the d'Arfey who was so handsomely rewarded by Charles II for his devotion to Charles I, were as helpful to her at this time as drugs or tonics. They soothed and distracted her, and in the intervals of her anxieties she discussed them with her few friends, including an old antiquary with a post in a museum. She kindly invited me to meet him and I had the impression that he was more interested in Mrs. Mount-faucon than in her archives. She must have had a good deal of masculine admiration in her day, and the crackling affability of a myopic octogenarian, the mottled skin of whose hands looked like gloves made of some other octo-genarian's mottled skin, was probably better than no male society at all.

Family affairs of my own made it necessary for me to be out of London for a couple of weeks. Directly I got back I went round to Duchess's Gate. I had a strange presentiment of crisis.

The Countess showed me into the drawing-room and Mrs. Mountfaucon rose at once from her writing-table, littered with what looked like bills, and came forward to meet me with both hands outstretched. I was surprised and yet, because of my foreboding, not altogether surprised to see that she was in mourning. I knew instantaneously from her bearing that it could not be for anybody whose death had caused her the deepest grief. Her mourning was deep enough, but it was stylish. She was wearing a smart black dress with black lace sleeves fitting tightly to her plump, white, and still not unshapely arms. On her head was a shady black hat with what looked like a purple quill lying on the brim. And round her neck was a choker of jet marbles.

"My dear Jane, you've heard, of course?"

" ?"

"Our poor, dear Mr. Basingfield!"

"No!"

"Quite suddenly. The night before last. I feel it very much. It seems the snapping of the very last link with my poor Morven. Nothing could have been more unexpected. He dined alone, it seems, quite frugally—a few beads of caviare, cold clear soup, a cut of salmon, some wisps of chicken, a bottle of Pouilly, a raspberry fool, and just a mouthful of his favorite cheese—*bleu d'Auvergne,* you know; I always used to try and get it for him when he came to lunch or dine with us here."

Her face seemed about to pucker into weeping, and I looked away, partly out of politeness, partly out of embarrassment, as her mouth made that curious chewing movement some people make when about to cry.

"No coffee!" she went on, with a not quite suppressed

tremor in her voice. And then, with control recovered, "He spent the evening, his man says, going through some papers. I expect, like most of us, he had had some money worries lately. And he went to bed quite early, having drunk, as usual, nothing but a glass of brandy and soda. When the man went to call him in the morning he was beyond any awakening in *this* world. He must have gone quite, quite peacefully in his sleep. Such a fortunate end. And he looked, the man said (and he seemed quite emotional), 'as innocent as a child.' But dare I say that Providence could perhaps have chosen a moment that would have seemed a shade less inconvenient for us— not that I question Its workings, Heaven forbid! But poor Mr. Basingfield was going, you know, to find out and explain to us exactly where we stand, and *that*, I rather fear, may be, through no fault of his—of that I'm sure— with one foot, I earnestly hope no more, in the soup."

I said I certainly hoped not, and asked whether Toby had been told.

"Oh, I telegraphed *instantly,* but no sooner had I done it than a wire arrived from him to say that he was on his way back. The wires must have crossed, like ships that pass in the night. . . . I expect his money has come to an end. Painting materials are so very expensive and he discards so many unfinished canvases. He sets himself such a very high standard. He aims at *perfection.* Of course I should hate him to be content with anything but his best."

I couldn't of course ask for news of Bella Mestiza, for I had no reason to think that Mrs. Mountfaucon knew of her existence, and every reason to presume that she did not.

"And now," she said, "I must hurry away. I feel it's almost wrong at such a time, but I had promised to take

Mildred Purbind—you remember meeting her? oh, and the humming-birds—!" She ducked her head, perhaps in case I should think her smile unfeeling, and I had a clear view of her hat. I was astonished to see that the feather was in fact a pen, with a trace of dried ink on the metal nib with which it was fitted. She lifted her head again, and went on, "Yes, I'm taking her, poor thing, as a little treat —she has such a very humdrum life at Chalfont—and Meliora Sperrow, to try and take her thoughts off her fibrositis, to see the new Greta Garbo. Toby is sure to want to know what it's like."

"I hope you don't mind my interrupting," I said, "but that beautiful feather in your hat looks almost like a pen."

"Oh, but it *is* a pen! I couldn't get the nib off, so I put it on the hat as it was. Do you think it matters awfully? It's such a fine broad feather, and purple, as you know, is a traditional mourning color. I felt that the black needed a *little* relief of some kind. I was very fond of Mr. Basingfield and I'm sure he wouldn't mind my not being wholly, utterly, in black. He was always so *understanding*."

In view of his distinction, I rather expected to hear of a memorial service for the Distinguished Ghost. Nothing was heard of one. He was buried in Shropshire, and Mrs. Mountfaucon felt unable to go to the funeral because she was expecting Toby back. In Toby's name and her own she ordered a handsome wreath.

When Toby returned, he seemed quite philosophical about the Rembrandt fiasco.

"Thank God we've got rid of the thing," he said. "Quite apart from that, we may have another financial cross to bear. We've got some money, or perhaps I'd better say we *had* some money, in America. Whether we've still got it won't appear until somebody has tidied up after the Distinguished Ghost, who chose, I must say, the moment of his exit with a want of tact he never showed before."

He was looking extremely well, sunned and salted by those Aegean afternoons, and with an air more confident and mature, which I attributed to Bella Mestiza. She, it appeared, had an engagement in Sofia, and would be returning to England in a few weeks' time. I must say that among my mixed feelings about this woman was a strong curiosity. When I asked Toby what her real name was, he looked a little shy and confused.

"As a matter of fact," he said, with just a hint of defiance in his voice, "she's a Mrs. Bunstable."

He looked at me apprehensively, as if I was going to make fun of this wildly unromantic name, and then grinned rather sheepishly.

"Oh," I said, with difficulty suppressing a loud hoot of laughter. (Bunstable!) "A widow?"

"No, she and her husband are separated. She says she doesn't know where he is now. He's white, and used to be in the Merchant Service."

"Was she fond of him?"

"I suppose so. She doesn't like talking about him. I think she had some idea once of settling down with him in a small house at Southsea or Southport or somewhere, and being respectable in a dull way, and neighborly, and very English, and having a family and I suppose it all fell through. She still has that side of her, a sort of Mildred Purbind side—but it's only one side."

"She didn't sound at all Purbindish in your letters. Has she got one of those lovely creamy café-au-lait skins and great big dark eyes?"

My voice sounded to me as if I had turned into a sisterly, sympathetic "good influence" after all, but I was perfectly well aware of a kind of resentment I felt against this woman who had so easily taken the place I could never have taken, though it had been open to me.

"Oh, she's not very dark," he said. "It's barely perceptible; but she can't help being color-conscious, and I suppose this leaning towards a dull imaginary model of an English housewife is a sort of compensation. And then, you see, she has to get her living by being a very different sort of person, an 'artiste' as she calls it, which means she has got to be smart and lively. And the getting of jobs seems to depend on a lot of what she calls 'contacts.' She seems to have one social life with theatrical and off-white friends and relations, and a tendency to jungle jinks; and another social life on more conventional lines, and this is all tied up with her child."

"Oh, there's a child?"

"Yes. A young boy. She keeps him at some sort of school in Surrey."

"What sort of school?"

"I can't quite make out. There seem to be boys of all ages from eight to eighteen. Very irregular. It must be a hotbed of vice. She's mad about him, and wants him to be a doctor. You know, social position and so on."

"H'm," I said. "But what about the home background and all that? Where, for instance, does he spend his holidays?"

"She has got a flat in Camden Town, and if she's there, he goes to her."

"And now, Toby, what about your plans?"

"I'm looking for a house. I must have room to paint."

And room, I thought, to receive Mrs. Bunstable. He could no doubt keep his mother from being jealous of his mistress by simply not telling her of Mrs. Bunstable's existence nor giving her any chance of finding it out. I had lately been reading *Dombey and Son,* and there flashed across my mind a passage against which I had put a mark. It was Cousin Feenix's observation that "in point of fact one does see, in this world—which is remarkable for devilish strange arrangements, and for being decidedly the most unintelligible thing within a man's experience— very odd conjunctions . . ." Yes, his liaison with Mrs. Bunstable seemed a very odd conjunction.

I asked him about his painting, and he immediately began to fidget in the way he always did when guilt was mixed with irritation. When he was merely irritated, the most characteristic sign of it (if he was sitting down) was the waggling of the foot of whichever leg was crossed over the other. But when he felt guilty as well, he avoided one's eyes, grew haughty, and began to stammer. He said he wanted to do a series of canvases of Balinese dancers. He had a quantity of photographs and some costumes and ornaments that he had brought back from Bali some years before, and he hoped to use Bella as a model.

I found it difficult to imagine an off-white mulatress, or whatever she was, who had first swum into my ken as having publicly kicked a cigarette out of the mouth of a total stranger, in the role of one of those formally trained, heavy-lidded, hieratically posturing, flexible-fingered, tragically graceful exquisites, but I didn't say so. Instead I inquired, perhaps tactlessly, about the painting he had been doing in Greece. He turned his head away, and began to stammer, in a rather lordly way, a complaint about the intensity of the light in Attica, which, he said, "killed" all color.

"Oh, come, Toby," I said. "You've known me long enough to be a bit franker than that. Didn't dalliance rather obtrude?"

He melteu at once into that infinitely endearing smile of his, the smile of a naughty boy.

God knows, and of course already then knew, Toby hadn't much else to smile about. How we all carry in ourselves the seeds of our destinies—how characters and events are inseparable—how, with one blow after another, we are driven, as a post is driven into the ground, deeper into the places prepared for us—*that* is what I'm trying to write about.

And now the Rembrandt fiasco rapidly receded from our minds, because there was soon something even more serious to think about. Not long after Toby's return I had invited him and his mother to dine with me, as they sometimes did, in my rather cramped quarters at Tregunter Road. I was already planning exactly what I should cook for them and what I should give them to drink when Toby rang up to ask if I would very much mind going to Duchess's Gate instead.

"Mother doesn't quite feel equal to going out," he said. "She has had rather an upset. I'll explain when you come." At this I could hear a fluster of pleadings and mutterings at the other end. "Hullo? Jane? Mother wants me to say that she knows you'll understand, though I can't imagine how you can understand something that hasn't been explained to you. . . . Oh, do shut up, mother! . . . Mother says she means that you're so understanding. . . ."

I had heard that before; I have heard it since. It only means that other people expect one to listen to their accounts of the messes they have got themselves into.

When I arrived at Duchess's Gate the first thing I noticed was that the Countess, who admitted me, was rather down in the mouth. The second thing was that Mrs. Mountfaucon was no longer in mourning, but was curiously constrained in manner. I kissed her affectionately.

"You must forgive me, Jane, if I'm not quite myself tonight." She was looking suddenly much older than usual, and her eyes were a little bloodshot. "The truth is that a most *harrowing* kettle of fish has come to light."

"A mixed metaphor, mother," said Toby sharply. "Kettles can hardly be said to come to light, or to harrow. Have a drink, Jane."

"The truth is," said Mrs. Mountfaucon simply, spreading out her little hands with the palms upward, "that we're quite, quite ruined."

"Ruin, my dear mother, is a relative term. The fact is, Jane, that old Basingfield simply made away with most of what was left of our money. The Distinguished Ghost was nothing more nor less than a crook."

"Oh hush, Toby! I'm sure he never meant—he didn't know—"

"Of course he knew very well what he was doing, mother! Of course he meant to do it!"

"Oh, Toby, *de mortuis*—"

"*De mortuis*, mother, *nil nisi bunkum!*"

I didn't know what to say: the news was a knockout. Mr. Basingfield was the last person I should have suspected of such behavior. I tried to think of any least sign he had given of not being the perfect trustee. All I could think of was his spectral appearances and disappearances, and his perhaps too emphatic insistence, when I had walked with him across the Park, on the need for Toby and his mother to be adaptable.

"I shall of course leave Duchess's Gate," Mrs. Mountfaucon was saying. "I've already given notice to Laceman." (That explained the Countess's low spirits.) "Mrs. Crumpsey says she's too old to begin a new job and if

133

she can't work for me she'll retire and go and live, bless her, with her sister in Derbyshire. I shall take a small flat somewhere and Toby will have to take a smaller house than he intended, and he'll have to be very, very careful."

This didn't sound like total ruin, and although I couldn't imagine Toby being very, very careful I was at once somewhat relieved: at least they wouldn't be selling matches in the gutter immediately.

"The extraordinary thing is," said Toby, "that nobody knows what our so-called trustee did with our money. In the last ten years the old swine seems to have taken something like fifty thousand and it's all gone, I suppose to some woman."

"Oh, Toby, hush!"

"Yes, my dear, hush indeed! I suppose you're telling us it was all just one big mistake. I'm afraid the mistake was made by your late husband in his choice of friends—but it's no good howling about that now. Only for God's sake don't make excuses for the old shark for whom you so promptly went into mourning, which I must admit was very becoming, and appropriate at least to our loss of fortune. I hope you'll ring up Harrods in the morning and order sack-cloth and ashes for two, so that we may repent in proper style our folly in trusting our trustee. If your first and more prudent husband can see what a mess we're in now, he must be whizzing round in his grave like a circular saw."

"Don't rub it in, Toby," I said. "You go rather far."

Mrs. Mountfaucon made a little whimpering noise and covered her face with her hands. Toby, possibly a little ashamed of his cruelty, turned away from her and began abruptly mixing another cocktail. He agitated the shaker with such vigor that he reminded me of people who seek to relieve tense feelings by smashing china. It turned out to be a very strong cocktail, and perhaps because of it dinner was a less uncheerful meal than it might have been.

Nothing more was said about Mr. Basingfield, and I do not recall ever having heard either of them allude to him again.

In that silence I find a certain grandeur. It must have been tempting for Toby to harp on the fact that Mr. Basingfield had been his stepfather's trusted friend. As for Mrs. Mountfaucon, she was a good Christian. However greatly wronged, she would I believe have sought excuses for whomsoever had wronged her. I have no doubt she prayed every day for forgiveness of her own peccadilloes on the grounds that she tried to forgive those who did her harm; and I have no doubt she believed that she must not judge lest she be judged. There is something to be said for Christianity. I think she must have been almost more shocked that the so gentlemanly Mr. Basingfield had betrayed a trust than by the consequences to herself. If religion sustained her in misfortune, it did not sustain her son, and if he had ever addressed the Deity to which she prayed, his tone would have been argumentative.

After dinner that night Toby did not talk about his own reverses of fortune, but about the war which he still exceptionally thought—for Hitler had not yet come to power—impending within the next few years. I suppose this advertence to public matters was a sort of sublimation. I had again very strongly, I remember, the feeling that his own destiny was linked to that of the society that had evolved him. A man who feels that there is something terminal about his own existence may easily envisage the world as failing with him: that is why old men habitually regard change as decay, and why they enlarge upon the decline of manners and morals and the poor prospects of the world they soon expect to leave. Toby was not an old man but he was an old man's son, and it was as if he unconsciously dreaded the coming of a new phase of civilization in which there would be no place for him. His recklessness, his sarcasm, his intelligence, and liveliness were signs that he was a man still young and vigorous, but his dark forebodings seemed to come from an ancestral voice within himself, prophesying war.

In the meantime civilization certainly had a place for him, and if it was a place of which a doctrinaire socialist could hardly have approved, what did that matter? And what does it matter now?

"War or no war," said his mother, "we must each of us have a roof over our heads, Toby. Tomorrow we'll begin house-hunting."

FIFTEEN

In those days house-hunting in London was not an ordeal, and without much trouble Toby found a house to suit his tastes and intentions. It was in that placid region bounded on the north by the Kensington Road, on the east by Palace Gate, on the west by Kensington Square, and to the south stopping short of those dark clumps of eighteen-seventyish cliff-dwellings of an outmoded pretentious-ness and only runnable, as houses, by slave labor no longer to be had.

Toby's choice was a little white stucco cottage, called by the agents a bijou residence, built a century or so earlier, and not in the least "dated," because it was neat, simple, decently proportioned, and manageable. It would always have made a pleasant abode for two or three people, with or without a contented cat or two, so long as it held together. I say "would have" because it received a direct hit in the middle of the Second World War, and in the light of a frosty full moon, so an eyewitness told me, it burst like a dry puff-ball. I passed the site the other day in late summer. For years now it has been thick with willow-herb, and just then it was releasing a glistening flight of silken emissaries, each silent seed rising in the cloudless afternoon with its promise of a rosy future.

When Toby moved to this pretty little nest of the time of William IV or perhaps of George IV, his mother moved to a two-roomed flat at Equerry Mansions in Westminster. From the establishment at Duchess's Gate it was easy to furnish these two new abodes, and it would have been easy to furnish more, except that a good many of their things were too big. I thought it strange, if these two were really anything like what Mrs. Mountfaucon called "ruined," that they didn't sell some of their treasures or at least some of their superfluities instead of putting them into storage for an indefinite period and at a ponderable expense.

For whom, I could not help wondering, and against what change of fortune, was Mrs. Mountfaucon holding on to these possessions? So far as I knew, she had no expectations of a windfall from any quarter. Did she imagine that her son would marry an heiress, become a best-selling painter, or protract his line? If so, I thought she was dreaming. The question remained unanswered, and the walls of a vast repository in a westerly suburb closed over a houseful of fine things, of marble and wood and silk and glass and gold, things hand-made as they were never likely to be made again, things evolved in taste and leisure, things with associations, like Pope's chair, the King of Saxony's presents, the Lely of Louise de Querouaille, and even those two portraits of Mrs. Mountfaucon and her son which had so impressed me on my very first visit to Duchess's Gate, and which were much too big either for a sixth-floor flat in Equerry Mansions or for Toby's little house in Navarino Grove.

I must say that when Toby had moved into his new abode it didn't look like that of a "ruined" man. He had done it up with the help of Butterball Evans, I should think at no small expense. I thought the decorations a shade too fashionable.

Looking out from the windows at the back one could see, behind the adjoining houses, little gardens with old pear-trees, trim carpets of lawn, and blackish, ferny rockeries. In the garden next door there was a decaying, weather-worn bust of, perhaps, Marcus Aurelius, much frequented by sparrows. The garden of Toby's cottage had been abolished just after the First World War, and on the site had been built a well-designed studio, approachable from the hall by a short, glass-covered passage.

Studios had been much in fashion in the twenties, when people with conventional antecedents and with more money than sense, people like some of Lydia Delap's followers, dabblers in music or sculpture, had pretended to be creative in them. They used them mostly for relaxing the social and moral standards of their parents, and regarded the possession of a studio as a symbol of emancipation and sophistication. Studios were the tents, so to speak, that marked the Flight into Bohemia.

Toby had engaged a daily woman to come in, as he said, "to rearrange the dust." No doubt she had soon discovered what I had noticed at Duchess's Gate, that he was hopelessly untidy. All his life servants had been tidying up after him. He had never been taught and had never bothered to put anything back in its proper place, and when he couldn't find what he wanted he had simply rung a bell. Now things were different. On the Empire sofa in his little drawing-room—a piece of furniture which terminated in brass swans' heads and was covered with striped yellow satin—there was soon a sort of high-water mark of French art magazines and unopened bills, interspersed with unsharpened pencils, over-ripe apples, half-empty packets of cigarettes, and unanswered invitation cards. In the fireplace a fetish from the Gold Coast held a dance program in its whitened wooden teeth. And beside a fine Pinwell water-color that hung over the mantelshelf he had already been jotting down telephone numbers on the white-and-gold wallpaper.

On the walls of his bedroom grotesque picture postcards, photographs cut from newspapers and magazines, and reproductions of works of art were soon pasted up haphazard, and among them were hastily scribbled addresses, reminders of engagements, a limerick in modern Greek, and snatches of the words and music of some American Negro songs of a kind at that time in vogue. Some of these, he told me, were in Bella Bunstable's repertoire; of others he had gramophone records. He seemed more than usually cheerful and was continually breaking into song.

> "Ashes to ashes and dust to dust [he would warble]
>   If you don' like ma figure
>   Tak' yo' hand off ma bust."

And there were phrases that seemed to haunt him as if they had been witty aphorisms—"Put a coin on the dresser before you start," or "De browner de berry, de sweeter de juice"; something about a character called "Ol' Poppa Jackson, de jelly-roll king"; and something else about a handy man, which seemed to be full of leering double meanings:

> "Yes, every mornin'
>   He's up before dawn
>   Trimmin' de rough edges
>   Off mah law-awn—
>   He's such a ha-a-andy man!"

It is natural to sing when one is cheerfully amorous, and the most trivial tunes, both music and words, become easily an expression of one's well-being, and become charged with private associations.

When he broke into these ditties I could not help being amused by the liveliness and skill with which he sang them and by the sauciness of his grimaces, but I felt somewhat detached, because they obviously meant a great deal more to him than they possibly could to me. I thought them just sexy buffooneries from Harlem. As I had never seen Bella Mestiza, or Bunstable, who was obviously the source from which he drew them, and as he himself seemed to become negroid when he sang them, I chose to forget his description of her looks and to think of her as fat, black, and steatopygous, with over-active sweat-glands, a mouth like a letter-box fitted with piano keys, and the whites of her eyes like hard-boiled eggs.

Sometimes, in less exuberant moods, Toby became European and graceful in his snatches of song. *"Viens dans ce bocage,"* he would plaintively implore, and he did not seem then to be addressing in his imagination this gross phantom he had evoked in mine, but some slender and doomed European, whom I saw as having a skin of the most delicate whiteness, particularly behind her ears and on the insides of her forearms. I seemed to see her helpless little wrists, arched insteps, and eyes bright with intelligence and desire but shadowed by some sad history. It was as if he were lamenting a *douceur de vivre* of which he had caught the last fragrance before it evaporated. At such times I was tempted to tell him that he ought to have stuck to singing after all, but I did not, because that might have seemed a reflection of his painting.

His unhappiness, his evident obsession with his Bella, his sociable habits, and dispersed interests (he was going, for instance, often at this time to the theater and the films) did not prevent him working hard and steadily. His studio was littered with enlargements of the photographs he had taken of Balinese dancers, with drawings he had made from them, and with unfinished canvases on which he seemed again and again to have tried to seize the unseizable.

It was the old story that many an artist short of mastery knows: an experience had been strongly felt, so deeply that it had become part of him, but struggle as he might, the form in which he must project it constantly eluded him. Something was needed to precipitate it, but that something was lacking, or there was some obstacle in the way. I tried to discover what that obstacle was, for I hoped to see it swept away, the vision cleared, and the hand freed. Sometimes I was disconcerted by signs of an exaggerated diffidence, which seemed to me associated with a sort of nihilism at the heart of him, a sort of hope-lessness. I thought then, and I still think, that he was haunted by that most fatal of unformulated suspicions—that the world didn't really need him and would need him less and less as time went on. It is a feeling that some people are bound to have when they belong to a declining order of society, when they have been uprooted, when they still have more property than responsibility, and do not belong closely enough to any community-within-the-community held together by common interests and practic-ing some degree of mutual aid.

Toby certainly worked hard at that house in Navarino Grove. He used to get up early and paint steadily for five or six hours, and he generally did some work in the after-noon or evening as well. If Mrs. Bunstable ever came to the house when I was there I was never allowed to catch a glimpse or sound of her. I always used to inquire about her, since he had from the first honored me with his con-fidences about her, and I always heard that she was very well. Then one day he said that she was out of a job and was hoping to get a small part in a film. From various small signs of spasmodic attempts at economy it looked as if he might be contributing to her support and finding it a strain.

A slight and typically bizarre train of events now took up his attention. It had to do with a console table, Butter-ball Evans, and a girl called Letty Tracy, of whom, up to this time, I had never heard. The beginning of the matter was that Butterball happened to say something to Toby about Letty Tracy. This was a shock to him, be-cause he knew them both but didn't know that they knew each other, and would rather, as they both knew him, have kept them apart. He now remembered that he had once, years before, lent Letty Tracy a console table, and it occurred to him that he would like to have it back. He didn't tell me whether he wanted it for his own house or to give to Mrs. Bunstable.

According to Toby, the table was a rare object made in Paris about 1820. He said it was elegantly proportioned and made of a rare wood with a satiny surface and very beautiful grain. I forget whether he had inherited or acquired it, but he had lent it to this Tracy girl at a time when he was liquidating some temporary dwelling-place of his—I think it had been a flat in Ebury Street. Letty Tracy, he said, was an "ash-blonde" whom he had known when she was at the Slade. She had later come into some money, and with what he regarded as a sorry want of originality had bought a cottage in Sussex. He told me it was called "Great Titlarks," and he thought this name a huge joke. She had much admired the table, and out of gratitude to her (he didn't say what he had to be grateful for) he had lent it to her. She had remained in her cottage ever since. She hardly ever visited London, had come to nothing as a painter, and apparently devoted all her time to entertaining guests, some of whom stayed at Great Titlarks for months at a time. Toby himself had had a standing invitation to go and stay with her, but had never done anything about it, and it was by now a long time since they had met or written to one another.

Having suddenly taken it into his head that he would like this table back, Toby was just going to write and ask Letty Tracy for it when he heard that Lilac Evans was going down to spend a week-end with her. Butterball seemed to him much too smart and mondaine to go and stay with so obscure a person as Letty, and he was suspicious and curious about her motive. He showed this plainly and I dare say she was amused by his agitation. She said that she was going mainly for some country air, she liked Letty

143

and admired her looks, and wanted to persuade her to do some modelling for a photographer of fashions. Toby had meant at first to ask Butterball to convey to Letty his hankering for his table, but then he changed his mind and said nothing; he thought it would be better to approach Letty directly about it.

He saw Butterball soon after her visit to Letty, and she gave him such a glowing account of it that he at once wanted to follow her example.

"The only thing is," she said, "I don't awfully like all her ideas about decoration. For instance, she has had all the furniture in her drawing-room enamelled strawberry-pink."

"*All?*" cried Toby. "*Pink,* did you say? Oh merciful heaven! *And* my console table?"

"*Your* console table? I did notice one, and a very pretty shape, but is it yours?"

"Yes, it's mine! That's what comes of lending good things to a bird-brain in a fair ground, a damned fair ground, in Sussex by the sea. I might have guessed that having failed to paint portraits Letty would start painting other people's furniture. I shall go down to Great Titlarks at once and cut her throat from ear to ear."

This was only rhetoric. He did go down, and she herself innocently drew his attention to the "improvement," as she outrageously called it, of the console table by several coats of strawberry-pink enamel.

"As a matter of fact," he said to her, "I think as it was only lent to you, you might have asked me first. I rather want it back, and it will be an appalling job having the paint removed, even if it's possible."

Letty had registered a kind of huffy astonishment and had insisted that she had quite taken it for granted that he had *given* her the table, otherwise of course she would never have dreamed, etc., etc. With rather a bad grace, she had expressed a reluctant willingness to return it to him, whereupon he had abruptly changed the subject and had not reverted to it.

Soon after his return to London her current young man had arrived for the week-end, a sub-lieutenant in the Navy who was, it seems, a good deal younger than herself. She must have told him about the table, because he presently took it upon himself to write, without her knowledge, to Toby, whom he had never met, a letter of singular egregiousness, in which he actually threatened Toby, if he took any further steps in the matter, with—of all things—a horse-whipping. Toby showed me the letter. It was so absurd that at first he thought it was some kind of joke, but when he realized that it was serious, he at once replied to it. When he told me he had done this, I said I thought he might have been wiser to get his lawyer to reply. He said he hadn't thought of that, but had kept a copy of his letter. I asked if I might see it, and this is what he had written:

Although I have never heard of you, you have written me an affected letter in which you, a puppy in uniform, pose romantically as the champion of a supposedly wronged woman. You may cease to concern yourself with my private affairs. Your intervention is insolent, and I can only suppose that your ignorance of the elements of civility must be attributed to the boyishness so noticeable in junior officers of the Royal Navy, an immaturity itself ascribable no doubt to the narrow specialization of a naval education. The standards of the gun-room, or wherever it is that you are confined with your equals in some poor semblance of civilized social intercourse, are not those of the world, and you are quite laughably far behind the times in your quaint allusion to the horse-whip—an obsolete stage property of mid-Victorian melodrama. Try and be your age, and of your age.

Your misplaced and clumsy attempt to be chivalrous has led you, I notice, to threaten me with violence. You bore me, but I do not fear you. I shall not trouble to inform the police, but if you are so rash as to show your face here I shall give you a sound drubbing, throw you out, and report your conduct to your commanding officer. He would no doubt give you the same advice which I give you, namely, Stick to your binnacles and bollards. In other words, Mind your own business.

Toby had evidently enjoyed composing this letter, and it was effective, because nothing more was heard of the young man. As for the table, Toby decided to leave it with the occupant of Great Titlarks. It had, as he said, been "ruined," and now he came to think of it, it did seem just possible that he might have allowed her to get an impression in the first place that he was giving and not just lending it to her. I restrained myself from saying sententiously "Neither a lender nor a borrower be," but I could not help thinking how like a man it was to try and get something away from one woman, of whom he had tired, in order to give it to another, with whom he was infatuated. I also suspected that Bella Mestiza, alias Mrs. Bunstable, was the sort of person who might well have approved of antique furniture being covered with strawberry-pink enamel. On the other hand, perhaps he had only wanted it back for his own use.

SIXTEEN

When Toby moved to Navarino Grove his mother had determined to remain within easy reach of Westminster Abbey. She liked making her devotions there, knew much about the Abbey's history and antiquities, and had long been on friendly terms with the vergers, a canon or two, and very likely with the Dean himself.

She took, as I have said, a flat in Equerry Mansions, a building smaller than Queen Anne's Mansions, less rococo than St. Ermin's, less austere-looking than Artillery Mansions, and less opulent-looking than St. James's Court. Equerry Mansions had been finished in time for Queen Victoria's Diamond Jubilee. Confident and solid, it is built of brick of a rather angry red and faced with a good deal of superfluous ornament that conforms to no style at all. The lack of proportion and harmony, together with the architect's inability to leave any space untrammelled, irritates the eye of a critical beholder and allows it no resting-place. The building's particular kind of ugliness makes it look as if it had been built some ten years earlier; it suggests the eighties at their most showy and aberrant.

As you go in, the hall, which ought to have been imposing in view of the building's purpose and pretensions, seems cramped, and is badly lighted and crowded with knobbly, fretted woodwork. At the time of Mrs. Mount-faucon's arrival the hall was presided over by the head hall-porter, an old soldier called Corby. Of more than medium height, with a solid figure, the face of an elder statesman, hair like stainless steel, and a complexion like a huntsman, he wore a dark green frock-coat with silver buttons and a row of medals always in a high state of polish. Polish was the outstanding characteristic of Corby himself. He had beautiful manners, the result, I should say, of a naturally fatherly disposition, a good digestion, an old-fashioned military training, a happy marriage, and a long association with the upper and upper middle classes when they were still definable and unmistakable and felt secure. If he made up to them because he knew it paid him to do so, he may also have made up to them because he liked them and believed in them: there was nothing sham, I will swear, about his urbanity and good nature. He and Mrs. Mountfaucon were very soon on the best of terms. Not only would they have understood and appreciated one another at sight, but she had quickly discovered that he had served in the same regiment as her second husband.

Whenever I went to see Mrs. Mountfaucon, Corby would conduct me deferentially to the lift and wait until I was inside and the liftman had shut the gate before with-drawing to his glazed office near the front door. The lift itself was coeval with the building. It ascended slowly, with a prolonged wheezing, sighing, and creaking, past slow Niagaras of over-elaborate wrought iron-work and vistas of lincrusta; and when it went down it seemed to swoop, causing one's insides to leave their moorings and hover over them. It was encumbered with a bevelled look-ing-glass in a carved frame and a small bench upholstered in shiny red leather. At the sixth floor it would stop with a sudden puffing noise, the liftman would throw open a large wrought-iron gate like a garden gate and shut it after me again with a smooth clash, and I would be left to make my way down a long, red-carpeted corridor to Mrs. Mountfaucon's flat, her "service" flat.

She would open the door herself and extend her arms in welcome. She was always wearing a biggish hat over her fleecy golden wig, generally a black hat, in the front of which she almost habitually wore a long silver brooch representing a horse at full gallop with Mazeppa. Toby liked her to wear this ornament, and as she always tried to seize her least chances of winning his approval, and as there was always the possibility of his coming to see her without previous notice, she liked to be ready for him. Her hats, and her style in general, seemed to me a shade too ample for her new setting. The flat consisted of a minimal hall, a small sitting-room with a balcony affording a not very distant view of the top of the Army and Navy Stores, a bedroom even smaller, and a bathroom so cramped that while sitting on the lavoratory-seat one could, had one not been single in purpose, at the same time and without contortion have paddled one's feet in the bath and washed one's hands in the basin. If these rooms were alarmingly disproportionate to their occupant and her habits and tastes, I must say I never heard her complain of them and she often praised them. I think she was finding it restful to live quite alone and to be free of many responsibilities that go with husbands and houses.

I remember very well my first visit to her at this place and the childlike delight with which she showed me the flat and explained its advantages, especially the balcony with its window-boxes. She showed me some of the flowers she was beginning to cultivate, and launched into reminiscences of gardening on the grand scale years before at Marsh. She showed me too how she had arranged some of her more treasured possessions, only a few of which had she now the space to display. We had already entered the era of the one-room flatlet, the caravan, the prefabricated shack, and the concentration camp, an era in which there is often more room for the pleasures of memory than for inherited objects of art.

"Because you've now finished our papers," she said, "(and what *splendid* work you've done, as I was telling the Keeper of Prints and Drawings only yesterday) I hope that won't mean, my dear Jane, that you're going to drop us. We have grown fond of you, you know, you're almost like one of the family. And Toby thinks the world of you. He has a good many acquaintances and friends, I don't even know who a great many of them are, and I'm afraid some of them are only friends in name. But you're different. You see, he *respects* you. He admires your judgment—"

"Oh!" I burst out. "How awful! It sounds as if I were a man, and an old one at that!"

"Oh, but Jane, if I may say so, most men would envy you your level-headedness."

"Oh, but that's not what a woman wants to be admired for—not this woman, at any rate—even if I *am* level-headed, which I doubt."

"But you didn't let me finish what I was saying. I was going to say, 'He admires your judgment, but he admires you for much more than that.' "

I said nothing.

"And he feels, I know, that you *believe* in him. . . . At present," she went off at a tangent, "it's a great anxiety to him to know where to turn for money. I do so hope he'll be able to find an opening for his talents that will bring him in enough to live on."

I see it all so clearly. The box-like little room with its bibelots, and "Daddy's" sword above the narrow chimney-piece, and the miniatures, and Mrs. Mountfaucon, sitting very upright in a small Empire chair, with her back to the light and Mazeppa fastened to her, and under the brim of her hat a straying curl or two of her golden wig catching such wan light as the french window could absorb from the Westminster sky, and her hands clasped before her in that characteristic attitude of supplication. It was from this moment, I think, that I first got it into my head that Toby was really short of money and had little prospect of earning much.

During the years that followed, the years during which it became rapidly plainer that the war he had so long foreseen could not be far off, Toby's concern about his income was seldom in abeyance. He tried various ways of making money, but his restless nature prevented him concentrating for long upon any one of them. He had sold two or three of his own paintings since he had moved to Navarino Grove, but diffidence, or lack of perseverance, or a delusion that he could make money quickly in some other way, had diverted him from continuing to paint.

The next time I saw his studio, it was a strange sight. Somebody (could it have been Bella Bunstable?) had put it into his head that he had it in him to become the English Walt Disney, or could at least produce a series of animated cartoons that would bring him money. He had managed to arouse a little curiosity in a film tycoon, and this personage had expressed a willingness to see what Toby could do; the technical processes and cost of producing such cartoons could be considered later. Toby had accordingly spent several days of almost uninterrupted work in "seeing what he could do." The result was that the studio was filled with drawings and adumbrations of human and animal "characters," and with strips, or sequences, showing them in various activities. He didn't seem keen to talk much about them, and from the few he showed me, I could have seen, if I hadn't already guessed, that he would never be a Disney. His creations quite lacked the common touch; some of them were very delicate, satirical, original; they would never do. He knew it; he knew that I knew it; and we did not pursue the subject.

One morning, some weeks later, I heard of somebody who wanted an illustrator for a book. I at once thought of Toby. I didn't telephone to him but decided to look in at Navarino Grove on my way elsewhere. I was admitted to the house by the charwoman, who showed me into the drawing-room. It was in disorder, even by Toby's standards. Some flowers in a vase ought to have been thrown away, on the floor there was a trail of unopened envelopes that looked as if they contained bills or ultimatums, and over them was a light powdering of dust. I was just thinking that the woman might have apologized for showing me into a room which she had not yet, and I should have thought not lately "done," when I noticed a fur coat lined with violet silk thrown over the back of a chair, and while I was looking at this coat I was surprised by a light soprano voice behind the folding doors which divided the drawing-room from Toby's bedroom. The voice was singing, with gusto:

> "How could Red Riding Hood
>   Have been so very good,
>   And still keep the wolf from the door?"

Then it gave way to humming, the humming of a mellifluous and contented bee, then it stopped for a moment or two, then suddenly I heard sung with great emphasis on the other side of the door:

"Who filled your ba-a-asket—"

then the door opened, and I heard, much louder:

"*If* I may a-a-ask it?"

then I found myself face to face with Bella Mestiza, alias Mrs. Bunstable, who exclaimed:

"Oh, I'm sorry!"

The first thing I noticed was that, as Toby had told me, she was hardly "colored" at all, at least so far as her skin was concerned; it was of hardly more than a deep creamy tint. Her complexion was clear and matt, like the petals of a dusky white rose more dusky than white, and she seemed to have little makeup except some oil on her eyelids and a salmon-pink lipstick. But her hair was quite negroid, and she wore it in a defiant upstanding bang or fuzz, as if all her southern pigmentation had rushed to her head in a flourish. Her eyes were bright and mobile, and she seemed extremely cheerful.

"I had *no idea* there was anybody here!" she cried, speaking with that over-emphatic animation not uncommon with certain women, notably some Jewish or American women, who behave as if everything depends on their keeping up a reputation for uncommon vitality. "I think you must be Jane. Of course I've heard such a lot about you from Toby—"

"And I about you," I said.

"I bet you have! But you know how it is with him, how he loves to keep his friends apart. Why, I don't even know who some of them *are*! I tell him he's just too

Oriental!" (I didn't quite get the point of this. Perhaps she meant that he would like to keep her in purdah if he could). "But anyway," she went on, "I'm glad we've met at *last,* and won't he get a shock when he finds out!"

At that moment a rapid tattoo was audible: it was Toby rushing downstairs in a pair, as it appeared, of heavy scarlet slippers from Morocco and a silk dressing-gown. He was drawing deeply at a cigarette just lighted in sheer agitation, I dare say, over the discovery that Bella and I had met. As he came into the room his eyes seemed enormous and for an instant half-hostile, half-panic-stricken.

"Mrs. Thingummy called out that there was somebody to see me, but of course she didn't say *who*. Bella, this is Jane."

"Oh, you're telling me! Why, we're already old chums!"

She pranced about the room, giving an impression of springiness, as though she might suddenly turn a cart-wheel. She was wearing a thin frock of dark, spotted foulard which fitted rather tightly to her elastic bust and trim hips. Skirts were being worn a bit longer than in the twenties, but hardly by her, and her legs were uncommonly shapely, though a bit on the muscular side.

"I don't suppose," she said, "Toby has told you about Jocky, that's my big son. He's just crazy about football and I'm on my way now to get him a new pair of football boots. Oh, the way that boy grows!"

Toby helped her into her coat. A bunch of artificial violets was fastened to the collar.

"Back before lunch!" she cried, giving him a playful slap, and "Au revoir!" she cried to me, and out she breezed.

"It's like having a whirlwind in the house," Toby said. "It must be her tropical blood."

He was looking at me quizzically, and longing, I believe, to ask me what I thought of her. I felt that if I was too enthusiastic he would prevent me seeing her again, and that if I was not enthusiastic enough he would be disappointed. I said I thought she was perfectly charming, that I had somehow expected her to be darker, and that she was obviously very fond of him.

"I'd like you to see Jocky," he said, after a pause. "I've practically adopted him. I wish to God I could make some money and sell some pictures or something. I think I shall have to give up this house."

"Oh, what a pity. You can't have been here six months yet."

"I know, but I simply can't afford it. And I can't see why, when mother only has a flat, I should have a house."

"The idea was, wasn't it, that you should have somewhere to paint?"

"H'm. I can't *draw* well enough. I ought to do nothing but draw for ten years, and I can't, because I must make some money somehow."

"You might write, Toby. I wish you'd write down some of your stories about your relations. If you don't, they'll be lost for ever, and they are too good to lose."

"Do you really think so? Well, I might. . . . But I've got some other ideas."

"I hope you're happy with Bella."

"I should be, if I had more money. I'm sorry to harp on the subject, and to think that I was brought up to the convention that one should never speak of it! But Bella's jobs are rather erratic, with hiatuses between; she doesn't get a penny now from her husband—and there's Jocky."

I began to think it might be a good thing that he had

these new incentives. They might turn him into something like a responsible family man. That would be something quite new.

SEVENTEEN

Glancing past Mrs. Mountfaucon I could see through the open french window a child's toy watering-can on the balcony.

"Ah, Jane, you're looking at my watering-can. You've no idea what a speech it provoked from our Toby. He calls it a doll's watering-can, and is *most* scornful. He says it's affected of me. He thought I had got it, I believe, to show him that one ought to cut one's coat according to one's cloth, or whatever the saying is. But of course I never try to preach at him. It would be hopeless, and there's no question at present, I'm afraid, of cutting any coats; we shall have to wear the ones we've got, until they drop off. It did seem, I must confess, a reasonable economy to buy such a small watering-can. I admit it's a mere toy. But as you see, my garden's not large, the balcony itself is *minute,* and I only have to refill the little can half a dozen times to water all my plants. . . . By the way, Toby has quite given up the idea of doing those animal cartoons. His heart wasn't in them at all."

"I wish he'd stick to his painting," I said.

"Oh, so do I! But he won't. And now he's off on quite a different track. And for this we have to thank an old acquaintance of his, a Miss Tracy. I keep seeing her face everywhere, and so do you, but I dare say you're quite unaware of it. One can't open an illustrated paper without seeing her showing off some new coat-and-skirt or evening frock, and now I see she's advertising those what-d'ye-call-'em cigarettes—you know, the advertisements that say, 'A tonic for your tonsils.' I understand that in fact she's a non-smoker."

"Tut," I said, wondering what on earth all this was leading up to.

"Miss Evans dug her up out of her country retreat and persuaded her to become a professional photographer's model, and now she's simply *coining* money. She has been talking to Toby—"

"Don't tell me he's going to be a photographer?"

Mrs. Mountfaucon recoiled slightly, as if I had suggested some incapacity on his part.

"No. I rather wish he were. So *paying*. No. She knows his extraordinary flair for style and she has persuaded him to become—you'll never guess—a milliner! It seems so funny for a man. He's already begun to attend a class, learning to make hats. But they say that at present his stitches are too large." She hid her face in her hands.

"Toby always likes to do things on the grand scale," I said. "And perhaps one of his stitches in time would save nine."

"You're making fun of him, cruel Jane. . . . My dear, it's a perfect conspiracy. Miss Evans, Miss Tracy, and I don't know who else—they've all encouraged him. They've put it into his head, I do believe, that he can set up on his own as a creator of fashions. They've promised to try and persuade other women to go to him and buy things, when he opens up on his own. What they *haven't* undertaken is to explain where on earth the capital is to come from."

"But surely it will take some time to learn the trade," I said. "And perhaps he'll get tired of it, before there's any question of his setting up on his own."

"Oh, my dear Jane, I'm afraid not. He's quite determined. I shall *have* to find the money for him. There'll be nothing for it but to sell the Crotchester cottages. They're all that's left."

I had no confidence at all in the project. It was true that Toby had a most uncommon sense of style. I didn't doubt his ability to design somewhat extravagant fashions, provided that he went through the necessary preliminary training. What I did not believe was that he had the capital, or the power of raising capital, or the persistence, or the commercial acumen to compete successfully in the world of high fashion. I myself knew little about it, so I didn't feel that it was for me to go out of my way to discourage him. Conceivably he could perform this difficult feat; he was brilliant and versatile. I contented myself with teasing him about his large stitches and assuring him that when he opened his shop I would buy my hats from him. In secret, I rather dreaded the prospect: I am a dimmish dresser, and I felt I could foresee the sort of hats Toby would design. I envisaged tam-o'-shanters of gold brocade skewered with porcupine quills, sombreros trimmed with skunk and lilies of the valley, bowlers of straw, and boaters of beaver.

The prospect, though alarming, seemed distant, and for some months that year I was away in the United States, cataloguing a collection of medieval manuscripts. When I got back I found not merely that Toby had not got tired of his scheme, not merely that he had "completed" his training, but that he was already looking about for a suitable showroom and workrooms for his business, his own business. I was flabbergasted, but said nothing.

In next to no time Mrs. Mountfaucon telephoned to say that he had found and taken a second floor in Hanover Square. More and more I seemed to be becoming her ally rather than her son's confidante, and I wasn't sure that I much relished the thought of becoming another caryatid to support, even if only morally, Toby's fecklessness.

Hanover Square! He always had such big ideas. With my natural caution I could not help wondering if a beginner ought not to begin in a smaller way, at some obscurer address. I said nothing, but asked Toby to lunch because I thought he might like to tell me about his plans. On the ground floor in Hanover Square was a dressmaker called Willy Trebizond—extremely smart, said Toby; the best-dressed woman in Europe (I forget who she was) bought some of her clothes from him. Toby perhaps hoped that he himself might in time tempt her to ascend to the second floor. On the first floor was a successful firm of interior decorators called Designing Women Ltd. Toby knew one of the partners. In fact it was she who had put him in the way of obtaining a lease of the floor above.

"She's a keen feminist," he told me, "and in planning interiors she has carried to an extreme the fashion for clinical starkness. Glass, rubber, and steel are almost the only materials she'll touch. If she uses textiles, they're coarse. If she uses wood, it has to be bleached. Everything has to be washable. Crevices have to be eliminated or stopped up like teeth. Corners have to be rounded, for fear no doubt that the dust, to which her clients must probably return sooner than they bargain for, may look in too soon and remind them of their destination."

For all this he had some Freudian explanation, which he uttered dryly, rolling a roguish eye. I forget what it was, but I think it had something to do with an infantile, if scarcely conscious, wish on the designing woman's part that somebody would sterilize her father.

I may say that when Mrs. Mountfaucon first heard the name of the firm in which this lady was a partner, she took it for a moment in the wrong sense, and from the shadow that passed over her face, like the shadow of a cloud over a full-blown pink-and-white peony, one might have guessed that she feared some irregular agency for bringing together representatives of the two sexes—a process that might well involve her son. But the cloud quickly passed, and she smiled brightly, as people generally did and were meant to do, at the facetiously ambiguous name of the firm.

When Toby had had time to settle down a little, I went to see him, finding my way up to the second floor in Hanover Square by following a trail of little name-plates of stainless steel, on which, in mauve letters, was engraved

toby—hats—accessories

He received me in what he called his showroom. It was a room of only moderate size with rather a low ceiling, and was furnished to give an impression of simple luxury. There was a long and handsome maple-wood desk in one corner, at which he could write checks and omit, if I knew him, to keep accounts. On it was an expanse of lavender-colored blotting-paper and a stack of expensive writing-paper with *toby—hats—accessories* embossed as a heading, again in mauve. There were several large looking-glasses in gilded frames, and one could see, out of the corner of one's eye, one's least movement faultlessly imitated in several places at once. The floor was covered with a thick dove-grey carpet. An Empire sofa, which I remembered having seen at Duchess's Gate, had been newly covered in striped lavender satin; on it lay some French fashion magazines. The walls and ceiling were powdered with tiny gilt stars, and on a carved and gilded side table lay two or three embryonic hats. I said I thought the whole effect pretty and professional-looking.

"Of course, it'll take time to build up a connection, but I'm busy getting my first collection ready. This is the workroom," he said, opening a door.

Two young women were discovered working at a table littered with millinery, and I was introduced to a trim, capable, cheerful-looking woman in her thirties.

"Miss Salterton, my manageress," said Toby. "I'm very lucky to have her here; she has immense experience and taste."

Miss Salterton did not contradict this.

"Well, we mustn't disturb you," said Toby, "and I have a thousand things to do myself."

I was not sorry to withdraw; I had noticed how brief and cold was Miss Salterton's professional glance at my, alas, all too ordinary hat. We went back to the showroom, and I saw that the first of the thousand things Toby had to do was to fling himself into a chair and light a cigarette.

"What do you think of her?"

"She looks very capable, Toby. But isn't she very expensive? Doesn't all this take a lot of capital?"

"She costs the earth, and so does everything else. The rent is colossal, the girls have to be paid, I have to advertise, and so on. How I shall get through the first year I haven't the faintest idea. When my collection is ready I shall give a party to show it, and I shall absolutely count on you to come."

"Of course I'll come."

"There's really nothing more I can do at the moment. Let me walk a little way with you."

I knew nothing of business and less than nothing of the selling of hats, but I felt that the whole scheme had an air of costly improvisation. The place was less like a smart hat-shop than a film-set for a smart hat-shop. Could there be a prospect of anything but failure? I found it hard to believe in Toby's "connections" and "collections" or in his head for business. I felt he was simply acting an absurd part, like a millionaire indulging a whim—but Toby was not a millionaire.

When Mrs. Mountfaucon heard that I had been round to Hanover Square she telephoned to me to ask what I thought. Her anxiety was evidently acute. I could not tell her bluntly that I thought the scheme a predestined failure. On the other hand, I didn't want to take the responsibility of buoying her up with false hopes. I said drearily that I rather hoped Toby wouldn't try and run before he had learned to walk, and that I did rather feel he might be making rather a lavish beginning, but I did of course realize that the sort of customers he was after must be received in a suitable setting.

"Of course, Jane, Toby has, you'll agree, such exquisite taste, such real originality—oh, if anybody ever *deserved* to succeed! You don't think he's too sanguine? I don't know *what* will happen if he fails, we can't raise another halfpenny. He *must* succeed!"

It was perfectly obvious that she didn't believe any more than I did in his chances of success, and yet there was such a spring of vitality in him that we both believed that in some way, sooner or later, he must succeed.

Before long I received an expensive engraved card of invitation:

toby requests the pleasure of your company at the showing of his summer collection of hats and accessories.

six to eight p.m. cocktails.

It was a perfect afternoon in mid-June when I went round to Hanover Square. There was a babble of voices, and I found in the showroom some thirty people, nearly all women. Toby, flushed with excitement, was wearing a new suit of dove-grey and in his buttonhole a gardenia. Mrs. Mountfaucon was dressed as if for a garden-party and wore a picture hat that her son designed for her; it was trimmed with gilt teasels. Lady Meliora was there, of course. She was dressed as if for a vicarage tea in the country and was carrying a tussore sunshade with an ivory handle in the shape of a greyhound's head.

I recognized various people I had met at one time or another at Duchess's Gate or elsewhere, including Hassan Okapi, an attaché at the Mesopotamian Legation, who believed himself a reincarnation of Proust; a best-selling Hungarian Jewish novelist; an elderly actress, adept at sinister, haggish, or witch-like parts, and accompanied by a daughter whose prolonged marriageableness was beginning to make her resolute animation a little fatiguing; an old country baronet, at whose gouty heels one was surprised not to see an old, spoiled spaniel; an Irish peer who wrote a gossip column; and the Barracuta Sisters, two svelte and good-natured black dancers who were having a success at that time. Mrs. Bunstable was not present.

Toby introduced me—and it must have been painful to him not to be keeping us apart—to Letty Tracy. I think I should have guessed who she was from Toby's once having described her as an ash-blonde. Her hair, her skin, her clothes, were all wan; only her lipstick and her bag were of a pale, dreamy pink. She was indeed a beauty and one couldn't wonder that Toby had half-forgiven her for monkeying with his console table.

Butterball Evans was present, wearing that habitual, purposeful graciousness one notices in some women who lead a busy public life. One felt that the urgent consciousness of agenda for the rest of the day, the need to appear interested in everybody and everything, the duty of being elegant and tactful, and the habit of assessing exactly the social and fashionable importance or unimportance of the occasion, were all jockeying for position behind her quick, translucent eyes.

Most of the company was made up of pretty, young or youngish women, expensively dressed. Goodness knows who they all were. Some of them, I imagined, might be members of what the gossip columns called "the younger married set." They looked avid for hats, and I hoped they were. Very strong cocktails were handed round by the two young persons from the workroom. They were dressed alike in a lot of fresh frills, like midinettes in a musical comedy, and seemed shy, anxious to please, and a little overawed. The noise was deafening, and I failed to hear what Lady Meliora and the Barracuta Sisters, cornered together, were finding to say to one another, but there seemed to be much.

Presently the workroom door opened, and a little posse of hired mannequins glided in to display Toby's "collection." The trouble was that the room was already full, so the mannequins, instead of being seen in proper focus, were seen in close-up, immediately and inextricably mingled with the guests, from whom they were not easily distinguishable except that their hats and "accessories" were mostly more *outré* and that they tended, so far as space allowed—and that wasn't far—to revolve slowly, to posture and prance with the preoccupied, graceful narcissism of their kind.

Until that afternoon I had been a little vague about the meaning of "accessories." I had mistily supposed that it meant—at least when combined with the word "hats"—appendages like veils, or adjustable clips in paste or metal. But now when I saw one of these slowly revolving, big-eyed beauties making sinuous movements with arms enclosed in long gloves made of string and trimmed with beads of coral, and another wearing a broad belt of blue leather set with alternate looking-glasses and bunches of artificial white currants, and a third carrying a bag made of something like cellophane to which there seemed to have been gummed a crucified vampire-bat of black patent-leather, I recognized not only the Toby touch, but the full significance of his word "accessories." Not that these objects were much more striking than some of those worn by the guests; nor were the wearers of the goods for sale in every case more fetching than the potential customers —indeed, I quickly found that almost the only way to distinguish between them was that the invited persons were carrying cocktail glasses or smoking cigarettes and the models were not.

There were loud cries of admiration. Toby came in for repeated congratulations. Astonishing hats on the heads of the mannequins were closely peered at as if they contained hidden treasure. In the general atmosphere of gorgeous climax Lady Meliora, who had by now self-protectively joined forces with the rural baronet, was seen to bend graciously towards Butterball Evans, whom she evidently mistook for a mannequin, and ask her to turn round for a moment in order that she (Lady Meliora) might have another look at Butterball's hat (it was a simple little cap made of hardly more than a coil or two of pale golden gauze, and must have come from one of the very best "houses" in Paris).

"I'm so glad you like it," I heard Butterball say over her shoulder in a curiously clear and penetrating voice, "but *don't* tell me you've taken me for one of the models. If so, I've never been so flattered in my life. I do think Toby's a born designer, don't you, and I should like to think this little hat is half as good as his own things."

"Ha, ha," said the delighted baronet, who seemed about to dig Lady Meliora in her well-corseted ribs, "that *was* a floater! But I'd have made the same mistake myself. Damned if I could tell t'other from which, when all the girls look so perfectly ripping. I've never been to one of these, what d'ye call 'em, hat shows before. I never knew one could get near so many lovelies at once. I shall certainly come again whenever I'm asked."

Butterball smiled smoothly and Lady Meliora's grip on her so ladylike sunshade seemed to have tightened a little; she looked more than ever like a daddy-long-legs in a cageful of tropical butterflies.

A certain strain was beginning to be perceptible in the perhaps by now too prolonged gush and twitter of approval, and one or two of the butterflies, as if their antennae had perceived it, began to make a slow pirouette of withdrawal towards the door by which they had entered. At the same moment, I could hear a voice saying to Toby, "My dear, *too* lovely! The smartest thing I've ever seen in my life! I can hardly bear to tear myself away, but I really must fly!" This struck a shiver of desolation through me, it seemed to ring so false. I don't know why, but I suddenly thought of that row of cottages at Crotchester, part of the proceeds of which had been so oddly converted into this, as I felt, hopeless party. I had never seen them, but I imagined them as forming part of a typical purlieu of a lesser cathedral town, as plain Victorian brick boxes with skipping children, slate roofs, brown teapots, old-age pensioners sitting and smoking, women hanging out the washing, and gardens transfigured by June into little paradises full of Canterbury bells and new potatoes. What a far cry from Hanover Square, and how difficult to connect the two scenes!

From this transient reverie I was awakened by the rapid breaking up of the party. I waited until everybody else had gone and I was alone with Toby and his mother, alone with them and the used glasses and the ashtrays full of cigarette-ends, and the air thick with the fading blended smell of cosmetics and good scent and alcohol and cigarette smoke, alone with them and the future.

"My dear Toby!" cried Mrs. Mountfaucon, who in spite of her age was never tired but always excited and stimulated by a party. "The whole thing was most *brilliantly* organized, it was a tremendous success! I congratulate you from the bottom of my heart."

She held out both her little, unpractical hands to him. He took and kissed them and then turned and flung open one of the windows as wide as it would go.

"Thank you, mother," he said. "The whole place reeks like a badger's den."

"Sett, dear."

"What, mother?"

"I said 'sett,' dear. It's called a badger's *sett*. A squirrel's *drey,* but a badger's *sett*."

"My dear mother, what an extraordinary moment to choose for a display of rustic pedantry. Anyway, it stinks."

She flung out her hands towards me in a beseeching gesture.

"And what did Jane think of it all?"

"I was simply dazzled," I said. "Toby, I do congratulate you."

He cast a quick suspicious look at me. Perhaps he thought I might be wanting to cultivate, without his knowledge, some of the women to whom I had been introduced. If so, nothing could have been less likely; they were much too hard and bright and worldly for me.

"It was obvious," I went on, "that everybody was immensely interested and impressed. I only hope that they'll follow up their compliments with some orders, and those with more orders, and that they'll rope in other people, and that they'll all pay their bills and that Toby will be quickly and permanently successful."

"If I had ten times the capital, and the looks of Clark Gable, and the prestige of Molyneux, and the business ability of Lord Nuffield, and Noel Coward's gift for giving many people exactly what they want exactly when they want it—"

"Well, then you wouldn't be Toby," I said.

"No, but I should be successful."

"If I may say so," I said (and I meant it), "it's already a unique success just to be you."

"What nice things you do say, Jane," said Mrs. Mountfaucon, "and I believe you really mean them. . . . And now let's begin to think of dinner. Toby has asked his invaluable Miss Salterton to join us, and there's some rather special champagne. I do think we've all earned it."

EIGHTEEN

"I've got no illusions about myself."

Toby had said it more than once. Up to a point it was true, but I shouldn't like to have to define the point.

He was seldom free, all the same, from what Amiel called *la nostalgie de l'irréalisable, maladie touchante qui n'est pourtant pas la sagesse.* His energy and his at times passionate efforts to attain an impossible joy and freedom helped to make him attractive to women, who instinctively recognized them as a malady, and yet, because that malady was essentially masculine, found it touching. I admit that it touched me.

I dare say Mrs. Bunstable found Toby attractive for a variety of other reasons. I don't doubt that the chief of them was that he was strongly, even violently, addicted to her—and I use the word "violently" with due regard for its meaning. It was certainly and rapidly becoming impossible for her to continue her attachment to him either for his money or his expectations of money.

The Hanover Square establishment lasted slightly less than six months. Toby got out of it with a formidable burden of debts. He was now, as he put it, "deeper in the financial soup" than he had ever been before. There were no more cottages to sell, and his chief remaining assets were his own abilities and resourcefulness. I must say I not only admired him for his lack of self-pity, I loved him for it—but I don't want to return more often than I can help to the subject of my own feelings.

He told me it would be impossible for him to keep up the house in Navarino Grove, and he had arranged to get out of it as soon as possible. He said he would take a bed-sitting-room somewhere and concentrate on earning some money. This was a time, I thought, when some of his friends ought to be doing something for him, but I doubt if they knew what a state he was in. I told him, as I always used to tell him, that he ought at all costs to stick to his painting. He said he knew I was right in theory, but in practice it was for the time being impossible.

Ever since their giving up of the house at Duchess's Gate and the winding up of my work on their papers I had been drifting away from both Toby and his mother. I don't mean that my sympathies and affections had drifted away from them, but my life inevitably became less closely entwined with theirs than it had been. I still kept my *pied-à-terre* in Tregunter Road, but I was often out of London and sometimes abroad, so I didn't always know how they were getting on. It was clear that since they had lost their money and were no longer able to entertain they had been dropped by a good many of their acquaintances, or rather of Toby's, because Mrs. Mountfaucon's Lady Meliora, her Mildred Purbind, and her little circle of ecclesiastics, amateurs of heraldry, faded museum officials, old country connections, and so on undoubtedly remained attached to her in various mild grades of adhesiveness. I myself had a horror of seeming to pay either Toby or his mother any less attention than I should have paid them if they had been able to go on living as before, so I made as unobtrusively as I could every effort to show that my feelings for them were not liable to fluctuate with their income. All the same I did get at times out of touch with them, and it was with a slight shock that I sometimes found how many weeks or even months had gone by since I had last seen one or both of them.

One morning I happened to be in Bayswater. I had been to see somebody in Palace Court, and I was walking past the Greek Cathedral towards Queen's Road (as it then was) when I saw in the distance an unmistakably familiar figure coming towards me down Ilchester Gardens. Toby had always been to a first-rate tailor, his shoes and shirts had always been made for him by the best makers, his ties successfully avoided a meek conventionality, and out of doors his bald head was generally covered by a jaunty chocolate-colored hat with a curve in its brim like the curve of a racehorse's nostril. His frightful untidiness had never extended to his clothes, which he always wore with an air, dandified but not foppish. He held himself well, without arrogance or swagger, and his gait was that of a *flâneur*. I imagine that people often walked like that in the eighteenth century.

As I now saw him coming towards me my heart, as they say, missed a beat. He had all his usual distinction, but perhaps he was walking a shade more quickly than usual, even with a touch of anxiety. The extraordinary thing about him was that he was carrying a large untidy bundle done up in what could only be a dirty bath-towel. As soon as he caught sight of me he waved the bundle gaily above his head and began to grin.

We asked each other what on earth we were doing there, and he explained that his bed-sitting-room was somewhere near by, just off Westbourne Grove. I asked him why he had picked on this particular quarter. He said it had always attracted him, he had a happy association with it from his childhood, and he liked its atmosphere. I quickly asked him to lunch, as I didn't want to put him to any expense; and he said he would be delighted if I would just allow him to leave his washing at the laundry, which was a few yards away, in Moscow Road. Toby carrying his own washing to the laundry! I could hardly believe it.

He led me to a little Italian restaurant at the north end of Queen's Road. There we sat, almost alone, in an Edwardian setting, facing each other over a trumpet-shaped, electro-plated vase containing a couple of carnations and some gypsophila, and overlooked by a wonderfully fussy overmantel, all nooks and crannies and brackets and little heart-shaped mirrors, with a cornice of fretwork peacocks. Half-overshadowed by a palm in a brass-bound jardinière we ate ravioli and zabaglione and drank Chianti. There was a delicious intimacy about this unplanned occasion. I was spellbound by Toby's high spirits and the pleasure he obviously took in amusing me. When I looked into his big, animated eyes, like those of a highly sophisticated stag, or followed the gestures of his impatient hands, my heart seemed to turn right over. I knew he mattered to me, and I knew that in a way I mattered to him—and more than ever I felt thankful that we had never gone to bed together.

"Do you remember Seddons?" he asked.

"Seddons, Seddons . . . Oh, not the butler you used to have, who was once 'nearly drunk'?"

"Yes. I ran into him a week or two ago, and gave him a drink over there at that pub on the corner, the Redan."

"Oh, Toby, doesn't that remind you of your father?"

"It does, a bit. And he told me he was making quite a good thing of the dogs."

"The dogs?"

"Greyhound racing, you know. He offered to take me. I'd never been. My dear Jane, it was most extraordinary, rather like a novel by Kafka—everybody going about so solemnly, bookies making the oddest signs to one another in a sort of deaf-and-dumb language but with almost epileptic haste, strange processions of men in white coats leading dogs, melodramatic lighting, preoccupied betting maniacs, and the whole proceeding almost wholly inscrutable from beginning to end."

"Did you win anything?"

"I lost two quid. Seddons insisted on my going again, and I more than made it up. He thinks he has got a system, and he wants me to go regularly and join him in a syndicate, but it's so appallingly boring, I've had to cry off. Gambling gives me the sort of feeling I had as a child when I used to build card-houses. Just when you get them to a good height, down they go, and you have to begin all over again. Nothing is so irksome as suspense: the monotony of it is indescribable."

I wanted to ask whether he had given any thought to going on with his painting, but I did not want to appear to nag, so I decided to say nothing about it unless he introduced the subject himself.

"I've been much troubled this last week or two," he said, "with anxiety dreams. I know it's hell to have to listen to other people's accounts of their dreams, but it's as if one had been through a trying experience—one has to tell somebody about it. Last night, for instance, I found myself obliged to catch a train, I didn't know why, or where to, I only knew it was important. I didn't know where the station was, and I don't know what country

I was in—it might have been South America. The buildings were rather nondescript and widely dispersed, and the station seemed to cover a vast acreage. There were many lines curving off into the distance. Judging by the shadows, it was late afternoon of a hot, dry day. There seemed to be a main platform where a good many people were waiting for an express, and there was a large book-stall with several entrances, and I wanted to get something to read. There was a vast number of books and papers in many languages, but I couldn't see anything I wanted. I know I hadn't got very much time and I hunted almost feverishly for a book or a paper. A young woman said, 'Can I help you?' and I explained that I had forgotten the name of the book I wanted. The express came in, filled up, and went out, and I looked at an indicator to find out about my own train. Somebody told me it was already waiting at the most distant platform of all and would be leaving in a few minutes.

"Instead of reaching it easily by a bridge or subway, I found myself trying hopelessly to hurry through deep, hot, dry sand full of sticks and tins and broken glass. I passed a group of natives, wearing big hats and squatting in the shadow of a building with closed shutters, and I asked them the way to the train. They talked volubly in an unknown language and pointed to the end of a high platform which jutted out into the sand like a jetty. This platform was very long, and at the far end I could see my train, rather aloof and unimportant, for it was only on some local branch line. It looked as if it might leave at any moment and I could see men and women in white moving near it.

"The immediate problem was to get on to the platform. The surface of it was level with my eyes, and there were no steps or footholds by which I could climb on to it. The side was as smooth as glass, and the top overhung it a little. I began to worry about my bare feet, which felt tender, and when I looked down I could see pieces of broken glass sticking out of the sand all round me. Fortunately two of the natives came and helped me up. I offered them a tip, and they were furious, drew knives, and brandished them, and called their companions to witness. For some reason or other, or no reason at all, this didn't alarm me in the least, it merely amused me, perhaps because I was so pleased to be on the platform at last. I smiled at them and then turned and ran in the direction of the train.

"The engine was very squat, with a tall funnel, from which rose a jet of silvery steam. I got an aesthetic pleasure from looking at it, but it took me some time still to reach the train. There was only one carriage, and when I got into it, with my heart beating fast, it was full of men, women, and children in white clothes. They all looked at me as if they had been waiting for me, and at that moment the train started. . . . Oh, Jane, what a bore for you! But how can I possibly convey the intensity of every moment, the *importance* of the whole thing! Of course I know exactly what these anxiety dreams mean. They simply mean that I ought to be painting, they're nothing to do with sex—it's just frustrated creativeness; I never dream when I'm painting."

"You're inviting me to nag at you," I said, "but I won't. You know my views."

"Yes, Jane, and you're right. But at the moment I'm trying to make some money. As a matter of fact, I'm writing a play."

"A play!" I exclaimed.

A rolling stone gathers no moss, but it may gather momentum. Already in retrospect Toby's life could be seen as a series of abandoned experiments. Avid for speed and the sense of power it may bring, he had rushed straight at Blenheim Palace and off and away again. As a speculator, he had been in a fur coat to Riga. In search of love, pleasure, art, new sensations, heaven knows what, he had been half-way round the world. He had been half-way, or further, towards becoming an opera-singer, and a painter, and had lately set out to be a high-flying milliner, and a maker of animated cartoons. He had been ready to present himself to me as a lover, and to Seddons as a gambler. He had always been something of a playboy, but seriousness was always breaking in. And now he was writing a play.

There was nothing wrong with the subject. The central character was well chosen—the notorious Lady Ellenborough. Toby soon showed that he had a perfect grasp of his theme. He had enthusiasm. He knew just the actress for the part, knew her personally, was writing the play for her, and had already "got her," as he said, "mad keen about it." He had even designed some of the scenery and costumes. He knew much about the theater, and possibly had some "stage sense" as well. He described a scene to me with such brilliance and wit that I could envisage it with intense pleasure. His eager account of the play was itself "as good as a play." But even while he was speaking I did not for a moment believe that he would ever finish it. I wonder if he himself believed he would.

"Good-bye, Toby," I said, "and be sure and keep me a front stall for the first night. I hope the play will run for years and make you a fortune."

Sometimes to talk to Toby was like talking to a child.

I knew he wanted to make money. That was obvious. But what else did he want? Variety? Yes. Fame? Probably. Perfection? Certainly. But was perfection in any way attainable? I doubted it, and I doubted whether it could be attainable along with the worldly success he seemed to crave for as well.

And where, in this constant renewal of energy, this change of direction, this gathering momentum, was the central truth about him? Looking back, I should say it was just there, in that very energy. From later experience and wider knowledge of people, I should say that there are persons whose appetite for life and whose temperament are such that they must throw themselves again and again into some new enterprise foredoomed to incompletion by their very restlessness. And I shouldn't dream of condemning that restlessness, which I see and admire as a passionate and acute apprehension of life. Even at the time of this encounter in Bayswater I had all the same come to the conclusion that Toby was likely to be constant in one thing at least—his attachment to Mrs. Bunstable.

The next time I saw him was at Tregunter Road. He had telephoned to invite himself to dinner, and arrived with an offering of flowers quite out of proportion to his reduced means. He seemed to be slightly agitated, and the reason soon came to light. Bella Bunstable had engaged herself to go on tour in South America. She would be absent for months, and he was going to miss her. He evidently wanted me to sympathize with him.

I remember once at a show of prize cattle hearing a wonderful woman who had nothing to do with farming remark that the difference between the cows and the bulls was so great that they seemed like two separate species—the cows so placid, milky-eyed, and soft-flanked, the bulls so ponderous, portentous, and power-conscious. Admittedly there is often less difference between men and women, especially in a civilization like ours which evolves intermediate types and individuals, but there were times when Toby's maleness made me feel as if I, as a woman, belonged to another and uncommonly distant planet. Did it not strike him as, well, a little crude that, having made or tried to make love to me not so very long before, he should now have made a date with me in order to let me understand that he was not going to like being without somebody he had made love to more lately? No, he was a man. But I could see that I was in a way honored by the confidence of a man so secretive. Our relationship was now such that I might almost have been his sister, and I believe he would have been surprised if I had at this time given him the slightest sign that I might not be altogether content with the role of sister-substitute. In fact I was not altogether discontented with it. All the same . . .

"And how's the play going?" I asked.

He was sitting with one leg over the other, and the words were hardly out of my mouth when his foot began to waggle frantically. With the loftiness he always assumed when he felt that he was perhaps being "got at" for having appeared to show weakness of purpose, he said, stammering slightly:

"T-two acts are finished. It's simply a matter of revising the third, and filling up a few gaps. As a matter of fact, I'm thinking of writing a novel."

"Oh! I *was* so looking forward to Lady Ellenborough. And everybody writes novels. Not," I hastened to say, "that I should expect a novel by you to lack originality."

"It won't be in the least autobiographical, but it will be about a man of our generation, suffering from the real sickness of our century—that sense of not belonging anywhere, of not being rooted, of not taking part in the life of a community. It would show a sort of hunt for a solution. He would lose, first, his innocence, then his illusions, then hope. First he would think sex the answer to everything, then love. The order is important—first, sex; then love. Then action. Then he would begin to think a bit. He would probably take up, one after the other and only to reject each in turn, Christianity, Marxism, and Art for Art's Sake. . . . I shall find it very difficult to let him give up Art for Art's Sake—I can't think of a single argument against it."

"And then?"

"And then in the end he would realize that in order to be a developed and civilized character he must stop fussing about himself and throw his weight entirely on the side of order and taste. The trouble will be to define order and taste."

"Dear Toby, forgive my saying so, but it doesn't sound in the least like a novel."

"It'll be picaresque, like *Candide*. I mean the hero will go through a whole succession of events, neatly contrived, I hope, and slightly startling."

"To be left cultivating his garden?"

"As it were."

The next day he telephoned to say that a friend of his had suggested that he should turn his play into a radio play. Radio plays, he said, raised many interesting new technical problems, and it was thought that they were going to have quite a future. He said he wanted my advice: should he go on with his play, or turn it first into a radio play, or begin his novel? I don't remember what I said. All I remember is that he did one day give me two acts of the play to read, and that they were brilliant. I doubt if he got far with the radio play, and I never heard that he made even a beginning with the novel. But

I was soon out of touch for some time with his literary aspirations, and with Toby himself, and with his mother, owing to preoccupations of my own.

NINETEEN

In the late summer of 1938 Mrs. Bunstable left for South America. So did Toby. The impending war had long been more evident to him than to many, and now he felt that it was near. He had no intention of running away from it, but for him, more plainly than for most, it loomed up as the end of the world which had made him and in which he could breathe and survive. Before it began he had things to do. He has left on record his opinion that his father, through knowledge of the vanity of things, became "insulated against activity" and "had refused to participate in man's struggle against Nature and against Fate"; but Toby himself, however clearly he understood how Nature and Fate were cornering him, was driven by his high spirits to wrestle with them. Yes, he had things to do, to enjoy, to make.

He sailed for Rio with Bella because he wanted to be with her as much as possible, because he was infatuated with her, and not least because he was afraid that some other man might come between them. He didn't intend, he told me, to go on tour with her, which he could not in any case have afforded: he would be in Rio with her when she opened her tour and again for a short time before she returned to England. In the interim he would remain in or near Rio, living as cheaply as possible and "painting," he alleged, "all day."

I sighed faintly when he said this. I was thinking of Greece, and of England, littered with his discarded, unfinished canvases. His thirst for the tropics, for warmth and color, might much more easily lead him, I thought, to lounging in the shade and lazing in the sea. As it happened, I was quite wrong. Bella and Brazil and the threat of war were to combine in releasing his long pent-up creativeness. He was to be freed, to expand, to work fruitfully. But I did not then know that that was what would happen, and when I saw him for the last time before he left, I could not hide my scepticism at his "This time, Jane, you'll see."

"I think I must go on being a little circumspect," I said. "Am I, by the way, right in thinking that your mother still doesn't even know of Bella's existence?"

"I suppose you are," he said, "but mother's a dark horse. She must know there's *somebody*. I've trained her not to pry, so I'm spared direct questions. But she has been saying things like 'How well and happy you're looking, Toby; you seem to have such poise nowadays, and I don't seem to irritate you so much as I used to.' She saw a photograph of Bella on my mantelpiece, and although she said nothing, she gave it one of those searching looks of hers."

"Have you ever thought of bringing them together?"

"Oh, God forbid. As you may have noticed, I'm not much of a bringer-together at the best of times."

"Your mother would never pry, but if she were ever

to ask me if I know to whom you are attached, or anything like that, what am I to say?"

"Oh, put her off gently—say I never tell you anything."

He asked me if I remembered suggesting that he should write down some of his stories of his own and his stepfather's family. A friend of his, whom he didn't name, had made the same suggestion to him, and had probably been impressed, as I had, by the way in which his acute mind transmuted, as if in a distorting mirror, facts into fantasies. I felt pretty sure that this projected book, if it were ever finished, would do for his relations much what he had once done for Lady Meliora's harmless old dog when he had described it to me. (The book did get finished, and it came out after his death, and was received with just the kind of appreciation on the part of just the kind of readers he would have wished for. I believe he was not responsible for its more than ambiguous title, *Curious Relations*, with its various suggestions of bizarre kinsfolk, strange narrations, unexpected reciprocities, and, to quote Cousin Feenix again, "odd conjunctions.")

No less sceptical than before, I put on what I hoped was a convincing act of encouragement and enthusiasm.

"Oh, do write it!" I said. "You know I've always thought your stories too good and too Tobyish to be lost."

He looked at me with large eyes as if trying to weigh up whether I meant what I said. The innocence, the directness, the luminosity of that hurt child's gaze was somehow more than I could bear; it seemed to melt my bones, and to divert it I abruptly changed the subject and asked what would happen to Bella Bunstable's son while she was away. I wondered if I ought to offer to take him to the Zoo or somewhere one day, but it seemed that everything had been arranged for his welfare during his mother's absence.

"My God, I wish Jocky was my child!" Toby suddenly exclaimed with a startling intensity. "I think the world of him. I'm so paternal and he's so promising that it puts me quite on edge to think of the things that might go wrong before he can mature."

"I suppose he doesn't know what he wants to be?"

"Oh, but of course he wants to be an airman. . . . He stole something at school and then lied about it, so they sent him to the school psychiatrist, who reported that he had 'perfect mental health.' Isn't that amazing?"

Toby's eyes glowed as if the child were his own and as if he were its mother rather than its father. I found this just faintly embarrassing.

"What a future for him!" Toby went on. "What a contrast to half the people we know! And now he has won the half-mile in the school sports, and he plays in the first football eleven. 'Perfect mental health'—isn't it a wonderful phrase? I can't get it out of my head."

So, I reflected, infatuation with the mother had been projected to include the child. What a pity he had not got a child of his own, on which he could lavish this fund of quasi-parental emotion.

"If the war begins quite soon," said Toby, "I shall come back at once; but if it doesn't, I shall be back early next year."

"In either case," I said, "I hope I shall hear from you. I loved your letters from Berlin and from Greece."

"To tell you the truth, Jane, I don't believe I shall write any letters. I have an idea that I'm going to be too busy."

"Yes, I know," I said, wagging my hips and doing a

few steps, "dancing the cachuca at Copacabana, etcetera, tra-la."

Away he went, and I must say the agitations over Munich, added to the complexities of everyday life, caused me to think less often of Toby than I might otherwise have done. Besides, to the general agitation a particular one of my own was added. I had lately met the man who eventually became my second husband. I did not then know what he felt about me, but I already knew what I felt about him, and to me, as if I had been some adolescent girl in love for the first time, the menace of war and perhaps invasion seemed a direct menace to a wholly unexpected and therefore all the more cherishable promise of private happiness. Between the menace and the promise I glowed with love even of the most obvious and shabby and trivial aspects of life in my native land. But I digress. . . .

I had no letters from Toby, but gay picture-postcards arrived at intervals. Late in October I thought I had better go round to Equerry Mansions to see how Mrs. Mountfaucon was getting on. At the front door I had a little confidential talk about her with Corby, the bemedalled hall-porter.

"She's all right, mind you," he said, "but it wouldn't surprise me if she isn't a bit too much on her own, that's what it is. She's getting on a bit, let's face it, and when we get on, you know, we want taking out of ourselves a bit, otherwise people go broody, as my old mother used to say. They don't like to feel that they don't matter to nobody no more. What Mrs. Mountfaucon wants is a bit of young company from time to time. That's why I'm glad to see you coming to see her, madam."

"Oh, Corby, that's very nice of you," I said, "but I'm

not exactly 'young company'. I wish I could come oftener. And how are things with you?"

"Well, times are changing, you know. We're getting a different sort in now, you know. Big fur coats, big shiny cars, big cigars, big waist-lines, and they don't want you to forget it." He had lowered his voice confidentially. "There's no getting away from it, they're not like the old-timers. I suppose it's not yet being used to what they've got, like. They like to complain a lot, just to show that they can buy what they want and order you about. Why," he again lowered his voice, "you wouldn't credit it, but we've got one upstairs rung down to me after midnight, on Thursday it was—after midnight, mind you—'Oh, porter,' she says, waking me out of me beauty sleep, 'there's a tap dripping something dreadful in my kitchen. I must have it stopped at once, or I shan't close me eyes all night.' Wouldn't credit it, would you? Why, if Mrs. Mountfaucon was flooded out and floating around like a cork she'd no more think of troubling anyone before morning—if it was *fire,* now, that's different."

This, the longest speech I had heard him make, was now interrupted by his duties, so he showed me into the lift, and up I went, reflecting on a dictum of my father's, "Be careful about listening to servants' gossip, especially other people's servants' gossip."

I made some remark to Mrs. Mountfaucon about Corby's affability.

"It seems an odd thing to say, Jane, but Corby's so *good,* he's almost like a brother to one. Oh dear, I do rather wish I had a brother at times. . . . Corby, you know, was in Morven's, my second husband's, regiment, though of course he didn't know him, only *of* him. Morven's men *worshipped* him. . . . And talking of Morven, I must tell you the drollest thing. On Sunday mornings

I always go to the morning service at the Abbey. I've got rather a special place, as they know me there. And near me, almost next to me, sits always old Lady Trunnion-James, the admiral's widow, a proud old thing—though I don't think she can reasonably be proud of either her dressmaker or her looks. She has a very straight back and a very high-bridged nose, but gracefulness, I fear, she has *not*. Oh, but I don't want to be unkind. . . ."

"Do go on," I said.

"The point is that she knows me very well by sight and by name, we worship the same God in the same place, but she only gives me the coldest of nods. She all but cuts me." (This instantly reminded me of 'Seddons, you were *nearly* drunk'.) It's a huge joke, really," she went on. "You see, I know *why*. One of Morven's brothers, who was in the Navy, married a barmaid, and Lady Trunnion-James thinks *I* am the barmaid! . . . Now wait, Jane! I don't expect you to say, 'Oh, how could she?' I hope I've got the feelings of a gentlewoman, but I know I don't *look* dowdy. I *do* go to a good dressmaker, and I *do* think, and even Toby allows, that Mélanie Galhauban has worked out some sort of style for me; and it just *doesn't* go with sad brown toques (cowpats, as dreadful Toby calls them), and serviceable dark hats with random trimmings, and wisps of fur not to be identified, and long narrow panels of senseless embroidery let into navy-blue coats-and-skirts, and shoes, such shoes, oh really out of the *Ark*! But there, I *am* being unkind, and I don't care two pins about being cut, it's so awfully *funny*!"

I think that was the nearest thing to an unkind speech I ever heard from Mrs. Mountfaucon, but I thought none the worse of her for it.

"Ah, now I know," I said, "where Toby gets his descriptive gifts from."

"Oh dear, I hope not, bless his heart, but of course he doesn't mean half he says. . . . My dear Jane, he seems to be extremely happy in Brazil. He's painting more freely and confidently, he says, than ever before. But he says he feels he's painting against time—of course he's worried, as we all are, that another war may break out. But he says something so striking—'I've suddenly ripened in the sun.' It quite haunts me. I do hope it's true."

TWENTY

It was a magic morning early in the year 1939. I was sitting in a large bright library lightly scented by clumps of hyacinth and narcissus. As the room got warmer the scent became stronger and headier. A lively fire leaped and crackled up the chimney, and out of doors the sun was shining through a flurry of snow. The sun on the snow made quite a glare in the room. From time to time the sun disappeared behind rapidly moving clouds, at times it shone again through driving snowflakes, then the wind seemed to drop and a real snowstorm would set in. All the flakes seemed to be of equal size and their circling or upward movements seemed to be obeying a complex rhythm, like that of a ballet. Some few flakes, detaching themselves from the rest, would approach the windows, hover for a moment as if looking in, and then drift away like frustrated moths. Then it would stop snowing altogether and I could see how the snow was already lying thickly and evenly, and the reflected radiance from the fallen snow filled the great room and gave me a sense of well-being and exaltation. I will admit that I had my own reason for feeling exalted. At the same time I had a faint sense of uneasiness, of foreboding, but as there seemed to be no reason for that, I put it out of my mind.

I was staying for a long week-end in the Cotswolds with some people whom I knew slightly. They had asked me to look through some uncatalogued seventeenth-century manuscripts in their library. It was an easy task in an agreeable setting. The standard of comfort was high, nobody talked of war or politics, and the house was full of beautiful things. This was Sunday morning and the other people staying in the house had gone out or were in some other room.

"Do I disturb you?" said my hostess, coming into the room. "I forget if I told you that Lydia Delap is coming over to lunch."

My heart at once began to beat more quickly, and I felt a slight contraction in the throat. I felt a little resentful of her, a little afraid, a little hostile. I suppose I had a deep-seated jealousy of her association with Toby long before I had known him. Unreasonable, perhaps, but such is human nature. Lydia was not a person I was likely to meet in the ordinary way. She didn't live in that part of the country, and it was pure chance that was now to bring us together.

She arrived with a rather faded male escort, and when we all assembled for a drink before lunch, and during the meal itself, I was able to get a good look at her. I am sorry to say that I saw what can only be called, though it is both vulgar and unkind to use such an expression, an "old bag." It was not that Lydia was more than middle-aged, but she had let herself go. At a time when many a woman of fifty or thereabouts contrives by good luck, temperate living, suitable activities, and a proper care for her appearance to look neat, shapely, flexible, and even quite appetizing, Lydia looked hopeless.

I remembered having been told by Toby that her visit to Scandinavia, after their fanciful jaunt to Berlin, had given her a taste for blond hyperborean types, and that she had later taken up with a Finnish masseur who had been killed in a skiing accident. (On hearing of it, Toby had allowed himself to murmur "Masseur's in de cold, cold ground. . . .") I remembered further his having told me that she had gone to live in the country ("If Sussex," he had said, "can still be so described") and had there put on what she imagined to be a kind of protective coloring, with a suggestion not merely of the open air and of tradition but of the sporting and the pious: he summed it up as "cubbin' and Communion." I knew that she had always had what people called "a thing"—to be more precise, a kind of bogus mysticism—about the good earth and all that. (There was a hint of it, I remember, in that passage I copied out from *Bones of Wonder*.) This "thing" I understood to be now combined with Anglo-Catholicism and an unconscious reversion to that country life of her childhood which she had abandoned for Bohemia. If she now wanted to appear like some conventional type of English country gentlewoman, the result was, to put it mildly, not exactly graceful.

Everything was wrong, from the foundation upwards. Foundation! Whatever she had or did not have on underneath, she looked uncorseted. Her loose, middle-aged spread was enclosed in a loosely cut tweed coat and skirt patterned in a large off-white and tobacco-brown check. The skirt, too short, too much in the fashion of ten years earlier, drew attention to her thickish legs in thin, expensive-looking, fawn-colored cashmere stockings, and her feet were in low-heeled brown brogues with fringed tongues. Under her coat she wore a loose, beige sweater with slack, dangling folds like the apparently quite unsupported bust beneath it. Pinned in the front of it was a gaudy plaque of painted wood, like some table-mat evolved by an amateur craftswoman and exhibited at a village bazaar. She had a string of false pearls round her (I do believe) once beautiful throat, a big false pearl in each ear, and on her head a large, flat, off-white beret with a cairngorm clasp at one side. She still wore her hair bobbed. Once abundant and coppery, it was now dry, straggling, and of an uneven gingery tint streaked with whitey-brown.

All this, if it had belonged to someone with an ordinary face and commonplace manner, would have hardly been worth recording in such detail, but it must be admitted that Lydia, whatever her little weaknesses, had been a beauty and a personality. Even in ruin her face was not commonplace. As for her manner, I don't believe it was any less affected than it had been.

One could not have ignored her face. It would have had a kind of fascination to an observant eye, even if the eye belonged to somebody who knew nothing about her; but I was surprised to see it so neglected, and the reflected snowlight did not censor its faults. The country character she now aimed to be ought to have had a ruddy, windswept look, autumnal perhaps but fresh-looking—at least with ordinary care of the skin. But Lydia's face was biscuity in color, flabby, and matt. The only cosmetic she seemed to have used was a most unusual lipstick, dark and with a bluish tinge, as if she had impulsively kissed a spoonful of mulberry jam. The effect was certainly odd and striking. Her eyelashes and eyebrows appeared almost colorless, and her cheeks and neck had sagged. She kept her head tilted back as if she had one vertebra missing or an insufficiency of skin on the nape of her neck. This idiosyncrasy and the aura of heavy bluish smoke from the Egyptian cigarette she was smoking gave her still the familiar yearning look which I had seen in photographs, drawings, and paintings of her; but it also thrust her round chin too much into notice, made her snub nose look even more insignificant than it was, and exposed too much of a throat that would have been better wrapped up in something or other; her sweater, I kept thinking, ought to have had a high neck.

After lunch we found ourselves together. I no longer felt afraid. What I did feel was a mixture of distaste and curiosity. I think Lydia generally did not like women, and she sat passively beside me on a big sofa, as if she were not interested in me and as if it were not worth her trouble to talk to me, or at least to be the first to speak. It had stopped snowing but there was no more sunshine; the sky had darkened, the wind had dropped, and the frozen hush outside seemed to be pressing against the windows.

Lydia produced a cigarette-case but didn't offer it to me. She helped herself to a cigarette, slipped it between her inky-looking lips, lighted it, put the case away in her handbag, and unexpectedly murmured, with a sidelong glance at me, "I hear that Toby d'Arfey has gone off to South America with a coal-black Negress."

"The things one hears," I said, with what was meant to be a weary, tolerant smile. I didn't see why I should give her the pleasure of a prompt and indignant denial.

"I have it on pretty good authority," she said, as if daring me to deny it.

"I do know that he has gone to South America," I said.

"You know him very well, don't you?"

"I'm sure you know him very much better than I do. You've known him much longer than I have."

"Yes, I've known him since he was a boy, just a boy." This was said in a dreamy, complacent, throaty purr, through a slow blue haze of cigarette smoke. "A boy of such immense promise. Promise and charm, such charm. . . . So you don't think it's true that he has gone off with a Negress? I hoped it was, I did hope it was. Do him such good."

"He has always had a penchant for colored people, hasn't he?"

"Oh, I know, I know. In Paris, long ago—oh, too long ago . . . Of course I'm older, much older, than Toby. I can't help thinking of him as a boy. He must be almost forty now, or more. But his mother—what a long battle that was. Do you think he has won at last, freed himself from her?"

"You mean she used to try and keep him tied to her apronstrings? *I've* never seen a sign of it," I said with emphasis. "Of course he's her only child, she's devoted to him, and he to her—she's his only near relation. But he bullies her dreadfully, keeps her in her place, orders her about, and has trained her thoroughly to do what she's told. Poor Mrs. Mountfaucon."

"*Poor* Mrs. Mountfaucon? I must say I'm amazed. I can't say I've ever thought of her as 'poor Mrs. Mountfaucon.' I've always thought of her as a dreadful incubus, and as an enemy of life—freedom—creativeness—everything!"

"Oh no, but surely—"

"She has always detested me, you know. But you must know, you know her so well."

"I went through their family papers for them. I'm an archivist by training," I explained. "I got very fond of them both."

"Oh, but she thought of me as a kidnapper, a corrupter, a sorceress, poison for her ewe-lamb."

"Now," I said, "*I* am the one who is amazed."

"Ah, you're being a loyal friend, you've got a loyal face. But how could one be loyal to both? How could one not take sides? She would have crushed the life out of him if she could. That immense possessiveness . . ."

"I'm still amazed."

"It's his mother, surely, who made him so secretive. He never would tell anybody anything about what he was doing, what made him unhappy or happy, or whom he had been seeing. It's as if he's always afraid of having the cup, any cup, dashed from his lips. You must have noticed that."

"Indeed yes, I have. But it would never have occurred to me to blame his mother. She says his father was exactly the same."

"Oh, you're loyal," she said in a broody murmur. "But *I'm* disillusioned. . . . Tell me, do you think they really were totally ruined by that defaulting trustee, that courtly old bore Eustace Basingfield? I couldn't make out. Toby seemed to hate to talk about it. No wonder, poor boy."

"Did you know Mr. Basingfield well?" I asked.

"Oh, he'd been about all my life. My father knew him well. They belonged to the same club, they had friends in common, and he used to stay with us when I was a child. I remember when I was very small being fascinated, I'm sure perversely, by his shoes. Such small, narrow feet for a man—my dear, they were like tea-leaves. And such exquisite, hand-made shoes. Fetishism, I know. At the age of five I was madly in love with him."

"I never saw anybody more distinguished-looking," I remarked, "but I've sometimes wondered what his motive was, in misapplying other people's money. He was apparently well off, and by no means young."

" 'Misapplying' is a nice word, too nice. I call it stealing, and I've a shrewd idea of the motive. It was a woman. Young enough to be his granddaughter. I saw them together once, and as he left surprisingly little when he died, I've no doubt he had settled some whacking great sum on her."

"Do you suppose," I asked, "that Toby and his mother know?"

"Who the woman is? I've no idea. But Toby knows her well. You must know her yourself, she's always about. Only don't ask me to name her."

"And do you suppose she knows where the money came from?"

"Well, when a man makes settlements on one, one doesn't ask where he got the money, but one generally has some idea where it came from."

At this point we were separated by our hostess. Making small-talk by the fire, I felt my face burning at the thought of the wrong done to my friends. I glanced away from Lydia, towards the darkening windows, and for the moment I thought of all men as only cruel and false and longed to hide myself anywhere out of the world.

I saw Lydia again for a moment or two as she was going away. I hardly disliked her any more. Often one hates people for what they seem to stand for, and because one doesn't know them; when one has met them, one's suspicions may melt away. If Lydia had still had her former hold over Toby, I dare say I should have disliked her even more after meeting her than before.

We were at the front door. Wrapped in a blanket of a coat with a big fur collar, a coat that hid her awful abandoned figure, she did look, with her mulberry lips and tired eyes, rather striking.

"Do let's meet again," she said in a husky voice and as if she meant it. It was a nice thing to say, even if she didn't mean it.

"Let's," I said, and I didn't mean it. "Being fond of Toby's such a link."

She smiled, and turned, and was swallowed up by the winter darkness.

As soon as I reached my room I said to myself, "Young enough to be his granddaughter—always about—you must know her." And then I remembered Mrs. Mountfaucon and Toby having discussed quite casually how a woman of their acquaintance and mine had bought a house in the country that would be rather expensive to run. Mrs. Mountfaucon had thought she must be "doing very well." Toby had said that she was no doubt being kept by some rich man and he wouldn't be surprised if it was a certain French millionaire racing-man. The woman in question was none other than Butterball Evans.

TWENTY-ONE

I cannot remember exactly when Toby got back from Brazil. It must have been in the spring of 1939. What I do remember is that he made a number of rather bitter jokes about returning to the sinking ship, and he said something about always liking to be on the spot whenever the Russians went through. In fact the first news I had had of him when he came back was from a nursing-home in Wimbeck Street, asking me to go and see him. It was thought, he said, that he had a tropical disease, and he was under observation. Whatever it was, he thoughtfully explained, there was no chance of my catching it from him.

I had found him looking far from well. He was sitting up in bed, surrounded by books and ashtrays heaped up with cigarette-ends. He had lost his usual fresh color, and his skin was of a pale primrose color. His eyes looked very large and dark. He seemed an impatient patient, but was otherwise in high spirits and full of the pleasures he had enjoyed in Brazil and the amount of painting he had done there. Bella was not yet back, but Jocky had been to see him, and had won a prize for a model airplane that he had made.

"That's the world we live in," said Toby. "Boys are

given prizes for making copies of lethal weapons. I hope you've arranged to be out of London for the duration, Jane?"

"You mean, if there's a war?"

"I don't mean *if,* I mean *when.* And it can't be long now."

"Oh no, I suppose I shall be in London," I said. "I'm more or less committed to a dim job in a Ministry."

"Unspeakable. So don't let's talk of it. Mother, by the way, refuses to leave the neighborhood of Westminster Abbey, which she seems to think is the headquarters of a benevolent Deity, or perhaps our tribal god."

"Toby, please don't say anything to disillusion her."

"My dear, I wouldn't *dream*—In any case, she's past disillusioning."

In the midst of this banter, I had a strong impression of an older Toby. He had indeed ripened in the sun. Bella, Brazil, and his brushes had somehow made him realize himself. I looked at him with a new respect. He gave me an impression of power. He seemed, as he had never quite seemed before, a complete and adult man.

I was much struck at this time by something I had often noticed before—I mean the way in which some people exaggerate hearsay about other people's misfortunes, particularly illness. Be sure that if you're on the verge of a mild nervous exhaustion and the doctor orders you a rest, certain persons who are ostensibly your friends will go about saying that you have gone out of your mind. A little trouble with your duodenum or gall-bladder will be represented as cancer, and a collar-bone fractured in a motor accident will give you the reputation, if not of mincemeat, at least of a bundle of broken ribs.

Perhaps this tendency to enlargement comes from nothing more than a wish to shine in conversation by uttering startling news. Toby's enigmatic condition certainly gave rise to it among his acquaintances. Somebody who scarcely knew him asked me if I had seen him lately, and before I could reply remarked, "I hear he had sunstroke in Brazil, and now has fits." I said he was having a little trouble with his digestion, which was expected to clear up quickly.

"Most unlikely," was the answer. "It's almost certain to be amoebic dysentery. And after that one is never quite the same again."

"Is anybody ever," I said with mild exasperation, "after anything?"

The truth was that the doctors seemed unable to decide what was wrong with Toby. They put his condition down to a short excursion he had made into the Brazilian hinterland, but they could not or would not define it.

"After all, it's *my* body," Toby said, "such as it is. And I've told them so, and that I've got a right to know what's wrong with it. I've explained that I'm quite capable of assimilating disagreeable facts without making a fuss. The nearest I can get from them in the way of plain speaking is 'A form of debility, you know. Not unusual for white men in the tropics—quite common in West Africa. We shall have to do a few tests. In the meantime you must rest, and we'll have to correct the tendency to anemia.' "

"Vague," I said.

"They obviously haven't the faintest idea what's the matter with me. They keep taking my water away to look at, as if they expected, with perseverance, to find alluvial gold in it. They've taken enough specimens of my blood to decorate a set of graduated lampshades with polka dots. And now they're thinking of taking all my teeth out, though I feel that my teeth are still much more use-

198

ful to me than they're likely to be to anybody else. I shall be sorry to part with them. It will make me feel like one of the witches in *Macbeth*. I've been thinking of a drawing I once saw in a French paper of a gross middle-aged man in bed with a tart. Beside her was a tumbler with a set of false teeth in it, and he was saying, *'Donnes-moi mes dents, chérie, je veux te mordre.'* "

As he said this he gave a brilliant smile, and I thought how white and strong his teeth looked. I noticed that he was chain-smoking and could guess how much he was feeling the strain of uncertainty about his condition, and the condition itself.

"I suppose one can get used to having no teeth," he said musingly. "I used to mind about being bald, but I hardly ever think of it now. It's supposed, you know, to be a sign of virility, and up to now I've had no complaints on that score, though I must say there have been times when one has almost wished that sex would leave one alone. Sometimes it has seemed a strange necessity, like having to shave, but so much more trouble and expense —such a *fuss*. . . . Yes, I shall be toothless as well as hairless. Yet my father must certainly have been bald for nearly half a century before he so unthinkingly became my father, and as he was seventy when I was born, I dare say he was toothless too."

I restrained the temptation to exert a pooh-poohing bedside manner, and said I hoped he was finding the nursing home comfortable.

"It may be, Jane; I don't know. I see it at present through liver-colored spectacles. The night nurse is breezy and takes a morbid interest in cricket. It's sad, isn't it, how in England everything comes back to cricket in the end? A game so bad for the character, and dangerous too. . . . Then the food here isn't good. I asked for salad yesterday and was brought a wet, outside leaf of lettuce, like blotting paper. I turned it over without enthusiasm. Lucky I did; there was quite a sizable slug underneath it. . . . Then there's some sort of Indian woman in the next room. She has a constant stream of visitors who chatter excitedly and incessantly as if they were getting her ready for suttee or something. But the night nurse says she's a *malade imaginaire,* so I expect it's much Urdu about nothing."

His pleasant flippancies are to me precious in retrospect, like memories of a picnic on a site later destroyed by an avalanche. Looming over us both, over us all, was the immense folly, fear, waste, and ruin of the impending war. And when it came we were all still in London. Mrs. Mountfaucon had no thought of budging from Equerry Mansions and made no fuss of any kind. Toby seemed to get better. He was out and about again, but not a good color and too easily tired. Bella Bunstable was back and intended to entertain the troops. As for me, I was sucked into my Ministry, like a straw into a backwater. The war soon destroyed not only the rhythm of all our lives but our sense of passing time, and when Toby had a relapse I realized with a shock how one had already got used to the war, just as one might get used to a bad leg, or living with a lunatic, or constant earthquakes, or all three.

TWENTY-TWO

"The doctor has sent him to a nursing home in Bayswater."

"Oh, my dear . . . These noisy nights! Oughtn't he to be in the country?" What Lady Meliora meant, though she had too much delicacy to say it, was that the nursing home might easily be hit by a bomb.

"I hardly know what to do for the best." Mrs. Mountfaucon was wringing her hands.

Lady Meliora was not a demonstrative woman, but she had lost, many years before, her only child. She now put out a long, thin forearm, almost skeletal in its refinement, and laid upon one of Mrs. Mountfaucon's plump wrists a long, thin hand in an old, clean glove. She only left it there for two or three seconds, and then withdrew it, as if she had been on the verge of an indiscretion; but that was long enough to produce an inarticulate sound, a sort of gulp, from Mrs. Mountfaucon. Almost instantaneously, Mrs. Mountfaucon must have resolved to pull herself together. She sat up very straight, put on a "brave" smile, and said:

"I don't want him to suspect for *one moment* that he may not recover."

"I know he's very brave, Susannah. Like his father. If only I thought it would give him the slightest pleasure, I would go and see him, but I know it would only irritate him. Don't, of course, tell him that I even thought of going. . . . Does it seem a good nursing home?"

"It's quiet, Meliora, I must say, with its thick carpets and such hideous stained-glass windows to deaden the light. The hall and the stairs and the waiting-room are gloom itself, and in the quietness the matron and nurses loom up like ghosts. . . . Oh, but Toby's nurse is anything but a ghost—so young and fresh, and they seem already to have quite an understanding."

"So long as she looks after him properly—"

"So long as she doesn't look after him too well! I hope she won't try and *get hold* of him. I've such a horror of the way nurses, *some* nurses, prey on their patients."

"Oh, *do* they?" I asked.

"I don't believe you've ever had a day's illness in your life, Susannah!" Lady Meliora perhaps wished to head her off the topic of predatory nurses.

"Not counting the time when Toby was born, I've had three days in bed in my life—so far."

"Oh, do touch every kind of wood, Susannah! The days were consecutive, I presume?" Lady Meliora asked with a delicious dryness.

"Oh, no," Mrs. Mountfaucon said, without a hint of complacency, "there were about twenty years between each of them, I'm thankful to say."

Her thoughts must have returned instantly to Toby and the danger of his being "got hold of."

"Meliora, don't you remember poor Sir George Fawnstalk, after his wife died? I must say she had one of the most *exquisite* figures I ever saw, a positive hourglass, with eyelashes like a Persian cat, and such blue, blue eyes. You remember how *he* was got hold of by a hospital nurse? She somehow spirited his money away, so that the wretched penniless nephew, with two sets of darling little twin daughters, only a year apart and as like as four pins, came into nothing but the title. . . . I suppose it can't be much of a life—a nurse's, I mean. Going to and fro at all hours with thermometers and bedpans, they must naturally want to hitch their drab little wagons to some ailing star. Then there was that old, old Miss Constance Crudence, the bishop's daughter, who was quite, quite helpless and alone, except for a niece who was after her money and clapped her into a little suburban nursing home. By the merest chance I went to see her—oh, and only just in time! It was a horrid little house, very new and dreadfully spick-and-span, with casement curtains, and cement gnomes in the front garden. I'd never seen them before, they seemed quite out of place. It had been started by two trained nurses who had set up together on their own. One was a female, short and thick-set, and bluff, like a man really, with square hands and short hair. The other, her husband, was a male nurse, pale but very strong-looking, with such long bony fingers, and such an unsmiling face, pouchy, rather, under the eyes. He tried to keep me out, and when I got in she tried to prevent me seeing the poor old thing, and then they tried to prevent me seeing her alone."

"Susannah, you've never told me this dreadful story. When did it happen?"

"I didn't tell you at the time because I didn't want to distress you; you had worries of your own just then. . . . Well, I don't know if they had any other patients at the time, but they'd certainly *got hold of* poor old Miss Crudence. She told me that this vile man had been trying to break her spirit by various means—for instance, by telling her the most filthy stories; by keeping her awake when she wanted to sleep; by jeering at her, telling her she would soon be dead, and so on. Then they were working on her to make over all her property to them, bit by bit. They used to say, 'Unless you sign this, or unless you give us your fur coat and your pearl brooch, you'll get no midday meals in future.' The niece never came to see her and she couldn't write and summon help because those two monsters intercepted her letters. If I hadn't moved her out immediately, they'd have had every rag and stick she possessed, including some very fine diamonds which had belonged to Mrs. Fitzherbert. Can you wonder that I have a horror of nurses?"

"No, my dear, but that was a very exceptional case."

"I don't believe the nurse is born," I put in, "who could get the better of Toby."

"Oh, but Jane, he's so ill, and nurses have their arts. This one has such very wide nostrils, an unhappy feature really, almost a deformity, and such a *bad sign*. I dread that she may throw her head back while I'm speaking to her; one almost feels that one would get a glimpse of her brains. And brains she certainly has. She necessarily spends so much time alone with him, she will tempt him to confide in her, and illness weakens one's will-power; it's just then that she might try and *get hold of* him. I daren't warn him, he would bite my head off; and of course I can say nothing to her, because he depends on her for every attention. In fact, I have already given her a jumper—not a present, really; more like a bribe."

I must confess that for once I was a little irritated by my dear Mrs. Mountfaucon in the role of tigress defending her young. I knew it was no good trying to reassure her by any direct means, so I simply said that if she thought it would do Toby any good, I would try and contrive to go and see him regularly, perhaps once a week.

She thanked me effusively, gave me his telephone number, and begged me to go as soon as I could. Evidently she had no fear whatever of my "getting hold of" him, and thought me as safe with him as if I had been his great-aunt. At the same time I think she hardly realized that I was already overworked and overwrought and that I badly needed rest in my very little spare time.

The nursing home was not in Bayswater. It was in Monteagle Gardens, a square in that vague region which is neither Holland Park nor Ladbroke Grove—at least it had been a square, but one side had already been made uninhabitable by bomb-blast. The whole square has since been demolished. The houses were grandiose, seven-storied, mid-Victorian follies, with cavernous basements, florid porticoes, and first-floor drawing-rooms with huge windows. Nearly all of them had been converted, twenty years or more before this time, into flats more or less inconvenient and unmanageable. Most were now empty and many were windowless. Some of the empty windows had been filled with hessian or cardboard, but even these makeshifts were already decaying and some were broken or torn.

The railings round the garden in the middle of the square had been removed, the shrubs had been damaged, and beneath them was a thick litter of dirty paper and other rubbish. The open space in the middle of the square was now a balloon site, and perhaps because the afternoon was rainy, with low, scudding clouds, the balloon was tethered to the ground. It looked like a dropsical, thin-skinned elephant, and was not fully inflated, so that its surface bellied and flapped slowly, as if it were breathing. This false appearance was almost the only hint of life in the whole square, except for some stunted shrubs.

Near the balloon was a hut for its attendants. The doors and windows were shut, and it appeared as deserted as the houses whose dirty and crumbling façades overhung it. There were no children playing in the street; they had all been "evacuated" to the country. There were none of those old ladies whom one would have expected to see still wandering purposefully along hereabouts to exercise their dogs. There was no traffic whatever, not a bicycle. Drab rain fell from the pewter-colored sky. The huge silent houses were waiting for the end.

I began to think there had been some mistake about the address, but when I came to the further side of the square I saw that one or two of the houses had curtains in the windows, and that these windows were not only intact but clean, and presently I came to the house I was looking for. It was in better repair than any of the others; it even looked spruce. The steps were spotless, the front door was painted a glossy olive-green, the brasswork of the bells, marked "Visitors" and "Night," was polished, and a gleaming brass plate bore the name of the nursing home.

I had only to wait a few seconds for the door to open, and I was admitted by a woman who seemed to be neither a nurse nor a servant, and had not the brisk and formal air of a receptionist. As she spoke she prodded about in her rather untidy red hair with the point of a long pencil, as if there might be some hole in her skull into which she might conveniently push it; perhaps it was her function to keep the books. She was dressed in a brown knitted garment and wore swinging earrings of imitation jade which aroused in me a feeling of deep melancholy. Her manner was impersonal, as might be that of a ghost who had learned to take eternity for granted. She said she would find out if I might see Mr. d'Arfey, and asked me to wait a moment in a small room at the back of the ground floor.

It was a terrible room, evidently clean, but with dark panelling and a thick carpet—terrible because without character. There was a window, but it was impossible to see out of it; the top half was of frosted glass and the lower of stained glass with a geometrical pattern in bistre and umber with floral motifs in puce. A large land-scape in a heavy frame hung over the chimneypiece; it might or might not have been a view in Scotland; it was devoid of style and supremely insipid. Some illustrated papers lay on the table; they were nearly a year old, but did not look as if they had been much used. Near them was an ashtray of dun-colored marble, and in it were four half-smoked cigarettes, heavily carmined with lipstick, the relics of some harrowing and recent vigil. I felt I was in hell, and the feeling was not diminished when the non-descript woman opened the door and directed me upstairs. There was no lift.

I found Toby in a comfortable room rather like a hotel bedroom, and likewise at the back of the house.

"I see you've also got stained glass up here," I said.

"I have no particular wish to see the view," he said. "I can imagine it only too well. But I have got a particular wish to take a hammer to that window."

It was more elaborate than the window downstairs. It might have been designed in the late eighties or early nineties. The centerpiece was a young woman after, per-haps, Walter Crane. She had a heavy, wavy coiffure, a short upper lip, a long neck, chaste draperies, and bare feet. She was tripping along in a sort of flower bed and spilling some khaki flowers out of her apron. Beneath her was an inscription in debased William Morris-ish let-tering:

         · · · · DAFFO-   AND · TAKE · · ·
    DILS · THAT · COME   THE · WINDS · OF ·
    BEFORE · THE · SWAL-   MARCH · WITH · BE-
    LOW · DARES · · ·   AUTY · · · · ·

" 'Dils that come,' " said Toby bitterly. " 'March with
be!' Oh, the disintegration of it! As if one were not
disintegrating quite fast enough oneself!"

"Oh, come, Toby," I said, looking round. "You might,
you know, have found yourself in a much colder-looking
and more antiseptic sort of room."

"It's not bleak, Jane, I grant you. But if you knew
what a bore I am, you might have hesitated to come and
see me."

"You know the answer to that," I said. "Bosh."

He had become very thin. His face had a waxy look
and an even, yellowish tinge.

"How's Bella?" I asked.

"How odd that you should ask."

"I don't see why. Is it in any way indiscreet?"

"Not in the least, my dear. As a matter of fact she was
here yesterday. And the result is I'm caught up in a perfect free-for-all of feminine antipathies. Bella was shown
up by a snooty maid who said something on the stairs that
annoyed her, and now the maid has put on an ostentatious
coolness in her manner to me. Then the extraordinarily
sympathetic nurse who looks after me came in while Bella
was here. Each obviously wished the other to blazes, and
the air seemed to crackle. And on top of that mother has
developed a violent jealousy of the nurse. Oh, Jane, do
please think of them all as perfect dears who would rather
die than alienate my affections from you! I couldn't bear
it if you were to add one more impulse of hostile possessiveness to this swarm of doting cross-purposes."

208

At that moment the air-raid warning sounded.

"I won't complain of that apes' chorus of pointless cacophony," he said. "*That* we all have to endure. But I should have thought a spirited rendering of 'Colonel Bogey' on the electric organ would have been more tonic."

I asked him one or two of the sort of questions one does ask of people in a nursing home. I asked for instance if he had any idea how long he would have to stay where he was.

"My dear Jane, if I were briskly dying beyond my means, I should know much more where I am. But I expect to take some time over a decline that I really can't afford."

"Surely there's a good chance of your getting better?"

"The doctors are so cagey, one never can judge. It's not dying that worries me particularly. After all, it's just like going through a busy turnstile, through which some remarkably interesting people have preceded one. You never know, one might catch up with them. How delightful if one came across Voltaire, I can't think of anybody I'd rather meet. No, it's not dying but being economically unable to be ill for a long time that's worrying me."

He did not pursue the subject but began to talk gaily and frivolously of other things, until the nurse came in and it was time for me to go. I liked her at once, and as she showed me downstairs, I said, "I'm so glad he's got *you* to look after him."

"His mother isn't," she said, with a pleasant smile, and waved wistfully to me over the banisters.

As I left the house the light was fading. The raid seemed to have come to nothing, and the silence would no doubt have been even more complete than before if it had not been broken by the balloon-minders in their hut, who were howling in a melancholy way "Roll out the

Barrel." As its windows had been blacked out against the approach of evening, the hut gave no other sign of life. The rain had stopped, and as I made my way round the square the howling stopped. I heard something rustling as I was passing one of the great gloomy houses. I glanced down into the area as I passed to see what might be the cause of it. The largest rat I have ever seen was looking up at me from the steps. Just then the all-clear sounded its false assurance. I suddenly realized that I was very tired, that there was no prospect of rest, and that millions of people in various parts of the world were in the same condition, and then my thoughts went back to Toby.

TWENTY-THREE

Mrs. Mountfaucon's anxieties about Toby were not diminished by the prospect of a long illness which could not be paid for. The weekly fees of the nursing home alone must have been far greater than their joint weekly income, and so far as I knew, they had no soluble capital left. In this unpleasant situation she suffered a stroke of bad fortune. Incendiary and explosive bombs fell one night upon the suburban depository where her and Toby's "things" were stored, and made short work of them.

Not a stick was left. Pope's chair, the Lely, some needle-work done by Lady Jane Grey, furniture, china, glass, everything had gone up in smoke.

I did not hear Mrs. Mountfaucon utter a single word of complaint. What is more, she did not utter any word of pious or philosophical resignation, and when I condoled with her, perhaps rather too effusively, she only said gently, "But, Jane, think of the *lives* that are being lost every day and every night—in Germany as well as here."

After this misfortune, all the same, she did sometimes begin a sentence with "About the time we lost our things —" or "After we lost our things—"

I told Toby how much I admired his mother's coolness in the face of adversity.

"It's that old-time religion," he said with a twinkle. "I mind the loss far more than she does. I have a conscien-tious objection to the destruction of pleasing trifles. It's lucky mother has got Pope's teapot in the flat. I'm afraid she's going to miss his chair; she'll be like a boxer de-prived of his straight left. Strictly between ourselves, I rather preferred the things that were *not* relics. I regret rather, among other things, the Boudin. My father bought it from Boudin himself."

Of all my memories of the war, I could dwell agree-ably—if one ever had a chance nowadays to dwell on one's memories—on the pleasant tranquil talks I had dur-ing my regular visits to Toby in the nursing home. A good many things were going on in his mind that I could not always fathom or even guess at, and he sometimes made remarks or took some line of discussion that sur-prised me. He read the papers more than before.

"I see a lot of stuff in the weeklies," he said one day, "about 'the modern dilemma,' 'the contemporary prob-lem,' and all that. It's mostly cant or twaddle. It seems to me there are only two 'modern problems' of any importance. The first is to keep populations down and to reduce them everywhere, and the second is to give people a sense of community, both locally and universally."

Another day he was irritated by some politician or public man who had written or spoken offensively about "intellectuals" and had generalized about their alleged attitude to the war.

"Of course there are pretentious intellectuals, silly ones, flabby ones, or ones with an eye to the main chance—but such people are to be found in any human group, they're not necessarily preponderant. The trouble with some intellectuals now is that they want to do what they can and yet haven't been helped to do what they're best fitted to do; they haven't the slightest illusion as to the importance of their own survival, they simply want to do what little they can."

Evidently by "they" he meant himself. An invalid, an intellectual, an artist, and a "museum piece," he seemed to be desperately trying to diminish the distance between himself and Mr. Everyman.

"Anybody worth calling an intellectual," he went on, "must have intellect enough to know that he only survives today by the grace of God and the heroism of the R.A.F."

The grace of God! The heroism of the R.A.F.! I could hardly believe my ears. It crossed my mind that if somebody had put Toby into a novel, they would never have thought of putting phrases like that into his mouth. He seemed to be speaking out of character; but he hadn't finished.

"There are moments," he went on, "when the men of the R.A.F. seem almost to belong to a different species to ourselves. The conditions of their life in another element,

their fantastic solitary feats in mid-air, the precariousness
of their lives, their boyish brotherhood, their inarticulate
philosophy, their strange slang—everything seems to put
them in a new category of humanity. . . . But I'm afraid
I'm being sentimental. They're simply ourselves, 'chosen
away to brightness.' In every airman is the embryo, if not
more, of an intellectual. In every intellectual—yes, even
in the silly, flabby ones—there must be the germ, quite
atrophied perhaps, of a Douglas Bader, a Cobber Kain,
a Sailor Malan. . . . We're all together, really, like a
swarm of bees. Some day, perhaps, people won't be so
limited, so one-sided. Some day acrobats may be philoso-
phers, and the other way about. . . . I can't fly, I can
hardly stand, but there must be *something* I can do."

For a moment I was too taken aback to say anything.

"But, Toby," I said gently, "you're ill, you can't do the
impossible."

"No," he said, grinning, and making as if to roll up his
sleeves, "but I'll have a go at it."

I knew this wasn't just bravado. I knew it was Toby
liberated, as never before, from himself. But it was not
like a religious conversion: I knew he still regarded war
as a monstrous outrage and folly. The point was that, ill
as he was, he could, morally at least, stand up to it and
face it. As if he knew what I was thinking, he began to
try and explain himself.

"In 1916," he said, "when I was sixteen, I came to the
conclusion that war was not merely disgusting but insane. I made up my mind that if the war went on long
enough to involve me, I would be a conchie. However,
it didn't, so I wasn't put to the test. Later I never gave
much thought to politics. One just took it for granted in
a vague way that nothing like the war could ever happen
again. As soon as it became clear that the same sort of

thing could happen again, I just lost interest in the future. Disgust with the world, that is to say, with the human race —or most of it—was what I felt. I was a complete defeatist: by that I mean that I felt that whatever happened the future would be intolerable. But about the time of Munich, under the immediate threat, I suddenly understood that I had an enormous affection for England. I don't mean patriotism exactly, I mean that one looked at ordinary people in buses, in shops, in the streets, silly, shoddy people many of them, and one saw their weaknesses, and one didn't in the least despise them, one pitied and liked them. One saw that they were threatened, and I knew that I was threatened too: I didn't feel isolated any longer."

"So you no longer felt defeatist?"

"I saw that one couldn't feel disgust with the human race without including oneself. If one didn't include oneself, one was taking up an attitude of superiority, absolutely untenable and unjustifiable. If one said, 'The world is insane,' one implied, 'But I am sane,' and one remembered that a lunatic thinks that *he's* right and everybody else is wrong. I still saw, and I still see, that there's a kind of mad virtue in complete pacificism, in passive resistance. The choice was between that and facing the fact that one was prepared to take up a gun and shoot a German as he entered or tried to enter the street one lived in. If I hadn't been ill when I got back from Rio, I should have tried to enlist. Do you believe me?"

"Yes. I believe you."

"You might reasonably say that it's easy for an invalid to profess belligerence, when he can't hold a gun— easy to breathe fire by proxy. But I'm old enough to know when I've made up my mind about anything, and I *had* made up my mind, not, God knows, that war is better

than peace, but that if one's own existence and the existence of one's own people, with all its faults, was threatened by an invasion of hooligans like the Nazis, bent on
destroying everything one was used to and believes in,
then there was only one thing for me to do, and that was
anything I possibly could do to help to keep them out
and knock them out. A bit late, wasn't I?"

"You were ill, Toby."

"Yes, I was. But with the enemy, I won't say at the
gate, but almost overhead, I had just got to the point of
accepting what most people take for granted—that if one
is attacked, one defends oneself. Do I now eat humble
pie and say that I'd been just an ineffectual intellectual?
I do not. I say that I had previously lost or never really
had that sense—call it primitive if you like—of being
part of a community which I needed and which needed me.
I had felt alone, and all of a sudden I no longer felt
alone, and now I don't feel in the least alone, and that's
why I don't really very much mind the idea of dying.
Herd instinct, I suppose."

It seemed to me as if the "Daddy" in Toby had asserted
himself. Just as Captain d'Arfey had dashed forward,
sword in hand, at the battle of the Alma, so Toby, but
for his illness, might now have been in uniform: I could
easily envisage him as a debonair tosser of a hand-grenade
into some enemy sanctum. But if "Daddy" was suddenly
in the ascendant, the feminine side of Toby was not absent, his mother's side, the patient, merciful side, anxious
not for personal glory but to protect and prolong life,
for life's sake—and that would mean the life of others
rather than his own. There is a place for anger, and there
is a place for mercy. "Daddy" and mother were both
right—and Toby was both. It was as if the old man and
the young woman had not quite fused in their offspring,

as if in Toby the young woman for ever looked up admiringly to the gallant old man, who was also Toby, and who, conscious of his manhood, was always ready to charge, even if necessary in a bath-chair, at the head of his men, and who could never be indifferent to feminine admiration.

I doubt whether Mrs. Mountfaucon had been allowed any hint of her son's trend of thought. She did indeed notice on the table by his bed that small wooden model of an airplane. Once when we had arrived simultaneously at the nursing home I had seen her looking rather vacantly at it, but with a slight pout, perhaps because she did not know where it had come from or what it meant, and because it seemed to hint at some side of his life, some personal relationship, that was kept hidden from her. Probably out of tact she asked no question about it. When she was not present Toby told me that Jocky Bunstable was now "mad about the R.A.F." I wondered to what extent the boy had influenced his views.

From his warlike aspirations Toby was apt to be suddenly and often diverted by the fusses constantly stirred up, I must admit, by members of my sex. Except for one very old gentleman, bulky, helpless, and querulous, and referred to by one of the nurses (so Toby told me) as "that old porpoise," Toby was for a time the only man under the roof, and a sort of bone of female contention.

One afternoon, after I had rung the bell, the front door was opened to me by the matron. She asked if she might have a word with me and led me into her office on the ground floor, opposite the waiting-room.

"I know our good patient is expecting you," she said, carefully shutting the door, "so I won't keep you a moment. It's just to say that if you *should* hear anything about a little upset we've had this morning, please don't say a word to Mr. d'Arfey about it. The peace of mind of a patient, as you know, is something that must be disturbed as little as possible."

I awaited enlightenment.

"I dare say it was quite inadvertent," the matron went on, "but Mr. d'Arfey's mother seems to have lost an earring, a pearl earring. She must have missed it just after her visit to him this morning, so she came back and rang the bell. It was answered by the char, who got it into her head that she was being accused of stealing-by-finding. She seems to have been rather rude to Mrs. Mountfaucon, and instead of coming to me the woman went to some of the staff to complain that *she* had been insulted, and she told them that they were all suspected too. Directly I heard of it, I of course at once phoned to Mrs. Mountfaucon, who was most apologetic and said she only asked the woman if she had seen the earring, and if not, if she would keep a look-out for it and ask others to do the same. Mrs. Mountfaucon said the woman must have misunderstood her, but quite an upset has been caused."

"I can't help thinking that your char must be too touchy," I said. "I know Mrs. Mountfaucon very well, and she's the most considerate and kindly person. She must naturally be upset at losing her pearl, all the more because she has had heavy losses lately from the bombing."

"I dare say, but somehow the damage was done, and one of my nurses came to me in such a state and complained that Mrs. Mountfaucon seemed to resent her care of Mr. d'Arfey and now seemed to think she had been stealing jewelry."

"What nonsense," I said. "I happen to know," I went on plausibly, "that Mrs. Mountfaucon is particularly grateful for the wonderful way you've been looking after her son here. She would never dream of accusing people unjustly, if at all, of stealing or anything else; she's just not that kind of woman."

"No, I'm sure she's not," the Matron said soothingly. "I hope everything will be all right now, but I shall certainly hope to hear that the earring has been found."

"The war makes people edgy, doesn't it?"

"It's very difficult in wartime," she said, "to get a reliable daily woman, and this one's honest and a worker, but, yes, a bit touchy, I must admit, especially since both her husband's tibias were fractured by blast. . . . It's just that I do want to keep any worry and fuss away from our patient. And now I mustn't keep you from him a moment longer. I'm sure he's expecting you, and if you're late he'll be anxious. I knew you'd understand," she said, with rather a grim smile, and she opened the door.

On my way upstairs I put my own interpretation on these trivialities. I felt sure that the staff, including the char, were conscious of Mrs. Mountfaucon's possessiveness in regard to Toby and perceived that she resented the necessity of his being dependent upon other women. I felt sure that her innocent inquiry of the charwoman had merely touched off a whole train of resentment.

Toby grinned at me as I entered his room. He was just putting down the telephone.

"I've been speaking to mother. I asked her if she had lost anything. Her answer was, 'Oh, thank heaven you've found it!' 'It,' I may say, was a pearl earring. Here it is. Mother brought me this morning some sort of opaque jelly that she'd made. I ate it just now and the earring was embedded in it. I nearly swallowed it. 'In future,' I said, 'when you use pearls for cooking, you should pound them first in a mortar.' "

TWENTY-FOUR

On a later visit, as I paused outside Toby's door, I heard music—enchanting, elegiac sounds of the kind that for the moment dissolve the threats and obstacles, the gritty struggles and the dingy pangs, of our everyday life, and seem to free the aspiring prisoner that lies locked up in the flesh. As the door opened and the music sounded more clearly, I recognized the voice of Maggie Teyte singing Debussy's settings of the *Fêtes Galantes*. Toby turned his large eyes towards me and waved a hand at a portable gramophone on the table by his bed.

"I couldn't think of anything I'd rather hear just at present," he said. "I've been playing them over and over again. Yesterday they sent me into a half-trance and I remembered a day by the sea when I was a child, a blue day, when I saw a triumph of Neptune in the Bristol Channel, tritons and nereids and dolphins dipping and sparkling and blowing conches that gave out intolerably beautiful notes. I didn't *think* I saw it, I did see it, and heard it all, and somehow it's all linked up with Maggie Teyte singing Debussy."

"Did you tell anybody about it at the time?"

"I don't think I did. Nobody would have believed me.

They'd just have said 'What an imaginative child,' or 'You beastly little liar. . . .' I don't think it could have been suggested to me by a picture. I doubt if I'd then seen anything with a subject of that kind. It was as if the sea was yielding up the images it had engendered long ago in the human unconscious, and was making real for me the mythology of its movements. Oh, what a day, and I was alone, and it was unbelievably bright, and I knew that behind me all the may trees were in flower. All was grace and clarity; it was a Botticelli moment, with deep, deep undertones. Oh Lord, I'm afraid that sounds like Vernon Lee."

I felt that I was hearing him

> "dwell on such dead themes, not as one who remembers,
> But rather as one who sees."

In fact I remember that very night I looked up the poem in which those lines occur, in the hope that it might help me to enter into his feelings. The lines refer to an aged person, but although Toby was only in what ought to have been the prime of life, he now saw the past with that remote and stereoscopic clarity peculiar to the old—except when he was re-creating those family legends which eventually appeared as *Curious Relations,* and then caricature was always breaking in.

When he said to me quite casually "I've practically decided to kill myself," I sat very still and said nothing. I was not in the least surprised. I noticed with great precision the things in the room, the gramophone, the books on the table, Jocky's airplane, a glass ornament he had brought from Brazil, the inscription on the stained-glass window, and especially his brocade dressing-gown, which hung over the back of a chair, and his slippers, which were trodden down at the heels.

I can imagine that someone who felt hostile to Toby or his memory might say in fact that he wished for death. That I should deny, but I would admit that he always had a distaste for life when it lacked splendor, color, pace, spirit, *panache,* style, idiosyncrasy; and I would further admit that his distaste had now hardened into disgust at the prospect of being slowly crushed by disease and poverty. He was like the owner of a once splendid house, now isolated in a declining neighborhood and past repair, who decides to leave.

When somebody who is evidently of sound mind decides on good grounds to quit this untidy world, there are not many dissuasive arguments that can be put forward without impertinence. Perhaps the most solid of them can be put like this: Don't do it unless you're absolutely sure that you may not still be happy, or helpful to other people who may need your help. Toby, however, had been told that he could not expect to recover, and he saw nothing ahead but costly discomfort, painful decay, and helplessness, so I did not attempt to argue with him. His chief argument was economic.

"This place," he said, "costs sixteen guineas a week. The money simply isn't there. I might be here for months or even years, and where is mother to find the money? She certainly *would* find it. She'd starve herself, beg, borrow, or almost steal to enable me to die between clean sheets in this appalling room. Obviously I can't allow it. She's tough, she may live for years: what about her old age? She'd be no good at selling newspapers. I'm sure all the best pitches are taken, she'd certainly muddle the change, and it wouldn't bring in sixteen guineas a week. . . . Could you get me a gun?"

"Too messy," I said.

He turned his eyes on me. They were very large and dark and questioning.

"I thought it might be the best way," he said. "But I suppose I could gas myself, drown myself, or jump out of a window. Hanging and poison I don't somehow fancy. I must say it would give me some satisfaction to smash this window before jumping out of it. The phrase 'March with be' is becoming almost intolerable. But probably there's no proper drop, just a flat roof, I expect, six feet below the window-sill. Or else one would fall plop through a skylight into the matron's bed or somewhere."

"Couldn't you put the whole thing off for a bit?" I said. "To listen to you, one would never know that you were ill at all."

"But look at me—as yellow as a guinea and as thin as a lath. I look like an unsuccessful fakir. And part of my back is turning a sort of puce color. Forgive these details. . . . There is, however, an alternative. They give me a drug, thanatol. It's supposed to, and does, make me sleep and lull my discomfort: one could hardly call it pain —yet. They give me two tablets every night. It occurred to me that I could save them up for a week or two, and then take the whole lot. Letty was here yesterday, and I asked her about it. Her father was a doctor, you know, and she once began to train as a nurse. She thought it a good plan, but she was surprised that my nurse doesn't stand over me when I take the stuff every night. I asked her if she thought ten days' supply would do the trick. She said it would kill a regiment. I've already saved last night's ration towards my little store. So don't bother about the gun. Can you come and see me about this time next week, before the ten days are up?"

A week later we said a final good-bye to one another.

His behavior struck such a perfect balance between coolness and emotion that my admiration for him did something to mitigate the occasion for me.

As I left the nursing home the air-raid sirens began to
keen, and I felt so utterly melancholy and at the same
time agitated that I went at once in search of a good
strong drink.

That was on a Wednesday. Toby was to take his ten
doses of thanatol on the Friday night. I wondered how
poor Mrs. Mountfaucon would stand the shock.

On the Saturday morning rather early, after a restless
night, I rang up the nursing home. The telephone was
answered by the matron. Trying to suppress any note of
urgency in my voice, I asked for news of Mr. d'Arfey.

"Oh, good morning, Mrs. Valance," she said, "I've just
been paying him my usual morning visit. I think he's looking remarkably bright and cheerful. He'd just been reading his letters, so perhaps he'd just had some good news.
He said he'd had a very good night. Oh yes, he's quite
comfortable this morning."

"Good," I said, and my voice sounded unfamiliar to
me. "Oh, good. . . . Do you think it would be all right
for me to come and see him this afternoon?"

"Oh, yes, *quite* all right. Visitors do him good, so long
as he doesn't overtire himself."

Evidently Toby had decided not to take the fatal dose.
Perhaps he *had* had good news of some kind. Perhaps some
money had come in unexpectedly from somewhere.

I sent him a telegram to say I was coming, and went
to the nursing home at the earliest possible moment in
the late afternoon. It was not without embarrassment
that I climbed the stairs.

"Jane!" he said, as I came into the room, and held out
his hand. I took it, and he gripped my hand tightly, and

kissed it with fervor. "Jane, I apologize profoundly, but I'm really not to blame. My God, what an anticlimax!"

As he spoke I looked searchingly at him. He looked almost well. His color seemed to have come back; he looked calm and rested; his eye looked healthily, not feverishly, bright.

"So you didn't take them after all," I said, murmuring discreetly. "Oh, what a blessing! Perhaps you'll get better and live for years."

I thought he looked at me a little oddly while I spoke.

"Didn't take them?" he said in a loud voice. "It's Lazarus *qui vous parle*! Of course I took them, the whole lot! And *look* at me! . . . You didn't think, you *couldn't* have thought, that I was going to funk it at the last moment?"

"You *took* them?" I said, gaping.

"The whole bloody lot! And what happened? I had the best night I've had for months, and I woke up this morning feeling on top of the world—though for one awful moment I thought that I was on top of the *next* world, and that there, too, they have abominable stained-glass windows in the taste of the eighteen-seventies and inscribed 'March with be.' I thought it might be a sort of punishment."

"It's incredible," I said. "You told me that Letty Tracy told you ten would be enough to kill a regiment."

"All I can say is, that I must be the equivalent of a brigade."

"All *I* can say is, Toby, that she can't have known what she was talking about."

"Oh, she knew all right. She knows all about thanatol."

"Well, how do you account for it? I can hardly imagine," I said, "what it's like to make one's exit and then find that one hasn't made it at all. Had the stuff gone stale? Had it lost its kick?"

"Not at all. In spite of the décor, this is quite an efficient nursing home. And so it ought to be, at the price. No, it's simply the old trouble, that I just don't respond to drugs. Mother's exactly the same: I get it from her. She's extremely healthy, as you know, and has never been ill in her life, but there have been times when she has been given sedatives and anaesthetics—and they just haven't worked. And we've both got very strong heads for drink. I don't think I've ever been properly drunk in my life—not what could be called as tight as a newt—though I've been pretty cheerful pretty often."

"But you must have known, you must have suspected, that this stuff, this thanatol or whatever it is, mightn't act as powerfully on you as on other people?"

"Why? I'd been taking it every night, and it had apparently sent me to sleep and soothed my nerves. I know its reputation—I know it's supposed to be fatal to take an overdose. I know doctors are very cagey about prescribing it. I know that I took last night what ought to have been very much more than a fatal dose. It never occurred to me that such a *quantity* could possibly fail, even with me. . . . I do feel such a fool, but I feel almost well today, better than I've felt for ages."

There are times when one glances at inanimate objects as if for comfort or reassurance, but at moments of crisis they sometimes disappoint one by looking further away than they really are, by looking irrelevant; or their indifference seems like hostility; or their old or happy associations become tinged with bitterness. I had few and by no means happy associations with the objects in this room, and they seemed, in a brief instant almost of hallucination, to be listening. The portable gramophone with a disc still in

225

place, the little wooden airplane, the distasteful female in the stained-glass window, a bottle of medicine on the mantelshelf, the tiles round the fireplace, the flowers in the vases, all seemed to be listening to Toby, waiting to hear what he was going to say next, as if they knew perfectly well that although he had not died in the night, a time and a place were appointed for his death, and a long succession of condemned men and women were destined to occupy the bed in which he lay.

"I've decided to get up," he said. "I shall leave this place and get mother to get me a room at Equerry Mansions."

He said this with that slight air of loftiness he assumed when he expected to be argued with.

"Oh," I said.

"It will be cheaper," he said emphatically.

"Yes."

"Oh, I know what you're thinking. You think I'm not well enough to move."

"I can't judge that, Toby."

"Not only will it be cheaper, but I've decided that I really can't die in this room—die *again,* I mean." And he gave a brilliantly mischievous smile.

"There's just one thing, Toby. Has your mother any idea—?"

"Oh, of course she knows quite well, but she would never admit it to herself or to anybody else. Some women, you know, have that faculty of knowing an unpleasant fact and refusing to recognize it—I mean 'recognize' in the sense that they would acknowledge a bow from a disagreeable acquaintance, or in the sense that a great Power recognizes an upstart government in a neighboring State. Mother, like many women, is, as you very well know, a double personality. Not a split one, but a double one—

one inside the other. Inside is the core, a hard-boiled realist, completely without illusions, sophisticated if you like,
full of North Country common sense and of worldly wis-
dom, strongly possessive, self-willed, even, in some in-
stinctive way, calculating."

"No," I said, "not calculating."

"Outside," he went on, taking no notice of the inter-
ruption, "is a kind of decorative husk—the husk of a
coquette, of a coquettish little girl whose every instinct is
to please and to attract, by an appearance of ingenuous-
ness, of innocence, modesty, of timidity and propriety,
obedient to polite convention, to the conventions of the
society and of the religion in which she was brought up.
You must often have noticed, when I've told some fairly
candid story, how she pretends to be shocked and at the
same time obviously enjoys it like anything. Now this
business of suicide. At heart, at the core, because she's a
realist, she knows that it's a sensible thing for me to kill
myself, perhaps the only sensible thing left for me to do.
And because she loves me, with a concentration of all her
capacity for love into mother-love (and it's no mean
capacity, she's a woman of feeling), she accepts, I'm sure,
the necessity of this violent act, which goes absolutely
against the life-giving function, the life-maintaining, life-
increasing function of her whole being, because she knows,
to put it simply, that it's better for me than any possible
alternative. But the husk says, 'Susannah, don't admit the
possibility that your son can commit suicide. The Christian
religion forbids it. It's unthinkable, in any case, that *your*
son, your only son, should take his own life. Put the
thought out of your mind. Above all, don't let him see
that you even admit the possibility.' "

He paused and leaned back, perhaps a little exhausted
by this speech.

"Well," I said, "the thanatol has made you very analytical. Your mind is far too clear to be put an end to."

It did just occur to me that he might now be contemplating putting an end to himself at Equerry Mansions, and the rather detached tone in which he had been describing his mother made me wonder whether he could be quite so heavy-handed as that. I certainly did not feel that I had the slightest right to advise him against any step he might be meaning to take, and I knew that his analysis of his mother was not in the least incompatible with his devotion to her and his wish to spare her distress. Devotion, in any case, can be a very mixed feeling.

We were silent for a few moments. Then he announced that he was sick of lying in bed and would get up and sit in the other armchair. I helped him into his dressing-gown and he had hardly sat down in the chair when there was a knock at the door. It opened, and there was Mrs. Mountfaucon.

"Oh, Toby—Jane—I'm disturbing you. I'll go away again."

"For God's sake, mother, let go of that handle and come in and sit down. What *is* disturbing is a woman who makes a half-baked entry into a room."

"Toby!" I protested. "You know your mother comes charmingly into a room. She only thought she might be interrupting us."

"We were only talking about the diplomatic policies of the nations," he said.

"A fib, I know," said his mother, "but never mind."

"The truth is," I said, "that I must really be going. Toby has been so entertaining that I quite forgot the time."

"Oh, but please don't go just because I've arrived, Jane. And I have such a sad piece of news."

228

"Suitable for an invalid," said Toby.

"Sad, but a most extraordinary coincidence. Just when we've so lately lost our Pope treasures, I've heard of the suicide of Professor Snade Leavenbread."

The reference to suicide was like that agonizingly friendly grip that somebody gives your arm where you have just been vaccinated.

"He was the *great* Pope expert, you remember," she said, wondering at our silence.

"He was in no sense great, mother."

"Well, dear, he knew a great deal about Pope, no living man knew more. He came to Marsh, Jane, to see our Pope things. I'm afraid Toby couldn't bear him; I think it was because Professor Leavenbread used the expression 'source material.' I'm so thankful he never knew that the things have been destroyed. It would have broken his heart."

"Bosh, mother."

"Toby, he *worshiped* anything that had even remotely to do with Pope."

Toby began wagging an irritable foot in a downtrodden slipper.

"Oh, poor man, I wonder what made him do it!" Mrs. Mountfaucon was wringing her hands.

"Surely, mother, just suddenly realizing that he was Professor Leavenbread was quite enough to make him do it."

"It may have been," I said. "But after all, Toby, he had been Professor Leavenbread for a long time."

"True," said Toby in his dryest voice. "But even a worm will turn."

And on that note I rose to go.

TWENTY-FIVE

The tempo of the war was getting quicker, the pressure and strain of everyday life were growing more complex and intense, and as for private life, my own had long since dwindled away under the stress of duty—at least it had been dwindling, but all of a sudden I had begun to live again. I had begun a new life, all the more exciting and precious because of the stresses and hazards under which it had come into being and was flowering. In short, I was meeting whenever I could the man who has since become my husband. Because, as I have said, it has been no part of my purpose to obtrude myself unduly into this book, and only to show myself in relation to Toby and his mother, I will do no more for the moment than recall the effect upon him of my new happiness, which I couldn't have hidden even if I had wanted to.

It was on one of my last visits to him in the nursing home that he looked at me even more intently than usual as I came in and said, "Jane, what has happened to you? I never saw anybody look so radiant. You must be in love. Why, you're getting quite pink in the face!"

I said guardedly that there might be something in what he said, as there generally was.

"My dear," he said, "the best of luck."

When I say that this was one of my last visits to him in the nursing home I don't mean that I gave up seeing him but that he had made up his mind to get up and leave it.

"My suicide plans are shelved for the moment," he said lightly, very much as one might say that one was rather thinking of giving up smoking, but not just for the present. Anybody who did not know him as well as I knew him might have thought him a man of words rather than deeds.

"I'm bored, Jane, with lying here and waiting to disintegrate. I've decided that I'm quite capable of working in some Ministry or other and doing something useful. For instance, I know French quite as well as English. My doctor nearly had kittens when I suggested my being dropped to the *maquis* by parachute, so I suppose I shall have to do translating or interpreting or propaganda or something."

He looked ghastly—the word is not too strong—and I couldn't imagine him capable of going every day to work in an office, especially in wartime conditions. The idea was to me grotesque and painful, and to change the subject I asked for news of Bella. He was a little evasive, but said that, like his mother and like me, she had visited him regularly. Like me? I had made up my mind that however important and urgent the new demands on my extremely scanty free time, I would not let Toby down. I knew that he would miss me if I appeared inconstant in my affection for him. I had already told my husband-to-be that I had been paying a weekly visit to a dying man and should contrive to go on seeing this person once a week. But when Toby got up, left the nursing home, and did in fact go to work in a government department, my obligations sounded less convincing. I thought I had better arrange for Toby and my intended to meet. Even if they hated one another at sight, each would know the shape of what he was hating. Somehow it was never possible to contrive a meeting; always one of us was prevented by duty or health or absence or some other cause.

My new orientation—or let me say my new love—had quite altered my perspective of Toby. My affection and admiration towards him were unchanged, and the ties of friendship that bound me to him and his mother were enduring. (I was going to write "everlasting," but my father's ghost must have been looking over my shoulder. My father deprecated hyperbole. He told me to be careful always to say what I meant, only to talk about what I knew, and to describe things exactly. That is what I have been trying to do in these pages.) But love, like illness, sets one apart and adrift. I might still be one of Toby's women, but I found a slight relief in the thought that I had now shrunk to my proper and long-delayed status—that of one of Toby's less important women. Of the more important there were only two—his mother and Bella—and it would no doubt be as much as his remaining energies could compass to keep them apart, and to keep each, so to speak, in her proper place. I liked to think that I was perhaps foremost on a list of whose length I was uncertain, but which would include Lydia Delap, Lilac Evans, Letty Tracy, and perhaps others.

My second husband *in posse* never failed to inquire about Toby, felt some curiosity about him, and twitted me with being a lady with a lamp. On a transatlantic flight (I will spare you any account of my anxieties) he met a man who knew Toby and the work Toby was doing. This man, he reported to me, had said that for Toby to be on his legs at all was "fantastic" and for him to be working was "a kind of crazy heroism." Toby was only able to work for a part of each day but his work was said to be valuable. I said I should like to repeat to Toby what had been said about him, but my own work took me out of London at that time, so I had to tell him in a letter. He made no comment.

I next saw him at Equerry Mansions. It was at the beginning of a grim-looking New Year which seemed to promise most people nothing so heroic as blood, sweat, and tears but rather boredom, fatigue, scarcity, and anxiety, those four drab Furies. Mrs. Mountfaucon had contrived a little dinner for the three of us and her goodness would have quite shut out the Furies for an hour or two had I not been obsessed by Toby's aspect. His skin was drawn over his bones, and even his smile was cadaverous. When he made jokes, I could hardly restrain myself from weeping. God alone knows how, and for whom, his mother was keeping up the pretense that he was fit to be up and about.

"You've heard, I dare say," he remarked quite casually after dinner, "that Lydia Delap has been killed in an air-raid?"

I hadn't heard it; the news startled me.

Mrs. Mountfaucon hid her face in her hands. Was she praying for Lydia's soul, or trying to hide the relief she could not help feeling, or trying to fight it down?

"Yes," said Toby. He was lighting a cigarette with a too bony hand, and the thought occurred to me that he might not be going to smoke many more cigarettes. "Yes, she was dressing for dinner in her flat near Cadogan Square, and a Polish colonel was to call for her. Of course it *would* be a Pole. When he arrived he found that her looking-glass had been shattered by blast. A dagger-shaped piece of glass had flown straight at her throat and pierced her jugular vein. . . . Poor Lydia, she was always a narcissist. I expect her looking-glass was tired of seeing so much of her and, alas, her crows'-feet, and so took its revenge. . . . I hear she had lately been hovering on the verge of that roomy old receptacle for flagging egoists, the Roman Catholic Church." He could still roll his eyes wickedly; he could still hide his real feelings.

"Poor soul," said Mrs. Mountfaucon. "Perhaps her vanity was her undoing."

"I can't believe, mother, that she was vainer than most of us."

"It might happen to any of us, Toby, but to be killed by one's own looking-glass—oh, what a dreadful poetic justice. . . . Somehow it reminds me of poor Mrs. What-on-earth-was-her-name (there's no doubt my memory's not what it was—not perhaps that it greatly matters), the most garrulous woman we ever knew."

"A woman," Toby explained, "who gabbled and rattled on for eighty years, contriving, from long practice, to be at the same time a fearful mischief-maker and a consummate bore. Then she had a stroke—"

"And lay for years," Mrs. Mountfaucon went on, "as mute as a fish. She was perfectly conscious and in a perfect rage, with her eyes looking utter stilettoes. It does seem as if Heaven sometimes punishes us for our weaknesses in the most precise way."

"Heaven punishes us anyway, mother—if indeed Heaven is the right name to apply to it."

"Poor Lydia," said his mother, as if in meditation.

"Don't be such a perfect humbug, mother. You know you're delighted to hear the last of her. It is I who have reason to miss her."

She made no reply, bit her lower lip, and looked quaintly at me, as if to say, "What can I do with him?"

Then, suddenly grave, she said, "Believe me, I was trying to understand my own faults more clearly, Toby. Perhaps God may punish me too in my vanity."

"No masochism here, please, mother. This isn't the confessional, you know. But perhaps one of these days, after the war, you'll have a very smart new hat from Galhauban Sœurs, and you'll be pleasantly enraging other members of your sex with the sight of it, and then a sudden puff of wind will blow it into the lake in St. James's Park."

"Fiend!"

But he had turned away and was looking into the fire, thinking of Lydia perhaps, and Paris in the nineteen-twenties, *his* twenties, and his lost youth. His face, colorless and so pitiably thin, looked haggard—but only for a moment; instinctively he set himself to entertain his hostess and his fellow-guest, his mother and myself, his constant and slightly anomalous girl-friend. That, too, seemed to me "a kind of crazy heroism."

The next time I saw him we were alone together, and he told me he was at the end of his strength and had again decided to kill himself. We had a practical talk about ways and means. Once more I said good-bye to him for ever.

"My poor Jane, it must fall to few of us to have to go through two affecting death-bed scenes with the same person. Perhaps I ought to have spared you this and just slipped away. But that wouldn't have been very polite."

He said other things. I don't care to reproduce them here, but I can hear every word as clearly at this moment as if it had just been uttered and I can recall the exact intonation of his voice.

Just as I was going he said, "I shan't make any mistakes this time. A bungled suicide, if I may venture upon an epigram, is the solecism of a lifetime. I shouldn't like it to be said of me, 'He was not without *savoir vivre,* but he showed a lack of *savoir mourir.'* "

TWENTY-SIX

The immediate effect upon Mrs. Mountfaucon of her son's death was to reduce her to a condition in which I hope never to see anybody again. I do not mean that there was anything ignoble about it; I mean that it was not easy to contemplate.

There are questions which such a woman in such a situation is likely to ask herself: Could I not have prevented this? Am I to blame for my son's end? "Was it for this the clay grew tall?" And, underneath all, the recurrent, the eternal, the eternally unanswered *Why?* The debate was not made public.

"Poor lady," said Corby, "she's taken it hard. The very next morning I saw her having her usual chat with the paper man on the corner. Just as if nothing had happened, but I reckon it's broke her heart. I wouldn't like to say Mr. d'Arfey oughtn't to have done it, but I can't help wishing he hadn't."

It was an early afternoon in May when we set out from Equerry Mansions for the funeral. I had told Mildred

Purbind over the telephone to hire a car. It was unwise of me; for some reason best known to herself she had simply asked Corby to get a taxi. It was a veteran, quite unsuitable for the longish drive. More big-brotherly than ever, Corby handed us four women into this box-like, moth-eaten, old rattletrap of a car, and we set out on the long journey to a suburban crematorium.

Mrs. Mountfaucon sat at the back, with Lady Meliora beside her. Mrs. Purbind and I sat facing them, almost knee to knee. The vibration of the vehicle was appalling, and we four passengers quivered as if we were undergoing some formidable slimming treatment or shock-therapy. I couldn't help wishing that some male mourner had been with us, but Mrs. Mountfaucon had wished the proceedings to be as private as possible. I think her motives in asking Mrs. Purbind had been two: to ensure the presence of some kind of living representative, however residual, of "the family"; and to help Mrs. Purbind's self-esteem. Being of a less kind disposition, I would not, in Mrs. Mountfaucon's position, have thought either of these considerations important.

Lady Meliora sat very upright, with a minute gold filigree bottle of smelling-salts in her left hand, which was enclosed in a dove-grey glove. The sinews which time had dried and loosened in her neck shivered as if in an ague or from some electrical current, and I tried not to stare at them. Mrs. Mountfaucon, with the big black brim of her hat pulled down over her averted and rather blood-shot eyes, sat back as far as she could in her corner, with a handkerchief of creamy old lace pressed against her lips as if to prevent any utterance. She too vibrated; she looked so passive and diminished that I found it harrowing.

Each of her three companions had different ideas, evidently, about the best way to behave. My idea—perhaps not the right one—was that silence was best. Lady Meliora's—which was probably better—was to put a calm face on things and make an occasional, casual-seeming remark about anything except what was occupying our minds: for instance, "The park looks such a wilderness without its railings," or "The sky seems quite thundery, doesn't it?" or "Do you feel any draught, Susannah?" As she was in the ordinary way anything but a prattler, these commonplace utterances required a real effort on her part. Unfortunately they were too sparse to cramp the relentless onset of Mildred Purbind, whose evangelical piety, dutiful attachment to the chief mourner, and sense of responsibility and of the occasion had caused her, alas, to attempt to interpret the intentions of the Deity and to advocate resignation to them. Her sermonizing —it was hardly less than that—was a series of clichés, and however well intentioned it may have been I should find it distasteful to reproduce in full her exact words. It is perhaps enough to say that they included, more than once, the dreadful expression "passing over" or it may have been "passing on," and, far more shocking, "Our Lord wants us to—," and "It is His will that—." This, added to the shaking of the taxi, made me feel something like nausea, and I was more than thankful when Lady Meliora suddenly exclaimed, with intensity but somehow not unkindly, "Oh, Mrs. Purbind, please! I hardly think you need continue, just for the present."

Mrs. Mountfaucon's mouth was quite hidden by the handkerchief. She did not move, but her old eyes moved. They glanced at Lady Meliora almost expressionlessly, and were like the eyes of an animal in a cage which looks, without fear or hope, at someone outside. Then they rested very, very distantly, for some tense seconds, upon Mrs.

Purbind, who unbelievably leaned forward and patted Mrs. Mountfaucon's knee. Then they slowly swivelled, and looked out of the window. So did I.

It was a beautiful afternoon. The taxi-man seemed to be taking us the leafiest way. As we went on, the whole sky to the southwest turned bluish-violet, bruise-colored, and against it the young-leaved trees and flowering shrubs, held in a sunny radiance from the south, streamed past in a many-colored stereoscopic clarity of detail. It had been raining, and the swishing sound of cool foliage flowing past the open window sounded like another shower. Sometimes against the purplish sky a laburnum was a shower of light, or an overhanging red may tree in full blossom, like a magnified detail of a Pre-Raphaelite picture, wafted almost overpoweringly in upon us its suggestive smell, coarse yet exquisite like some of life's intensest moments. Great heads and bunches of lilac drooped and hung over walls and fences, saturated like sponges with dew-like raindrops and their own nectar, intolerably sweet, the white and the dark Persian especially on this day making me think of death. And when from time to time we found ourselves in dreary treeless roads of shops and traffic-lights, they seemed unreal, so strong had been the impression made by the richness of spring. The intermittent pale green light filtered through leaves and cast upon Mrs. Mountfaucon seemed the light of truth. She had remained silent the whole time.

As we approached the crematorium the sun came out.

"Oh, the sun!" murmured Lady Meliora.

"Like a sign from Heaven," said Mrs. Purbind.

I could have murdered her. I could at that moment have agreed how right Toby had been about her. I remembered the humming-birds, which he had cremated without her knowing; and now, without his knowing, she was about to attend *his* cremation. It was the kind of grim joke he would have enjoyed.

We crunched over the gravel path into the chapel, where we filed into a pew near the front. Toby's coffin, in a raised position, was only a few feet away from us, and a surpliced clergyman, who seemed thoroughly undenominational, led us in a not very impressive service. A good thing, perhaps; the prose of the Anglican burial service ravages the feelings.

Mrs. Mountfaucon was kneeling with her face in her hands. Suddenly she lifted her head, glanced behind her, and gave a little shriek. The clergyman paused, glanced at her, and instantly resumed his monologue: I expect he was used to emotional upsets in his small and specialized congregations. She had at once hidden her face again in her hands. I had thought that there was nobody present besides ourselves. I glanced discreetly out of the tail of my eye, and there, right at the back, whom should I see but Lilac Evans, in a plain black suit and little black turban, excessively smart. To say I was surprised would be an understatement; I was puzzled.

Mrs. Mountfaucon did not raise her head again until the critical and somehow always slightly absurd moment when with a wheezing and creaking, rather like the internal preparations made by some ancient clock about to strike the hour, the coffin began to amble slowly towards an orifice which swallowed it and was then closed off by two small folding doors that flapped shut together; they reminded me of a cuckoo clock. I had no feeling that that was the last of Toby, I had such an acute sense of his character, I might say of the presence of his character, and I was thinking what fun he would have made of the whole proceeding.

"So good of you to come," Mrs. Mountfaucon said to

Butterball Evans afterwards with a falsely sweet smile and an awful finality: without waiting for an answer she headed rapidly for the taxi. We drove away in brilliant sunshine, and Mrs. Mountfaucon talked in quite a detached way with all of us about matters that had little or no connection with the occasion.

Later, when it was time to leave Equerry Mansions, Mildred Purbind was gently but unanimously discouraged from acting upon her kind offer to remain with Mrs. Mountfaucon for the evening. No such discouragement was provoked by her suggestion that she might in that case be well advised to take a certain train from Marylebone, or perhaps it was Baker Street, which she had mentioned previously as a more convenient one than some others. There was nothing clumsy or irritating, there was even something affecting and genuinely daughter-like about her farewell to Mrs. Mountfaucon. Mildred always meant well; like herself, that was only too plain: but, as my father used to say, "It's not enough to *mean* well."

Life always has its Mildreds, breeds and needs them. After a great expense of time and trouble they come tripping forward with a large montage of the wrong sort of humming-birds. They are sometimes people who sometimes really do think more of the interests of others than of their own. Let us try and respect them, try and like them; they are probably the salt of the earth. All the same, a little salt goes a long way.

I admit that I have throughout these pages spoken condescendingly of Mildred. I dare say it is odious of me and I know she made me feel class-conscious. I can at least plead that I defended her against Toby.

After she had gone to catch her convenient train, Lady Meliora and I both offered to stay with Mrs. Mountfaucon, but she said she thought she would rather be alone and knew we would understand. So we left Equerry Mansions together, and dispirited. I was longing, as I have seldom longed, for a drink. I told Lady Meliora I was feeling a little faint and proposed to go and rest for a few minutes at Martlet's Hotel near by. It was, and still is, a smallish, quiet, old-fashioned place of the utmost respectability, and I was known there. Martlet's was the sort of hotel where old, dim, displaced country peers, and the widows of bishops and the sort of people who used to employ a female archivist like myself used to go because their parents had been there before them, and sometimes at the reception desk they would unexpectedly meet their own grown-up children and exclaim happily at finding that they were occupying adjoining rooms.

"Oh, Martlet's," said Lady Meliora. "How clever of you. Do you suppose they're very full? I was wondering, if you had no other special plans, whether we couldn't have a little dinner there together, quite early. A little hot soup and some sherry, and you'll soon feel better, and so shall I. It hasn't been a very comfortable afternoon."

So we bent our steps towards Martlet's, agreeing that it was difficult to ask people to meals nowadays under one's own roof, that there was so little to be bought and nobody to cook it, that the days were drawing out, that bombing was a public nuisance, and so on. But after sherry and soup—even hotel soup, even hotel soup in wartime, we felt slightly restored, and we held a little inquest on Toby. I understood better than ever before what a good, if limited, woman Lady Meliora was. And then we naturally touched upon the problem of Mrs. Mountfaucon's immediate future.

"I've been wanting to ask you," I said, "what you thought of that strange little scene at the crematorium this afternoon. Why did Lilac Evans turn up? And why was Mrs. Mountfaucon so upset?"

From my conversation with Lydia Delap I thought I knew the answer to the second of these questions.

"I think I can throw a little light on the matter," said Lady Meliora, "though I have only met Miss Evans once before, and then quite accidentally—it was at that party he gave in Hanover Square, for his hats and things, you remember?"

"Hats and accessories."

"Exactly. Poor Toby was cornered and had to introduce us, because he had no alternative. He did so hate his acquaintances to know one another." She gave a wan, wise smile. "She's very smart, isn't she? She carries herself very well, and with a figure like that I'm sure she has been amply repaid for all the trouble she has taken with her appearance."

The acidity of this observation I did not at once fully perceive, until I recalled a slight stress on the word "repaid."

"Oh well, it *is* part of her profession," I said rather lamely, "to be almost too well dressed."

"Oh, I'm sure it is," said Lady Meliora ambiguously, as if by "profession" I had meant the oldest profession.

"I'm not sure that it was very tactful of her to turn up this afternoon," I said, "and in such very chic mourning. I imagine that she was never really one of Toby's closest friends."

"Oh, wasn't she? That I can't judge. They certainly saw a lot of one another at one time, and at one time it was even rumored that they might be going to marry."

"Oh, I never knew that. In any case," I said, "I'm

very much in her debt. It was she who introduced me to Toby and his mother. I might otherwise never have known them."

Lady Meliora put on a pair of glasses and contemplated some mince on a plate that had just been put in front of her. It was scanty and of dubious provenance, and accompanied by a little heap of overcooked spinach and two chlorotic potatoes, described as "new."

"I suppose Martlet's are doing their best," she said, putting her spectacles back in their case, "but it's not an impressive best. . . . I can only think that Miss Evans somehow found out the place and time of the funeral, didn't know that it was going to be private, imagined that there were going to be quite a number of other people present, and attended, let us hope, for the sort of reason one does have when one attends a funeral."

"But still I can't see why Mrs. Mountfaucon should have shrieked when she saw her."

"I know why she shrieked, and I can see that you don't. I'm not sure whether it's right for me to tell you, because I do so hate to repeat any kind of slanderous report about anybody, especially when I've got no means of knowing whether it's true. But I think I'd better tell you, because you're a close friend of the family—oh dear, I suppose we can hardly call it a family now. I know you can be counted upon not to repeat a word of all this."

I murmured a suitable formula.

"After Mr. Basingfield's death it was discovered, you remember, that he had misappropriated the funds entrusted to him and had as good as ruined poor Susannah and Toby. The suggestion reached Susannah, I don't know from what quarter, that in fact a great part of the money had been settled upon Miss Evans and that she was in fact Mr. Basingfield's mistress."

I don't know if it was dishonest of me, but I gave her no inkling that what she had to say was not altogether new to me.

"But I thought they scarcely knew each other!" I said. "I suppose they may have met occasionally at dinner parties at Duchess's Gate."

"They're said to have been seen together in France on two separate occasions, once in a theater in Paris, and once dining together at a very expensive restaurant at Cannes. . . . Oh, look, half a tinned peach and a spoonful of vanilla ice—what magnificence! . . . Not that that proves anything about their incomes."

"But if that suggestion was true, do you suppose that she knew where the money was coming from?"

"I don't suppose she could have had any idea at that time, but she *might* have guessed after Mr. Basingfield's death, when it became known, presumably even to her, that he had ruined poor Susannah and Toby."

"But surely she would then have tried to make some restitution?"

"Not necessarily. That would have been to admit that she had been Mr. Basingfield's mistress—or shall we say his titular mistress, for after all he must have been getting on for eighty. Besides, a woman of the world, of *her* world, who has considerable sums of money settled upon her, does not, I imagine, wish to question their origin any more than she wishes to advertise it, at least when she has made a fool of such an old man. Nor, certainly, would she wish to part with them."

"What a horrible idea the whole thing is. Do you think she's so grasping? Do you mean that if somebody went to her and said that Toby might not have killed himself if he had had more money, or if he had been sure that his mother would not have been progressively impoverished by the expenses of his illness—do you think she would have refused to help?"

"I think," said Lady Meliora, "that to go and ask her for money and to suggest what can hardly be proved—that she was wrongfully enriched by Mr. Basingfield—would be to lay oneself open not only to a drastic snub but possibly to the threat of an action for slander. The world is the world, after all. Besides, as I say, there's no proof either that he did settle the money on her, or, if he did, that she in fact knew where it had come from. Mr. Basingfield seems in any case to have been quite well off and to have lived quite comfortably."

"What I've never been able to understand," I said, "is why Toby and his mother didn't bring an action against Mr. Basingfield's executors or estate for fraudulent conversion. I never liked to broach the subject with them, it's such a painful one."

"I dare say they took advice, but I imagine these things are difficult to prove, and that when money is once dispersed—perhaps by gift and with no transactions on paper at all—it may well be impossible to recover. Besides, it was Mr. Basingfield, not his executors, who stole the money. . . . The coffee, it seems to me, is not at all bad. Let's have some more. My doctor insists that it's rank poison for me, but I refuse to go through life on nothing but insipidities, especially when there's all this row going on at nights. There are those wretched guns at it again."

I insisted later, during a desultory air-raid, on seeing her home in a taxi, and she asked me to come and have tea with her one day if I could. She didn't perhaps quite realize how tied I was to my duties:

little short of a funeral would have let me out that very day.

"I've got one or two things that might interest you," she was saying, as she got out of the taxi. "For instance, the grant of a manor by Richard II to one of his favorites, who came to a bad end—if it doesn't get bombed in the meantime. And I've got an enfeoffment—"

"And I've got a wife and two kids," said the taxi-man irritably. "Come on, lady," he said to me, "let's get going. Jerry's dropping a bit too much scrap-iron tonight to 'ang about in."

TWENTY-SEVEN

"She does seem to have settled down after a fashion," said Corby of Mrs. Mountfaucon.

Though her flat was small, it was large enough to contain some remains of her personal treasures and belongings, and it had the advantage of that small balcony with its window-boxes. When I went to see her she showed me her flowers. They were obviously tended very carefully. Her manner was faintly like that of a lady of the manor showing one round her large country garden and more than slightly like that of a little girl showing proudly the patch of garden which she has been allowed to call her own and in which she has raised some struggling nasturtiums and a tuft or two of pansies and geraniums. It was with something very like coyness that she showed me her new toy watering-can. Its predecessor had begun to leak and Corby had assured her that it was not worth mending.

"It's *pre-war*," she said almost archly, "and just the right size, don't you think, for my diminutive garden? The man at the Stores said it was the very last one, and he had no idea when they would be having them again. I said I thought it unlikely that I should be wanting another, and that if this was in fact the last one I thought I deserved it, as Daddy had been one of the very first customers there, a sort of foundation member. He looked at me open-mouthed, and I'm sure he didn't believe a word I was saying. That's one of the things I notice about getting old, people often haven't the faintest idea what one's talking about, or, if they have, it bores them to distraction. You'd think the man would have been *interested* in such an old connection with the Stores, but they get such different assistants in wartime, and I suppose he's only temporary. He gave himself such an air of doing me a great favor, but after all I might have gone to Harrods or Hamley's for my little watering-can, and I'm sure they would have been delighted to sell me one—that is, if they *had* one. I felt almost hurt."

Ageing people who live alone are apt to become preoccupied with trifles, and with routine. The nap after luncheon, the evening cordial, and the timely pill become, or are believed by them to have become, essential to the body. So, too, their minds and spirits seem to need the comforts of habit, a ritual of everyday regularities—things like automatic attention at fixed times to the wireless news and the weather report, daily application to newspaper, crossword puzzle, or detective story, and periodical indulgence in some hobby. Mrs. Mountfaucon had no wireless set and paid little attention to the papers. Neither war nor peace could restore to her what she had lost, her background, her youth, her husbands, her money, her interest in clothes, her hopes, her fears. The only books she seemed to read were about English history, national or local. I couldn't imagine her keeping, like Lady Meliora, a dog, or indeed any other pet. Her tiny garden was something for her to cherish, she was not friendless, she still had her religion and her natural sociability.

Every morning she went to the early service at Westminster Abbey, every Sunday she went there to matins—and every Sunday, to her perennial amusement, she was pointedly ignored, except for a cold and distant nod, by that other regular worshiper, the admiral's unsinkable widow, old Lady Trunnion-James. But Mrs. Mountfaucon had stolen a march on this stiff-necked old thing, because she had for long been on terms of affability with various canons and vergers and so on, and was allowed to give voluntary help on weekdays towards the maintenance of the place. I rather think she polished some special brasses or dusted some special marbles. She told me how she had acted as a guide to American and other sightseers, and once I found her mending with gold and colored threads and silks a worn patch on an antique chasuble. She was a wonderful needlewoman and had been somehow associated with the Royal School of Needlework.

I cannot judge to what extent these activities alleviated her solitude. It must in any case have been lessened by frequent contact with Lady Meliora, by occasional visits from Mrs. Purbind, and, I hope, by my now and then going to see her or taking her out to a meal and a play.

Then she had various people she saw every day and took an interest in—Corby, for instance; one or two people in shops; and the old man who sold papers at a corner on the way to the Abbey, who called her "Ma" and received presents of various home comforts for his sick wife. She still corresponded with Mrs. Crumpsey and with the Countess, now always referred to as "poor Laceman," and she was still in touch with one or two old retainers or tenants in the country, or with their offspring.

More real to her was the memory of Toby, and she told me she was hoping to plan a small exhibition of the pictures he had painted in Brazil. I said I had never seen them and asked where they were. She said they were in storage but the management of Equerry Mansions were kindly going to allow her to store them for a few weeks in an empty flat next to her own until she could arrange for their public exhibition. Would I not like to see them when they arrived? I jumped at the chance; I was very curious to see what they were like.

I'm not quite sure what I had expected, but I was not prepared for the powerful impression the pictures made upon me. Mrs. Mountfaucon had had them all framed, but there was no room in the empty flat to hang them, so they were stacked against the walls. Most of them were landscapes and still-lifes of a tropical exuberance, so that to see them was to lose oneself in a lavish dream of the exotic. Mrs. Mountfaucon handed me a list of them in Toby's handwriting. "The Bay of Botafogo," I read. "Gavea: The Botanical Gardens." "Chirimoyas." "The Mangue Canal." "Wild Chocolate and Heliconias." "Jardim d'Acclimacão." "Avocados, Grenadillas, and Papayas." "In the Organ Mountains."

I had always thought that the Organ Mountains sounded sublime. I imagined them echoing, resonant, with crags like clusters of pipes above bottomless gorges choked with lianas, saturated with primeval warmth and moisture, and reeking with the vanilla smell of clustered, pendulous orchids: Toby's view of them, rather surprisingly, was less exuberant than this. Chirimoyas, it appeared, were a kind of fruit. They looked like gigantic green mulberries, and in the picture some of them were cut open, showing delicate whitish flesh, with a savor, no doubt, of some deliciously artificial paradise. In his view of the Mangue Canal Toby had solved the problem of presenting a not too rigid geometry of tall palms and their reflections, and, by affording some glimpses of passers-by and loungers in the double *avenida* which evidently ran parallel to the canal, had introduced a somehow slightly mysterious "human interest."

"You're not saying much, Jane. What do you really think of them?"

"I'm amazed and delighted," I truthfully said. "They seem to me unlike anything else. Each seems successful in its own way, and they all go together as if they were parts of a whole. They're the most successful, beautiful, and—what shall I say?—integrated pictures of Toby's I've ever seen. What's more, they're all finished, and yet not overworked. They're so fresh, they look like the work of a happy man, with absolute control of his medium—such freedom of touch, almost mastery, I should say."

I wasn't piling it on to please her. That was what I thought and still think. While I was speaking she was stooping over some pictures with their faces turned to the wall, and when I stopped speaking she looked up, but said nothing. She was biting her lip, and her eyes looked baggy. She stood up, and I took her in my arms, and kissed her gently on the cheek, and as I did so I thought that nobody else was likely to have done so lately, except possibly Lady Meliora.

"It's such a blessing," I said, "that he was so wonderfully able to justify his own faith in his own talent, after all those false starts—hats, and everything. These pictures prove that he really did make good as a painter."

Mrs. Mountfaucon made a small convulsive noise, thrust herself out of my arms, turned away to the window, and dabbed at her eyes and nose with an extremely small handkerchief. I rather dreaded an emotional speech from her just at that moment, so I rustled the paper that bore the list of the pictures, and said, "But I haven't seen them all yet, have I? It says here 'Portrait of Bella' and 'Portrait of a Boy.'"

"They're not here, they're in my rooms next door. I want you to see them, Jane. I'm not sure whether they ought to be exhibited with the rest or not; they're rather separate. Let's go and look at them and perhaps you would give me your advice."

She locked the door and we went back to her flat. Presently she emerged from her bedroom with the two portraits and propped them up where we could both see them.

"You know who Bella is, I expect?"

"Yes," I said. "I've met her."

"Well, I had never met her until last week, when I asked her to come and see me. I didn't ask her to bring the boy; in any case he's in the Air Force and is away training somewhere."

"If I may say so," I said, "I don't really see why you need have asked her to bring the boy with her."

She did not reply at once, but looked at me quizzically, with her head a little on one side.

"You know the boy too, Jane?"

"I've never seen him, but I've heard Toby talk about him. He took quite an interest in him."

"Indeed, yes, a *great* interest, it seems. My poor son, you know, had *nothing* to leave, not a penny, only his pictures and some few trifles. But he left a note for me to open after his death. (It was mentioned, you may remember, at the inquest.) In it he asked me to do what I could for Mrs. Bunstable and her son. 'She has done more for me than I can express,' he said, 'and I have always taken a sort of godfatherly interest in her boy, though in fact I'm not his godfather.' I puzzled over that a good deal."

"You *had* known," I asked, "of Mrs. Bunstable's existence?"

"I had guessed that there was *somebody,* but I hadn't known who she was, and I must say now that I do know I could wish her a prettier surname. I conclude, from what she has told me and by putting two and two only too easily together, that she had been Toby's mistress for some years, and that it was with her that he went to Brazil. I have no doubt that she was fond of him for his own sake because, poor dear, he can't have had a sixpence to spend on her in these last years."

"What did you think of her?"

"I think she's still a striking-looking woman, in rather a bold way. Full of vitality—a little too much, perhaps —and with character and common sense. Oh, but somehow," she clasped her hands towards me as if beseeching me to agree, "not nearly *fine* enough for our Toby!"

"Well, I don't know that I'd give her full marks, certainly, for refinement, or shall I say fineness."

"No, Jane, of course you wouldn't. Good-hearted, no doubt, she is. I try not to mind that she's a mulatress, a cabaret dancer, and another man's wife, but oh, I wouldn't have chosen *her* for the part she played in his life."

"No, perhaps not," I said. "But isn't it always rather a toss-up whether mothers like their sons' choice of wives, or lovers? I'm sure Bella was good for him, and I should think disinterestedly fond of him."

"Oh, I do hope you're right. But now tell me, what do you think of these two portraits?"

I said I thought they were excellent. I thought, but did not say, that the roguish or playful aspect of Bella was perhaps too much stressed. I then said that I couldn't judge whether Jocky's portrait was like him, because I had never seen him.

"He has fine eyes," said Mrs. Mountfaucon, "if the portrait is like him. In fact it's altogether a finer face than his mother's. Neater bones, and a rather haunting expression. . . . Do you think it possible that he was Toby's son?"

"Good heavens, no; impossible!" I declared. "It never occurred to me. Toby never met Mrs. Bunstable until the boy was quite big. Toby himself told me long ago that the father was in the merchant navy. Why, I even remember him saying that he wished the boy *was* his."

Mrs. Mountfaucon looked intently at me, with a searching, focused, almost fanatical gaze.

"Oh, but Jane, how can one be sure? That strange remark about not being the boy's godfather—and how *can* one know exactly when they first met? I've gazed and gazed at the portrait, and I do really think that it has somehow a faint look of Toby—something about the eyes, and the mouth."

"I'm sure you're imagining it," I said. "I'm sure it's *quite* impossible. . . . Did you hint at all to Bella what you were thinking?"

"I treated her, I hope, with the utmost friendliness and I gave her every opening to tell me anything she wanted to tell me. She talked without stopping but never so much as came near to the least shadow of claiming, as she so easily might, and with pride, that Toby was the child's father."

"Of course not. She might have done so if she had been a grasping woman who wanted to get something out of you. But the fact that she didn't proves among other things that it's just a wild supposition on your part."

"Oh, Jane, in a way I'm relieved to hear you say that! And yet, and yet . . . Well, I told Mrs. Bunstable that Toby had nothing to leave her. She knew it only too well. I told her that I am reduced to living on a small income from trust money, which is all that's left of our fortune, but that I would like her, because I know Toby would have wished it, to have the proceeds of the exhibition of his pictures, if there are any, for the benefit of her son. She protested most *volubly,* and I thought all the better of her for that, but of course I insisted that Toby wished it. So that was that."

"And will you see her again?"

"Well, Jane, when she went away she said, I thought rather impulsively, 'Oh, you darling, why did Toby never let me see you until now?' I said he probably thought it more seemly for us not to meet. But of course that wasn't the real reason. The real reason was that he would have thought we were going to plot something against him . . . I shall send her a ticket for the private view. But I shall ask *you* to go with me, dear Jane. And when are you going to bring your fiancé to see me?"

"Alas," I said, "he's still in Washington, and he may have to go to Delhi."

TWENTY-EIGHT

I knew Mrs. Bunstable was voluble, but I was hardly prepared for the flood of words in which she engulfed me. I had run into her one day in Oxford Street and she had asked me to dine with her one evening at a Chinese restaurant, as we could "talk quietly" there. Over the rather sloshy wartime chop-suey she let fly.

"You knew him; I knew him; nobody knew him. I believe he was quite different with every person he knew. Oh, and didn't he hate his friends to know each other! I'll say! Perhaps he thought they'd talk against him, plot against him, leave him in the lurch—I don't know what. And what a lot of different Tobys, even when you did know him! Sometimes he was like a child, so innocent and playful, and naughty like a child. But he was a man, yes, a real man, *I'll* say he was—though he had a bit of woman in him too. Ah, there was nobody ever like him, not in my life, and there'll never be anybody like him again. I loved that man, but *you* don't know, nobody'll ever know, what I went through with him. . . . Would you say he was a jealous man?"

"Yes," I said, "I would. He was."

"You're telling me! He wasn't just jealous, he was mad

256

with jealousy! If I said that he embarrassed me with his jealousy, then I *would* have my foot on the soft pedal, the softest pedal ever invented. When I went on tour I had to write to him every day, yes, every day, even if it was only a postcard, *me,* me that hates writing letters. Talk? I don't mind talking, I'm not at a loss for words, I can gag along impromptu, but it's funny, put a pen in my hand and I just don't know what to say. But did he believe me? Not Toby—he thought I was stalling. He said I never gave him any news. 'News?' I said. 'I never studied to be a journalist.' And was he wild! He said I never told him anything.

"Where it all began was when he ran into me one day in Charing Cross Road with one of the boys, Jed La Selva. You must have heard Jed and his band, he's been a lot on the air this last year or two. He used to be my accompanist at the Pick-me-Up, and that wasn't yesterday, and the best I ever had. I've known Jed for years and I don't suppose there's ever a month, or less, when I don't see him, and his sweet little wife too. Mind you, Jed's got what it takes, you know what I mean, you can't help noticing him, and of course Toby must jump to conclusions. The next thing I knew, there was a heat wave, mid-July it must have been, I remember I was expecting my son Jocky home from school, and I had a lot to get ready, so I set the alarm for five o'clock. Off it went, and up I got, I was half-awake anyway, and I went to the window and drew the curtains and looked out through the net curtains to see if the weather was going to hold. (I grew up on a farm, though you mightn't believe it, and I know a thing or two about weather.) Of course there was nobody about at that time of day, though there wasn't a cloud in the sky, when suddenly I saw somebody moving on the other side of the street. It was Toby!

"I couldn't believe my eyes, though I've yet to catch them lying to me. I knew in a flash what was in his head. He thought he might see Jed sneaking out from my apartment early in the morning. Can you beat it? My heart ached for him but I was so furious I determined to take no notice of him. Why, if the neighbors had seen him (and have you ever known neighbors miss anything?) they might have thought he was a detective, and there was no doubt which house he was watching. Why, his eyes were glued to my address just like your eyes would be to a bridge hand if you found you'd been dealt four aces. You do play bridge, don't you? But anyway you get my meaning. I'll spare you the whole story. What I went through with Toby—well, it would take as long to tell as it did to happen, and even then nobody *could* understand."

"Did he get any better," I asked, "as time went on?"

"My dear, he did *not*."

"But you don't mean that he was constantly prowling about and watching your comings and goings?"

"I do mean it, and I mean that history repeats itself. A year, two years later, I can't remember now, my husband was on a visit to me. We'd had a late night, but I never could help waking up early in the morning, and when I wake up I like to get up. 'Mental cruelty,' my husband used to call it. Anyway I peeped out early in the morning, without drawing the curtains, to see what sort of day it was going to be, and I was amazed to see Toby standing on the other side of the road a little way up, where there's a big warehouse with a sort of archway. Of course the gates were closed, I don't suppose it was much after five, and it was a fine summer's morning, and there he was, lurking, and fidgeting, and pulling away at a cigarette even at that time of the morning. I wonder he never got nicotine poisoning.

"My dear, I was worried sick, but I couldn't help laughing, I won't say up my sleeve but into my bedroom curtains. I know it's the oldest and corniest scene in the world, but all the same we all know how awkward it is for a woman who's in bed with her lover to be surprised by her husband—yes, but what about *this* poor girl, in bed with her husband, and surprised by her lover?"

She burst into a peal of laughter and slapped her thighs like some jolly fishwife, and I half expected her to get up and break into a few high kicks and pirouettes. Two Chinese waiters, one an old man, the other a boy, glanced in her direction, but without moving their heads, without any change of expression, and without speaking.

"I had to think quickly, my dear soul, I can tell you, and thinking quickly is not what you expect to have to do just at that time of the morning. I didn't go back to bed, not me, I went and gave myself a good sloosh with cold water to get the old brain ticking over. . . . Did you know I had a husband? Of course we've been separated for years, couldn't quite hit it off, so it seemed better. Not a bit, not one little bit, I will say, of hard feeling on either side. He's human, believe you me—nobody more. Well, every now and again, every two or three years I should say, Sammy—that's my husband—would show up, just for old time's sake, and to see Jocky and me and make plans for the boy's future. He always used to tell me a bit beforehand when he was coming along, so that we could make a date, though of course if I was on tour there wouldn't be a date, except once, when by the strangest chance he docked at Genoa where I was doing a short season in cabaret. *This* time he rang me one evening and asked if he could come round right away. I didn't see why not. The only thing was, I'd meant to have my hair washed and I knew it was looking like a bundle of hay or something. *Was* I worried? But I needn't have. The first thing Sammy ever said the very first time he ever clapped eyes on me was 'Oh, what a lovely head of hair!' Some men are like that, aren't they? Sammy's got a thing about hair. I don't want to brag but it always was springy—oh, my, even if I do say it myself, it was a lovely fuzz!"

"Was?" I put in. "It can't have been lovelier or fuzzier than it is now."

"Oh, you are *nice*!" She patted my hand and at once went on with her story. "And now, when I knew Sam was coming, I was so worried because there wasn't time to have it washed, and bless me if the very first thing he said wasn't, 'Sugar, how lovely your hair's looking!' Maybe it didn't mean a thing, maybe it was just like saying 'How d'you do?' or 'What a fine day.' Maybe it was just another move in the love-dance of the Great Crested Girl-catcher or what-have-you, but I lapped it up, my dear, I lapped it up, and did I pat my back hair? It's something, oh it *is* something when the man who's left you always comes back again—well, you know, for *more.* . . .

"Well, isn't it? I know you might say I was just being made a convenience of, so to speak, but I can't help it, I like to be wanted by Sammy, to go on being wanted by him, to know that he's about somewhere in the world, and for me to know, and for him to know, that I'm about somewhere too. Funny, isn't it? And after all, he *is* the father of the boy, and though it may be just one great big peep at the obvious, that's a bond that nothing can break. Well, there I was in a very pretty fix. Thank God Toby didn't see me and I hadn't drawn the curtains, but as I took another peep I saw him looking up: if I *had* drawn them he would have come and rung my bell, I'll take my oath.

"Oh, those impatient rings of Toby's at the bell! He used to ring always two longs and one short, but as often as not the short was a long too. Talk of impatience! I used to think the bell would explode or something, he seemed to push it so much harder than anybody else. Nobody else ever sent me express letters marked *Urgent:* nobody else ever sent me express letters at all. (That was before I had the phone, of course.) Yes, I remember now, he did once push somebody's front door bell in so hard that it stuck. There was quite a scene, everybody thought the house was on fire. My dear, I had to think quickly. Sam's a man that likes to sleep late of a morning, especially after a night before, which is what *we'd* had."

Here Bella rolled her eyes with a horribly roguish allure, as if she were enacting one of her cabaret turns. At any moment, to stress a point, she might have burst into song and dance.

"And what, *je te demande,* would Sam have thought if he was roused up all startled at five in the morning by two longs and a short, or more likely three longs, with the third the longest of all? I should think he'd have thought the ship had sprung a leak and all hands to the pumps!"

She threw back her head and slapped the edge of the table with both hands.

"But I suppose," I said, "as you and your husband are separated, he doesn't expect you to live like a nun? He couldn't reasonably expect you to make a whole-time job out of looking forward to seeing him again."

"Maybe not. Sam's reasonable enough. As I said, he's human. But what would he have thought of a bald man with big eyes and an upper-class accent, rootling us both

261

out of dreamland at cock-crow, and making a scene, which Toby certainly would have done."

"Would he? A scene?"

"Scene is not the word!" She glanced round, aware at last that she had been attracting some attention. "I suppose I'm talking too loud. Do you think people can hear? . . . Scene? My dear, he'd have made Othello look like a chorus-boy! I'll tell you just what would have happened. First, two longs and a short—or rather two longs and a much longer, shrill enough to wake the dead. *Scene two:* Sam wakes up and shouts 'What the hell's that?' Without stopping to explain I jump into my scarlet mules that Toby got me from Morocco and wrap me in my wrap as I take the stairs in two hops like a kangaroo. *Scene three:* I open the door and say 'Toby! What *has* happened?' Toby puts on his enigmatic smile, says 'Aren't you pleased to see me?' and glides into the hall before I can stop him. Out of the question to try and bar the way: he would have known at once that I had a man upstairs. No alternative but to show pleasure at seeing him, walk slowly upstairs taking his arm, and try and explain that I have been and still ought to be in bed *with my husband.*"

"Delicate situation," I said.

"*Scene four:* Wait, this isn't easy to imagine. Let me think. . . . Do you realize that jealousy *is* a kind of madness, and that Toby—I don't think he'd have *said* anything, not at first, at any rate. I think his eyes would have looked about twice as big as usual, and he would have put on an I-thought-as-much smile: you know, cynical, triumphant, like a lunatic who has been saying for years that enemies masquerading as friends have been putting frogs in the porridge, and then one fine morning suddenly *does* find a frog in his porridge. You know?"

"You put it very well."

"So far I see it all clearly. But *Scene five*? By this time, obviously, Sam, who's used after years at sea to sudden alarms at odd moments, has pulled on his pants and come out to see what's up. Oh, yes, I see it quite clearly. Sam, with tousled hair and bare feet, comes out in singlet and pants and finds me, a prey to indecision, looking earnestly at Toby on the landing. By this time Toby has let go of my arm—you'd have thought it was *me* that was the frog in the porridge—and still wearing his most horrid smile, he finds himself face to face with Sam.

"*Scene six.* Everything depends now on who moves first. I, of course, am the Eternal Feminine and unconsciously or rather hopefully half-expect them to start bashing each other, so that I can wait, throbbing, to drape myself like a scarf round the bleeding neck of the winner. . . . But life doesn't always run true to type, does it? First of all, Toby, jealous or not, is a gentleman. He sees dimly that he has disturbed a couple in bed at an unearthly hour without the slightest excuse except that he little suspected they would be husband and wife. Sam, having got over the first shock of being disturbed, is surprised to see anybody, amazed by Toby, and tries to size him up, waits to hear what he wants, and if Toby's excuse isn't reasonable, is ready to make a row. To me—yes, me—it will fall to improvise some patter that will save the situation, which is already past saving. So you see, by *Scene seven* I should have to give up. Things would just happen. There would be words at least, and words wouldn't help."

"All this," I said, "is not what actually happened, but entirely what you *imagined* might happen?"

"Oh, my dear, I don't know about 'entirely!' . . . I was there at my window, just weighing up whether to make a clean breast one way or the other, or both, when I peeped out again and saw Toby being approached by a policeman, yes, and obviously questioned. They were having a discussion or an argument, Toby pointed at my window, and the policeman looked to see where he was pointing, and then they went on talking. Then Toby lighted a cigarette and looked as if he was trying to explain what he was doing, loitering about like that in the early morning. Toby began pointing at the pavement, as if he was saying that he had a right to be there, and the policeman shook his head and looked annoyed. My guess is, he told Toby that if he didn't move on he'd charge him with loitering with intent, or causing an obstruction, or something. Anyway Toby, waving his arms about and protesting violently, went away."

"Oh, what a relief!" I said. "So your husband knew nothing of Toby, nor Toby of your husband. . . . I suppose you never saw Toby hanging about like that again?"

"Oh, yes, I did." A solemn expression came over her face, her eyes seemed to dilate and grow moister, and she sighed deeply. "I saw him once in the winter, in the afternoon, when it was raining and just getting dark, when he was already very ill, and I threw on a coat and went straight out and spoke to him. I said 'What *are* you doing, Toby? Why didn't you come and ring the bell?' He came in and I made tea but he wouldn't tell me for some time why he had been hanging about. Then he said he wanted to be near me, but was a sick man, and didn't want to 'inflict' himself on me. 'Inflict!' I asked him if he thought I might be entertaining some other man, a secret lover or something. He said if I had been, any other man would have been worth more to me than he was in his present state; but that even if I was alone, why should I be bothered with him, a man with no money, no health, and no prospects?"

Bella's eyes swam, and then, clenching her fist and beating it against her forehead, she said vehemently, "My God, what a dance he led me with his suspicions and his jealousy, but I wish he were here by my side right now, and I'd go through it all again, gladly, gladly!"

TWENTY-NINE

The exhibition of Toby's paintings was to be held at the Cadmium Gallery, only a few steps from Bond Street. One of its directors was Calzoni, whom I remembered from the old days of the Rembrandt agitation at Duchess's Gate. Mrs. Mountfaucon had succeeded in arousing his interest in Toby's paintings. I did not know and I did not like to ask her what financial arrangements she had made with him. Possibly by some desperate measure she had raised some money to subsidize the exhibition, but she would naturally have liked people to think that various galleries had competed for the privilege of showing her son's pictures. What is certain is that if the pictures had been mediocre they would not have been shown at that particular gallery. Like other art dealers Calzoni had to make the most of fashions in painting, but unlike some dealers he never dealt in pretentious rubbish.

I had already engaged myself to go with Mrs. Mountfaucon to the private view. It was a long time since I had

265

been to the Cadmium Gallery, but I remembered once going there long ago with Toby. It was on a winter afternoon, and inside there was an even light and an even temperature. Nobody besides ourselves was present except Calzoni himself, and a very old gentleman with spats, an ivory-handled walking-stick, a spotted cravat, and eyeglasses on a black ribbon, to whom he was showing a small picture. The old gentleman was evidently very deaf.

"And what are you asking for that?" we heard him ask in a penetrating voice, as he waved his eyeglasses at the picture.

"I'm afraid it's not for sale," we heard Calzoni say, quite distinctly.

"What?" shrilled the old gentleman. "Well, it's a pretty thing—very pretty little thing—but I think you're asking too much, a great deal too much."

"I said it's *not for sale* !" Calzoni repeated, loudly, with emphasis and a touch of impatience. "The owner's taking it away tomorrow."

"Corot? I don't question that it's a Corot!" the old gentleman testily boomed. "I'm not questioning it at all. Any fool can see that it's a Corot. But it's not any fool that'll give you your price. You're asking too much. These fancy prices are inflated, you know, won't last, can't possibly last." He shook his head knowingly. "Ah, you dealers, you dealers!"

Calzoni almost lost his temper. In order to keep it he tried to smile and only succeeded in wearing a furious grin. "I said, I'm afraid it's NOT FOR SALE !"

"Well, then, my dear feller," said the old gentleman, "why on earth didn't you say so in the first place?"

This little scene had given Toby and me an unholy joy, the quintessence of which came from the fact that the little picture was not in the least like a Corot and could not possibly have been taken for one by anybody who knew the front of a picture from the back. Calzoni's final despairing gesture, when he threw up his hands, white and bony hands, and grinned horribly over the top of them, was like some delicious moment in a Molière comedy.

I remembered Calzoni as a man of medium height, rather quick and supple in his movements, with mobile eyes, well dressed in a mode becoming to a well-to-do picture dealer, that is to say, in a morning suit, with a pearl in his tie. He had a smooth, plausible manner and was given to confident expressions of opinion about pictures. I believe his opinion carried weight, and that he loved pictures for their own sake as well as for their value. But now, when I arrived very early at the gallery with Mrs. Mountfaucon, and when I saw what time had done to Calzoni, how much and how soon it had altered him, my amused recollection faded and I felt a chill draught from the grave. I hurriedly looked at my own reflection in a glass, and all in a flash I thought it was time that I settled down, and I felt a pang of an awful recurrent anxiety that my husband-to-be might be killed in some accident of war, and might never live to be my husband. But I forgot about that as soon as I looked again at Calzoni. He seemed quite to have lost his resilience. He stooped a little, his forehead was lined, and he had formidable purplish pouches under his eyes—kidney trouble, perhaps. But habit and manners kept him going, and he began bowing us towards the pictures with a confident persuasiveness, as if he were going to try and sell us one.

"Oh," cried Mrs. Mountfaucon," a picture is already sold!" She ran forwards as if to make sure that the little red spot was not an hallucination. "Oh, *who* could have bought it?"

"I think anybody with taste would be glad to buy it," said Calzoni, not quite getting her meaning. "I think it's one of the best pictures in the show."

"No, no, I didn't mean that; but mayn't one know, Mr. Calzoni, the name of the buyer?" She had clasped her hands pleadingly together, in her little-girl style.

"By all means. The lady was here when we opened at half-past nine—just half an hour ago—a lady with a dog and a muff, almost a Gainsborough subject. Stately manners, you know, but very pleasant. She made up her mind quickly and at once wrote out a check. Let me see, she gave her name as Lady Meliora Sperrow . . . oh, excuse me one moment."

And before we could say anything, he had turned aside to speak to his secretary, a soignée young woman in black satin and pearls.

"Well, why didn't you tell me at the time?" we heard him say petulantly. "It's too late now." And returning to us, he said, "I have just heard that the buyer of this picture wished her identity to be kept secret. So if you please, we will treat the information as confidential."

"Oh, dear, good Meliora!" Mrs. Mountfaucon exclaimed. "How like her to buy it—to be the very first—and to try and hide her identity! Pictures mean nothing to her, and my poor Toby was *odious* to her. It's an act of pure goodness, bless her heart."

"And an act of good judgment, natural discrimination perhaps," said Calzoni. "But please—"

"I won't breathe a word, not a word—but how difficult to pretend I don't know!"

"*And* a good investment," he said.

"Oh, you really believe that?"

I sauntered away from them because I wanted to choose a picture for myself. Mrs. Mountfaucon had tried to give me one but I had refused to accept it. I had said that I would rather buy one in the exhibition. I thought it would have pleased Toby that I should wish, for his sake, to benefit Jocky Bunstable. I had already half-determined to buy one of the views of the Organ Mountains, and in due course I did buy it, but for the moment I was unable to concentrate because of a certain anxiety.

I was very anxious, largely for Mrs. Mountfaucon's sake, that the exhibition should succeed. It was not a good time for selling pictures by an unknown painter. The war was in a critical and dangerous phase, and I could hardly get hold of anybody who was in London and willing and able to go and see the pictures and at the same time likely to buy one. I had in any case hardly any contacts with dealers or collectors. I had written a sort of begging letter to the only art critic I knew, an amiable man whom I had occasionally met at dinner parties and who, like other sorts of critics, was apt, at least in conversation, to put artists in their places with the dreadful sureness of a separator of sheep from goats; he had a dry, crackling voice like the sound of a bonfire of canvases by failed aspirants to fame. I had not much hope of him. Apart from him, I had written and telephoned round to two or three faintly likely people. And I had told a white lie.

Since the far-off day when Butterball Evans had asked me round to Wilton Place for a drink, in order to tell me about Toby and Mrs. Mountfaucon, I had sometimes seen her for a moment or two in other people's houses or in public but I had hardly ever been alone with her or been more than once or twice to her flat. She still lived there—when she was not at her more recently acquired house in the country—and I took it into my head that there was no reason why she should not be encouraged to take an interest in the Toby exhibition and to buy one of his pictures. It was my intention to appeal to her better nature.

I may say I dreaded going to see her. When I first knew her, I had always been very conscious of being an un-smart muniment-girl; now, after years of clothes rationing and war-weariness, I was conscious of being the un-smart office drudge that the war had made me, though I had never "let myself go" and had naturally tried, so far as I could, to look my best. What was a great deal more embarrassing than my inability to look smart was to go and see her with the suspicion that she had been enriched by the damnable old man who had robbed my friends, and not to know for certain whether it was true. And then there had been that scene at the crematorium. I couldn't face her over the telephone, so I wrote and asked her if I might look in for a drink one evening, as there was something I wanted to tell her about. Her secretary replied, fixing a date, and when the date came I looked at myself in the glass more critically than usual and went round to Wilton Place.

The same French maid let me in. She was perceptibly older. We exchanged a word or two about bombs, which in those days added another useful general topic to that of the weather.

"What a pretty hat," said Butterball, glancing at the old gray straw mushroom on my head. "I do so hate hatlessness, don't you, in London, except for the *very* young. Do have a cigarette. What will you drink?"

With a costly rustling of her simple and exquisitely made blue-black silk frock she fluttered her beautifully kept fingers over too great a variety of bottles, rather like an organist fingering the stops of his instrument and inquiring what to play.

"What a very odd business that was at poor Toby's cremation," she said, after we had swapped a little small talk. "Perhaps I oughtn't to have gone. I only heard of the proceedings quite by chance. I was always fond of Toby, you know, but I'm afraid his mother never took to me much. I felt I'd like to go, and I didn't want to bother her, and it never occurred to me that she might *mind* my going. I certainly never thought she'd scream when she saw me, and then snub me on the top of that. I put it down to the stress of her feelings in her bereavement."

"Toby's death was really a knock-out to her," I said. "She hardly sees anybody now."

"I expect she sees *you*."

"Oh, well," I said, "I saw such a lot of them, going through their papers, you know, after you so kindly brought us together. . . . As a matter of fact, it's something to do with Toby that I wanted to ask you about."

She had been prancing around, but now, as if a sudden stress of emotion had made her weak at the knees, she sat down, gracefully enough, but for her rather abruptly; she was not given to impulsive movements. Did she think I was going to make some allusion, direct or oblique, to his loss of fortune? I was.

"The fact is," I said, "he did a lot of painting in Brazil, and there's going to be an exhibition."

"No! I never thought he had it in him. He painted so well, such decorative pictures, such technique, such ideas —but he never seemed to finish anything. And now a show! I *am* glad."

"But the thing is," I went on, "this is not a good time for selling pictures, and one does want it to be a success."

"Of course. He'd have loved a success. He deserved one. Where is it to be?"

"At that gallery of Calzoni's, the Cadmium."

"A very good place. I'll certainly see that we have photographs and a notice in *Style*."

"Oh, do. And if you could tell people about it, and get them to go; and if possible get them to *buy* something . . . As I expect you know, Mrs. Mountfaucon's extremely hard up."

"As hard up as all that?" she said, and turned away and put out her hand for her half-finished drink. Somehow the way she spoke and turned aside came nearer than anything to convincing me that she knew the source of old Basingfield's benefactions to herself. "She still lives quite comfortably, surely? Only the other day, as I was driving past in a taxi, I saw her coming out of Westminster Abbey in a vast great black picture-hat. It had Galhauban Sœurs written all over it."

"Pre-war," I said, "I feel sure." It was on the tip of my tongue to say "Her trustee defaulted, old Basingfield, you know, and not a penny was recovered," but I couldn't bring myself to say it. Was it cowardice? I don't know. If I had said it, I might have done anything but further my immediate purpose, which was to help to make Toby's show a success. "She lives," I said with some warmth, "in a crow's-nest of a little flat at the top of Equerry Mansions, on some wretched little annuity, and I should think by the time she has paid the rent there's very little over."

"But did Toby leave nothing?"

"So far as I know, not a sixpence."

"Good God," she said, and after a pause, "I'd very much like, anyway, to have one of Toby's pictures."

"I'll see that you get a card for the private view."

"Oh, Calzoni always sends me a card automatically," she said, with perhaps just a shade of condescension.

Of course he does, I thought, because you're a useful contact-woman; and that's why I'm here.

"Perhaps it would be best," I said, as I got up to go, "if you happen to run into Mrs. Mountfaucon, not to let her know that you've seen me. I don't want her to think I've been canvassing for Toby's pictures. I'd like her to think that they're a powerful magnet in themselves."

"My dear, if I do run into her, she'll probably shriek again. I won't say a word about you, and if I *do* buy a picture I'll go further, I'll buy it in an assumed name and tell Calzoni to say that I'm a Peruvian connoisseur on a visit to London."

As it happened, she and Mrs. Mountfaucon did not meet. Mrs. Mountfaucon hung about the gallery most of the morning on the view-day. There were very few visitors indeed and no sales, except one to me. I took Mrs. Mountfaucon out to lunch, and when we entered the gallery afterwards Calzoni told us, with animation, that one single buyer had taken no fewer than six of the pictures—a South American visitor, he said, called Gonzalez de Gomez, who was reputed to be forming a very choice collection of modern pictures in Lima. Mrs. Mountfaucon was enraptured.

"Oh, my dear Toby!" she said, clasping her hands. "Just what he would have wished. He was so happy in Brazil, which can't be far from Lima, can it?"

But when she expressed a wish to meet this distinguished collector, Calzoni said unfortunately he was flying to Lisbon immediately.

I don't know whether Butterball Gonzalez de Gomez bought the pictures because she liked them or because she felt that the price she paid for them was a kind of minimal conscience-money. I do know that it had been worth while for me to go and see her.

Early in the afternoon more people began to arrive. Lady Meliora came back. Letty Tracy arrived, in uniform, with a cheerful, young, and bemedalled lieutenant-commander—conceivably the very man to whom Toby had once written that letter of his, at the time of the row over the console table. Mrs. Purbind appeared, was out of her element, and clung to Mrs. Mountfaucon and to me for protection. Bella Bunstable stepped in, dressed, one would have said, for a race-meeting in Trinidad, and with dangling earrings. She saw two women looking earnestly at her portrait and nudged her way up to them to eavesdrop. She came back laughing and told us that one woman had said to the other, "I'm as fond of salad as anybody, but my doctor won't allow me any more olive-oil and so now I use liquid paraffin as a salad dressing." So much for human vanity.

I saw one or two women who had been at the opening of Toby's hat-shop, and at one time I was slightly irritated by the presence of a group of some of those whom I had thought of as Toby's "other" women. In spite of whatever precautions he may have taken to keep them apart, most of them seemed to know one another. They hadn't bought his hats and they didn't buy his pictures. They tended to get into a huddle with their backs to the pictures and after a backward or sideward glance or two they would utter a gushing remark or two:

"Charming!"

"That wonderful yellow!"

"It makes one long to go up the Amazon."

Then they began to talk excitedly about other things

and at one time the room began to buzz like a cocktail party.

Some quite friendly notices appeared in the Press, and one of them showed some understanding. After ten days only two of the pictures remained unsold.

THIRTY

The Toby exhibition was the last important social occasion in Mrs. Mountfaucon's life. It had been a great satisfaction to her, but after it she seemed to relax her grip on life. Every morning she went as usual to the early service at Westminster Abbey, pausing on the way for the usual conversation with the paper-seller who called her "Ma," and on the way back for a few words with Corby.

"The days go by so quickly," she remarked to me. "I dare say I seem like an idle old woman, but I don't want to be *perfectly* useless, and the days seem to be full of little duties, and yet I don't know what there is to show for them. Poor Mrs. Crumpsey has died of heart failure. I feel it so much, she was a true friend."

After condoling with her, I asked if she had any news of the Countess.

"Poor thing, she has a post with two old sisters at Barnes. 'I can only manage light duties now,' she wrote.

I suppose I ought to ask her to come and see me, but somehow I dread that she may begin on her obsession, about her right to a title, and all that. Old Colonel Flory, who seems to have the whole history of the peerage at his fingers' ends and is the *greatest* swell in heraldic circles, told me there might be something in her pretensions but he thought it would be a great mistake to tell her so, as it might go to her head, and she has no means to support her claim. I assured him that the whole business had gone to her head years ago and was firmly fixed there. The house where she lives, she says, almost overlooks Ranelagh, which has gone to rack and ruin—and *allotments*! A sad thought for me, I remember so well the first time I saw Morven playing polo there. He had such a wonderful seat, but I little thought then that I should one day be his wife."

After my engagement was announced, I took my husband-to-be to see Mrs. Mountfaucon. They got on very well, and she promised to come to our wedding. It was soon after that that she had her accident. One afternoon she had been watering her little balcony-garden and as she stepped back into her little drawing-room she tripped and fell, broke her leg, and knocked her head against the leg of a chair. She was unconscious for a long time, and when she came to, was only with the greatest difficulty able to drag herself into the other room to telephone for help. Shocked, exhausted, chilled, and in great pain, she was removed to a nursing-home.

As soon as I heard what had happened I hurried round to see her. When I was shown into her room, she was sitting up in bed, *without her wig*. I had never seen her without it before. I had never seen her before as what she now was, an old, tired woman, yes, an old, old woman with a little thin white hair on her naked-looking head, a head shaped noticeably like her son's.

She held out both hands to me in welcome. I kissed her as usual, and as she made no allusion to her wiglessness I naturally affected not to notice it. But I could not help remembering how she had said, when we had heard of Lydia Delap's dramatic end, "Perhaps God may punish me too in my vanity." Vanity? Wigless, childless, without fortune, lonely, without prospects of companions, she behaved with all her usual sweetness. I trust she felt the resignation and the hope she would have liked to feel as a Christian, because she did not recover, and was dead in a few days. One can never judge, but I should have said she had nothing more to live for.

Her executor told me that in her will she left all sorts of treasures to a variety of persons, but nearly all of these bequests were phantoms; the things had long since been sold, destroyed, given away, stolen, or lost. The will had been made at a date after the bomb damage to the repository, and the only explanation seemed to be that she was unmethodical and so preoccupied with other matters that she simply could not remember what she still had and what no longer existed. Her possessions had become so much part of her personality that she could hardly have envisaged herself without them. And so it happens that if I want to know the time I can never consult the watch that was presented to Sir Ferdinand d'Arfey by Catherine the Great, although dear Susannah Mountfaucon had intended to make it possible for me to do so. For all I know Toby had sold it in order to buy football boots or model airplanes for Jocky Bunstable, or some ornament for Jocky's mother.

Soon after Mrs. Mountfaucon's death some impulse took me westwards to look for Ranelagh, where I had never been and where she had watched her second husband playing polo in some far-off age. It was not an agreeable day, but I was in a forward-looking and happy frame of mind. The date of my wedding had been fixed, and *my* second husband was returning to London by air in two days' time. I felt I wanted to be alone, and to walk musingly about in some place where I had never been. I carried a walking-stick in case I met a bag-snatcher or sex maniac.

What a strange afternoon it is to remember. It was in May 1945. There was an easterly wind and an overcast sky, and with only vague ideas of direction I found myself walking along the embankment, or towing-path, from Putney Bridge. After a time I came to a broken-down fence behind which was the tottering skeleton of what might have once been a two-storied boathouse. Red tiles had fallen or were about to fall from its rickety roof, like red playing cards face downwards. I went through an opening in the fence and found myself in a sunken road and confronted with some festoons of barbed wire and some warning notices. I paid no attention to these, and found myself in what I suppose was Barn Elms Park.

I wandered about at random. After years of constraint it was healing to do so. All the open spaces, including no doubt the former polo-grounds, were given over to the allotments which the Countess had spoken of, and here and there people were working in them. The house was evidently in military occupation, and stray soldiers could be seen in the distance, walking in an aimless-looking way among some huts or out-buildings. Here and there ranges of wooden structures which seemed once to have been stables, pavilions, or summer-houses were falling to pieces. Walls or beams bulged or sagged, roofs were open to the sky or still half-covered with tiles, paintwork was faded or blistered, weeds flourished everywhere. Tradition, order, and grace were evidently taboo here, or unknown.

At every step the ghosts of old pleasures rose up more thickly, especially in the garden. Untrimmed hedges of box and yew enclosed neglected paths that led to an ivied grotto here, and there a garden temple. Glancing inside I saw that the walls had been scribbled over and the floor had all too plainly been used for purposes not originally intended.

Roses and rhododendrons in flower were besieged by tall uncut grass and rankly springing nettles. A water-logged boat had slouched down into the black water of the lake, which was unexpectedly spanned by a curved scarlet bridge, set up no doubt in imitation of some famous red lacquered bridge in the days of the Japanese Exhibition or perhaps even earlier. I walked on to it with caution, because some of the planks were missing or rotting.

Garden sculpture, mostly damaged, was to be seen here and there—two putti with a dolphin in a lily pond; a stone urn cast from its pedestal, upside down, and half-hidden in long grass; a stone shepherdess with a broken arm, face downwards in some nettles. A high wall of irregular rustic stonework at the end of the lake was covered with pink valerian, and over part of it an elder-tree was displaying its flowers, like lace handkerchiefs spread out to dry.

In the distance there were always a few drab figures, stooping as absorbedly in the allotments as if they were deaf mutes, against a background of some rotting white-painted wooden pavilion with a collapsed and tottering roof. A few vague figures in khaki drifted idly about near a dismembered aircraft in an open space, near some dirty tents.

From the river, where I had noticed before entering the

park that a drab and sparse regatta of some kind was being held, occasional faint bursts of cheering could be heard, under the gray sky and beyond the continual fluttering of new leaves. Again I came face to face with barbed wire and warning notices. I was tired, and the whole scene seemed to become more and more dreamlike, with its atmosphere of isolation and prohibition, of claustrophobia almost, of dislocation, disorder, and decay, and of life, human life, new life, worrying its way through the remains of a pleasure-ground, through the vestiges of privilege and leisure and ornament, to seek bare survival and subsistance.

I imagined the still youthful Susannah, with her husband Captain d'Arfey, on the crest of the wave of her life and of the imperialist age, strolling in an elaborate toilette on some resonant Edwardian afternoon towards the polo ground, and thoughtfully twirling her parasol while watching Morven Mountfaucon distinguishing himself—the polo ground where now a tired slut in a dirty cardigan was grubbing about among pea-sticks and cabbage stalks to help to feed her perhaps equally unlovely and unnecessary young. Unlovely? Unnecessary? Who on earth was I to judge? Just as beneath the conscious mind there is the incalculable unconscious in all its violence, crudity, and glamor, so beneath the level of the minority, the more conscious members of a nation or community, there seethes the vast mass of "ordinary" people, fertile, unpredictable, in all its potency and potentiality, the breeding-ground of all genius. Out of that mass long ago had emerged people like the Mountfaucons and the d'Arfeys, and now they had faded from view, and there would never be anything like them again.

"What a pity if there's going to be nobody to carry on

the name," Mrs. Mountfaucon had once said to Toby, meaning the name of d'Arfey.

"My dear mother," he had replied, "it seems to me that quite enough names are being carried on as things are. The telephone book is swelling visibly, and the country is grossly overpopulated."

I am of Toby's generation, I am old enough to remember Edwardian sights and sounds, the ambience of the fortunate in the nineteen-hundreds; and I had lived to see the pea-sticks on the polo ground. I had survived so far, unlike poor Toby, and I was still young enough to be on the happy verge of building a new life, not in the least like what I had known before. But on that extraordinary afternoon my heart was wrung with memories of my dead friends.

Toby's life seemed to have been the expression of an insatiable appetite for something unattainable, something that included peace and power and order, something of the confidence that his ancestors may be supposed to have sometimes had, in the eighteenth century for instance, and that even his own father had had, a consciousness of a natural place in an apparently ordered society. What his life had lacked, biologically, was that power of adaptation which Mr. Basingfield had, in his cynical way, seen—and foreseen—the need of. What he had mostly lacked, in the worldly sense, was singleness of purpose fortified by methodical ambition. Some would regard this deficiency as a fatal flaw, but if Toby had had an eye to any main chance, he would not have been himself, his unique self.

Though his ways of life might have seemed wasteful—of money, of talent, of vital fire, of moral energy—it will not do to complain that there is little to show for a man's or a woman's life, because the influence of every life works and goes on working in a variety of other hearts and heads, and its workings cannot be measured. Toby was a civilized man. He was always on the side of creators against destroyers, he was an enemy of the banal, and if he had strayed in search of easy amusement, he knew and always returned towards what was enduring and vigorous and best. He had independence of judgment, he had shown courage, passion, and wit; and, as his mother used to say, he would do the right thing in an emergency. He did not see life steadily or whole (who does?) but he "saw life" and threw himself into it with appetite. The surface of his life had the swimming iridescence of a bubble, a bubble threatened by the rough winds of a world in transition and revolution; and threatened also from within by the pressure of its hardly contained sphere of impatience. Tense and luminous and tinted, it floated gaily along until it burst. Its color and its erratic movements, against a heavy background of gathering and threatening clouds, were constantly surprising; but the bubble was shapely and gay and not harmful, whereas the storm was amorphous, threatening, and too vast to understand. As I looked back, that one precarious life seemed to me even in its frivolity to have had a certain grandeur, like a joke made on the scaffold by a man about to be put to death as a punishment not for what he has done or not done but for what he is.